"What you need is someone to take you in hand,"

he grated, his long strides taking him to within a foot of her. "If your father hadn't been so busy all his life perfecting the art of being a bastard, he might have found time to do it."

God, he made her so mad! She wanted to... Her eyes fell on his chest, on the silver necklace lying so lovingly in the hollow of his throat. "You think I need to be taken in hand?" she asked faintly.

"Yes" was his quick response.

Her glance moved down his smooth chest, down past his navel to the hint of black hair at the open waistband of his loose jeans. "The job's open," she found herself whispering, her eyes darting to his face. "Want to apply?"

Dear Reader,

Welcome to another month of fine reading from Silhouette Intimate Moments. And what better way to start off the month than with an American Hero title from Marilyn Pappano, a book that's also the beginning of a new miniseries, Southern Knights. Hero Michael Bennett and his friends Remy and Smith are all dedicated to upholding the law—and to loving the right lady. And in *Michael's Gift*, she turns out to be the one woman he wishes she wasn't. To know more, you'll just have to read this terrific story.

The month continues with *Snow Bride*, the newest from bestselling writer Dallas Schulze. Then it's on to *Wild Horses, Wild Men*, from Ann Williams; *Waking Nightmare*, from highly regarded newcomer Alicia Scott; *Breaking the Rules*, Ruth Wind's Intimate Moments debut; and *Hear No Evil*, a suspenseful novel from brand-new author Susan Drake. I think you'll enjoy each and every one of these books—and that you'll be looking for more equally exciting reading next month and in the months to come. So look no further than Silhouette Intimate Moments, where, each and every month, we're proud to bring you writers we consider among the finest in the genre today.

Enjoy!

Leslie J. Wainger
Senior Editor and Editorial Coordinator

Please address questions and book requests to:
Silhouette Reader Service
U.S.: 3010 Walden Ave., P.O. Box 1325, Buffalo, NY 14269
Canadian: P.O. Box 609, Fort Erie, Ont. L2A 5X3

WILD HORSES, WILD MEN

Ann Williams

Published by Silhouette Books

America's Publisher of Contemporary Romance

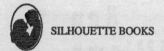 SILHOUETTE BOOKS

ISBN 0-373-07585-5

WILD HORSES, WILD MEN

Printed in U.S.A.

Books by Ann Williams

Silhouette Intimate Moments

Devil in Disguise #302
Loving Lies #335
Haunted by the Past #358
What Lindsey Knew #384
Angel on My Shoulder #408
Without Warning #436
Shades of Wyoming #468
Cold, Cold Heart #487
Wild Horses, Wild Men #585

ANN WILLIAMS

gave up her career as a nurse, then as the owner and proprietor of a bookstore, in order to pursue her writing full-time. She was born and married in Indiana, and after a number of years in Texas, she now lives in Arizona with her husband of twenty-four years and their children.

Reading, writing, crocheting, classical music and a good romantic movie are among her diverse loves. Her dream is to one day move to a cabin in the Carolina mountains with her husband and "write to my heart's content."

This is for my daughters,
Pamela Watson,
Melissa Buckner and
Kristina Myers.

And thank you,
Sam and Mary Ann Buckingham
and John Pharris,
for taking the time to
explain things to a greenhorn.

Chapter 1

Nora Peebles snorted for the third time since entering the store and Lee Ann knew something was definitely wrong. Nora was known throughout the county for broadcasting her displeasure in just such a manner. Only things that pleased her were accepted in stony silence.

"Is something wrong with the material, Mrs. Peebles?" Lee Ann asked with a slight smile. She fought hard to control her impatience, knowing that if she didn't find out what was bothering her, the woman was likely to continue standing in the same spot, snorting like a nervous filly, until closing time.

Nora withdrew her long bony, sun-darkened fingers from the bolt of bright gingham she was kneading and threw the younger woman a sharp glance. "The material's fine," she answered crisply, studying Lee Ann's face through partially narrowed lids.

Expecting a caustic retort, concerning the material's long list of shortcomings, Lee Ann was momentarily at a loss. "Oh—well, I'm glad."

Nora was a woman who got around to things in her own good time, so Lee Ann waited, still expecting a diatribe at any moment. But it seemed Nora wasn't in a garrulous mood.

Apparently, she wanted the reason for her ill humor to be dragged from her. All too familiar with the woman's peculiar ways, and knowing there was no polite way of getting out of it, Lee Ann reluctantly obliged.

"I believe it's been more than a week since I've seen you in town," she said in a pleasant conversational tone. "Have you been ill?"

"No," Nora replied evenly, shrewdly assessing Lee Ann's expression. "I've been just fine. Dad's a bit under the weather though," she added as an afterthought.

Nora lived with her husband of forty years, whom she ruled with an iron glove on the one hand and treated like a child on the other. She'd called him Dad as long as Lee Ann could remember, though their union had never been blessed with children.

"I see," Lee Ann said. "Well, I hope he's soon feeling better." Again she hesitated, but Nora only stared at her unwaveringly, the thin bloodless lips pressed firmly together.

After what seemed like hours, but was only a few moments later, Lee Ann cleared her throat and gave the older woman a thin smile. She was beginning to feel like a bug pinned beneath a microscope. What was wrong with the old harridan this morning?

"Well, I must say," Nora said, suddenly bursting into speech, "you sure seem to be taking it real calm-like."

Lee Ann folded her hands at her waist and said, "I beg your pardon?"

"I *said*," the older woman repeated in a voice loud enough to raise the dead, "you sure are taking it calm-like."

"Taking what calm-li—*calmly?*"

Raising a coarse gray eyebrow, Nora answered, "The news that that murdering half-breed has come sneaking back to town."

Before her mind could assimilate the woman's spiteful words, Lee Ann caught a glimpse of Jennifer, her assistant, entering the store from the back room, and turned toward the other woman helplessly.

Jennifer took one look at Lee Ann's face and hurried forward. "May I help you find something, Mrs. Peebles?" she asked graciously, stepping neatly into the fray. "You know," she added quickly, "just the other day, we received a shipment of that soft candy Mr. Peebles likes so much." Taking the woman's arm lightly, she continued, "If you'll come this way, I'll show you where we've put it."

Before leaving with Jennifer, Nora fired a parting shot in Lee Ann's direction. "I notice that he waited to return until your father was safely out of town."

Jennifer stepped closer to the woman. Her touch still light, but with a hint of steel behind it, she exerted enough pressure to turn Nora toward the front of the store.

She had no idea what had taken place between the two women, or what the half-heard comment from Nora as she'd entered the room had meant, but the frozen expression on Lee Ann's face was enough to tell her something was definitely wrong. And Lee Ann was her friend. She wasn't about to stand by and let this nosy old busybody upset her.

The fact that anything the woman said could upset Lee Ann surprised her. An emotional person herself, Jennifer had always admired the other woman's calm demeanor and self-control. So whatever Nora had been going on about must have been something that had touched a deep chord somewhere inside her friend. Jennifer's curiosity was thoroughly aroused, but before it could be satisfied, she had to placate and then get rid of the town gossip.

While Nora was distracted, Lee Ann withdrew to the back of the store. In the room that served as both office and storeroom, she lowered herself carefully onto the scarred wooden chair, behind the heavy oak desk.

Lee Ann loved managing the store, because it left little time for her to think about her personal life—which hardly existed. When she'd returned from college with a degree in business management, her father had put her in charge of running the Hanly General Store. The store had been in her mother's family for over fifty years. And though Wade Newley hadn't wanted to sell it, it held no interest for him.

Lee Ann figured he'd dumped it in her lap to keep her out of his hair now that he had no control over what she did with her days; it would ensure that he had more time for the ranch and time to follow his son's rodeo career. Whether it was because he trusted her, or because he simply didn't want to be bothered, Wade left all decisions concerning the store in her capable hands and that suited her just fine.

Anyway, it gave her something to do, and she liked the sense of independence it afforded her.

However, as much as she liked what she did, and though in the beginning she had worked seven days a week to develop the business into the kind of place most in keeping with what her grandparents had had in mind, before long she'd discovered the need for a little time to herself. And so she'd called Jennifer, who also had a degree in business management, to come help her. And she'd hired the wife of the former manager to work on the weekends, leaving her some free time.

Normally she would only sit down while filling out order forms or counting receipts, but she took no note of the paperwork spread out over the ink-stained blotter. The phrase, *"murdering half-breed"* had released long-suppressed memories. Like pictures on a movie reel, they scrolled across her mind's eye, blinding her to all but their seductive images.

Was it true? After all these years—after all that had happened—had *he* really come back?

"Are you all right?"

Lee Ann gave a slight start, took an unsteady breath and nodded. "I'm fine," she said, hoping she'd successfully disguised the true nature of her feelings.

But it seemed Jennifer wasn't satisfied with that.

"What was that all about?" Coming to lean against the corner of the desk, she folded her arms over her breasts and eyed her friend curiously.

Lee Ann considered feigning ignorance, but soon cast that idea aside, knowing how tenacious the other woman could be when her curiosity was aroused.

"I'm not certain," she murmured vaguely, wondering what she could say to appease Jennifer and at the same time not have to explain about things she wasn't ready to discuss. She needed time to consider Nora's outrageous statement.

Maybe it wasn't true. *Maybe it was.* But she wasn't ready to talk about it—*about him*—to anyone.

Pressing a long dark curl behind one small ear, she met Jennifer's questioning glance and said with a slight shrug, "You know Nora, she's always going on about something or other."

"I know her," Jennifer agreed, "but I don't usually hear her allude to murder. That *is* what I heard her say, isn't it?"

Getting to her feet, Lee Ann turned to survey the shelves above her head. "You know," she said ruefully, keeping her back to Jennifer's searching gaze, "I hate to mention this, but it's inventory time again."

"Lee Ann!" Jennifer wailed, straightening from the desk and throwing her hands out in a gesture of protest.

"All right," Lee Ann said brusquely. They had been friends since their freshman year in college. And though reticent with others about personal matters, they'd always shared the momentous events in their lives with each other— no matter how unpleasant the details. Realizing she wasn't going to get away with suppressing the truth—at least not completely, she said, "You did hear murder mentioned."

She faced her friend. "But Nora is a very shortsighted woman," she reminded her, and then continued almost angrily, "She tends to believe exactly what she wants to believe—whether there's any real basis for it or not."

Jennifer waved aside Lee Ann's assessment of Nora's character. "Are you going to explain, or let me die of curiosity?"

After a lengthy pause, Lee Ann muttered, "No," surprising herself almost as much as she'd probably surprised her friend.

After a moment in which she was very likely trying to digest the blunt refusal, Jennifer said, "Look, I can see Nora has upset you—"

"I'm not upset," Lee Ann retorted curtly, warning signals flashing in her stormy gray eyes. She turned away, and when she turned back, her expression had undergone another quick change, returning to its normally pleasant, unruffled mien.

"I'm sorry," she said contritely, not wanting to hurt her friend's feelings. "I didn't mean to snap at you. It's just—"

"It's all right," Jennifer interrupted with what Lee Ann knew was a falsely bright smile. "You don't have to tell me anything."

Lee Ann saw the distress in her friend's dark eyes and felt about two inches tall. "Jen?"

The other woman shrugged without meeting Lee Ann's eyes. "It really isn't any of my business." Turning away, she strode toward the door.

"It isn't that." Lee Ann stopped her with the words, "It's just . . . I don't know what to tell you."

Jennifer slowly turned back. "What do you mean?"

Lee Ann lifted one narrow shoulder and shook her dark head without answering. Nora's caustic comments had brought up a chapter in her life she'd put behind her. For a brief time, recent events had brought it to the fore. Then, like all things over but not quite finished, it had faded to an uneasy memory in the dim recesses of her mind.

"Do you know this 'half-breed murderer' Nora was talking about?" Jennifer asked.

Lee Ann's thin figure grew taut, but she replied evenly, "I know him."

"Is he a friend of yours?"

"Someone with whom I used to be friends," Lee Ann corrected.

"Has he been in prison?"

Lee Ann turned away without answering, busying herself with moving things around unnecessarily on the shelves, keeping her back to the other woman, while she sorted past events in her mind.

"Well, are you going to answer me? Who is he? Is he a murderer, or not? And Nora mentioned your father. What does he have to do with it?"

The sound of heavy feet striding across the wooden plank sidewalk, outside the front of the store, echoed loudly in the otherwise silent room.

"His name is Tyler Yancy. And I don't know," Lee Ann finally said softly.

"You don't know—what?"

"I don't know why he's come back to town."

"You know," Jennifer said wryly, "you're only adding to my curiosity."

"I know." Lee Ann gave a half smile and bit her lower lip.

"But you still aren't talking. Right?"

Slipping cold fingers into the pockets of her gray twill slacks, Lee Ann responded, "I can't, not until I know for certain why he's back—*if* he's back.

"Don't be angry with me, Jen," she added quickly on a pleading note. "It's all part of something that started a long time ago." She hesitated before adding, "And ended with my brother's death."

"Your brother! But I thought your brother died in an accident."

"He did. A rodeo accident. But some people—my father among them—believe his death was deliberately engineered to look like an accident."

"You mean someone—this friend of yours—*killed* him?"

"I didn't say that," Lee Ann responded sharply.

"But according to you, your father thinks he did," Jennifer persisted. After a momentary pause, she added with a probing stare at Lee Ann's unhappy face, "But you don't, do you?"

This was the very question Lee Ann had hoped to avoid. For a long moment, she studied the floor in silence. Then, throwing a brief glance of uncertainty in Jennifer's direction, she gave her head a slight shake.

"Was that a no?"

"That was…I don't know," Lee Ann murmured faintly. "I don't know what to believe… No—that isn't true. I don't think Tyler killed my brother. He couldn't have done such a terrible thing."

"Why not?"

"Because…" A soft light entered the gray eyes as her thoughts turned inward. "You'd have to know him, like I once knew him—seen the gentleness in him—to understand.

"He had a way with animals." She smiled at the memory. "I used to watch him practice for the rodeo. He could communicate with animals in a way no one else could. But when I mentioned it, he'd laugh it off, say it was nothing special, that being an untamed creature himself, they spoke the same language."

"What did he mean about being an untamed creature?" Jennifer asked with a slight frown.

A cloud passed over Lee Ann's face. "He's Indian on his mother's side. All through school the kids taunted him about it. They called him half-breed and savage. The whole town made certain he never forgot for a moment that he wasn't *white,*" she added bitterly.

"Animals are not people," Jennifer said softly.

"What did you say?" Lee Ann looked up.

"Just because he was kind to animals," Jennifer explained, "that doesn't necessarily mean he would be the same with people."

"You don't know what you're talking about," Lee Ann retorted sharply, refusing to admit that her brother had been one of the worse transgressors.

"If everyone thinks the man is guilty—everyone except you, then why isn't he in jail?"

"He was," Lee Ann admitted. "They arrested him almost immediately after my brother's accident. But the authorities had to let him go because of lack of evidence."

"That doesn't necessarily mean he's innocent—"

"Don't you think I know that?" Lee Ann whirled away.

What infuriated her most was that everyone in town had immediately gone along with her father's verdict of guilt. And all of them, her father included, assumed she went along with it, too. Still, to be perfectly fair to her father, she had to admit she'd been accustomed to deferring to his judgment in most things, just to keep the peace. *Until now.*

"Lee Ann—"

"Can we please just let it drop?" she said passionately.

"I can," Jennifer said astutely, "but can you?"

Lee Ann held her breath as Jennifer left the room, a pang of guilt, and some other less easily defined emotion, making her chest feel tight. In all the years of their friendship, they'd never come this close to having a fight.

For the rest of the day, Jennifer kept their conversations, few as they were, restricted to business matters. As for Lee

Ann, her friend's last question rang loudly inside her head, right alongside Nora Peebles's assertion that Ty Yancy had returned to town knowing her father was not in residence at the moment. And the day dragged on.

Not that there wasn't plenty of work to keep her mind off things she didn't want to remember, but with the entrance of nearly every customer that day, the past reared its ugly head. It seemed the whole town had heard a version of Nora Peebles's news, and everyone was determined to let Lee Ann know they knew, and to see if they could gauge her reaction to the situation.

Six o'clock finally rolled around. Lee Ann bid a restrained goodbye to Jennifer and hurried out the door. She began the fifteen-mile drive home with a heavy heart. She'd have given a lot to have been able to clear her mind, just pretend the whole day had never happened.

But she couldn't, any more than she could put the memory of Tyler Yancy out of her heart. And the good Lord knows she'd tried to do that for twelve years. Even going so far as to getting engaged in college. But nothing had worked. He haunted her dreams as vividly now as when she'd been an impressionable adolescent and he'd been a swaggering teenager.

She'd been little more than a child the first time she'd laid eyes on him. Well, not quite a child, more like an emotionally underdeveloped twelve-year-old. Most girls that age were developing a more adult relationship with their mothers, learning about the facts of life and how those facts would affect them personally. But her mother had died when Lee Ann was born and she'd learned about becoming a woman from their housekeeper, Francine. The woman hung on to every word Lee Ann's father spoke as though it were gospel, but had little time for a gawky young girl starved for attention.

Lee Ann knew her father would have fired the woman, if she had complained about her, and hired someone else to take her place with little or no thought for the house-keeper's feelings. Wade Newley didn't like dissension any-where on the ranch. The people who worked for Wade were worth their money only so long as things went smoothly for him.

But Lee Ann never complained, and the woman stayed on—probably hoping for a marriage proposal—until after Lee Ann had graduated from college and returned home. By then, apparently, Francine had realized she was never go-ing to be more to Lee Ann's father than a fixture in his home, easily replaced at his discretion.

If the truth be known, there was precious little that meant much to the Great Wade Newley, outside of the ranch and his only son. The Great Wade Newley. That's how her brother had always prefaced anything he had to say about their father.

Poor Les. A talented man in his own right, destined to be overshadowed by a larger-than-life father. Even in the one area he had loved more than life. Rodeo.

Several years back, the name Wade Newley had been on everyone's lips. He'd won more championship titles and more money in his short rodeo career than any other cow-boy on the circuit. Until a bull with a vindictive streak put an end to his lofty career.

But that hadn't stopped Wade for long. He had simply taken the money he'd saved and approached rodeo from the other end of the arena. He became a rodeo stockbreeder.

As for Les, he tried a lot of things while he was growing up, football, track, polo. He wasn't very good at any of them and nothing interested him like rodeo. So he made the decision to become more famous than his father, and set about letting nothing get in his way.

There had always been a streak of competition between the boy and his father. Lee Ann wasn't certain, but she sus-pected that her father had deliberately fostered it. The one thing she knew for sure was that her father and brother were far too busy getting at each other, when not actively involved in running the ranch, to take more than a passing interest in a little girl.

For the most part, she guessed she must have been pretty wild as a youngster. She remembered spending most of her time, when she wasn't in school, out on the range with her father's hired hands. Up until then, it seemed she'd spent the greater part of her life trying to find things to keep her out of her father's and brother's way. But no matter how hard she tried, she was at that awkward age, where everything either spilled or got broken, and all she managed most of the time was to annoy them.

But that was before she caught the interest of Smokey, her father's ranch foreman. One night, after finding her sitting around the campfire with the other ranch hands dipping snuff and playing poker—and winning—he decided to take her under his wing.

At first, the other wranglers had been wary of a child, and a female one at that, hanging around. But it wasn't long before they realized she expected no special treatment. And after she'd learned the ropes, she worked alongside the men, doing as much work as a child her size and age was capable of doing, and without so much as a grumble.

While her brother demanded respect from the men, Lee Ann earned it. Lee Ann was one of them in a way her brother could never be.

If her father knew where she spent the long days of summer, and any vacation she spent at home throughout the school year, he made no comment about it. It was obvious that his interest lay in his older child, the son who would carry on after him.

And then one day, Ty Yancy had come riding onto the ranch and Lee Ann finally found a focus for her youthful adoration. She knew right away that his was a free spirit, as wild and untamed as the horses he broke for her father.

Would their first meeting ever fade from her memory?

Even now she could see him mounted on his horse, Gray Sock. The shoulder-length hair as dark as a blackbird's wing, gleaming in the sunlight. In worn jeans and boots, chest bare, his only adornment a silver chain with a silver war-shield suspended from it, he'd come galloping into her life like some hero in one of the romance novels she sometimes found Francine reading.

She'd seen him once or twice at school a couple of years back, before her father had decided to send her to boarding school, and she'd heard his name mentioned by her brother, who had nothing good to say about him. But the flesh-and-blood entity, mounted so regally before her, had little to do with the picture she'd built of him in her mind.

The wicked glint in the almond-shaped eyes, which should have been black, but were more green than hazel, drew her like a bee to a flower. And the streak of recklessness in everything he did, from the way he rode a horse, to the way he challenged her brother with a glance, made him her hero.

In retrospect, she wondered if that's what had first attracted her to him. He was unlike anyone she'd ever met—and her brother didn't like him. At age twelve, that in itself was enough to get Ty into her good books. In fact, Ty embodied everything she'd ever longed to be, yet was too afraid—

The sudden blare of a horn jerked Lee Ann into the present as a white low-rider truck swerved out around her, too close for comfort, kicking up rocks and dust. Momentarily thrown off balance, Lee Ann instinctively trod on the brake, causing her own vehicle to skid on the hard-packed dirt road.

The car came to a jerking halt, its headlights pointed across the road. It took a moment for Lee Ann to assess that she was only shaken up and the car had come to no great harm. Which was good, because it was her father's car. Her own was in the shop getting the brakes fixed.

Glancing through the windshield, she noted that the headlights were now pointed down an overgrown lane, where weeds and thick brambles strangled one another in an attempt to keep trespassers out.

Broken Heart Ranch. It had been owned by the Yancy family since the early 1800s. Once the most prosperous ranch for miles in either direction, it had outshone her own father's Willow's Rest. But hard times had taken their toll. During her childhood, it had barely made a living for its owner, and now it lay abandoned, as it had for many years.

Was *he* there?

It wasn't a question that should have concerned her. Life had placed Ty Yancy far outside her realm, and common sense told her to leave it that way.

Lee Ann's fingers inched toward the key in the ignition. The stalled engine suddenly came to life and the front wheels bumped as the car moved forward.

She meant to turn the steering wheel in the direction of home, but, somehow, the car had passed over the banked dirt at the side of the road and was headed down the lane. Weeds slapped at its sides. No doubt ruining the paint job, she realized guiltily. Her father would be furious when he returned home and saw—

Her thoughts choked off abruptly. She had arrived. The headlights picked out three wagon wheels, centered in what had once been a circular driveway. According to legend, those wheels had been taken from the prairie schooner Josiah Yancy had driven west to the Montana Territory long before the mining boom of the 1860s.

The fourth wheel had disappeared sometime that first summer, along with Josiah, who'd been taken by the Piegan Indians, the true Montana Blackfeet. He was never seen again, but his wife and seven children had stayed on to make the place a home. And they'd fought whoever and whatever they'd had to fight in order to keep the land and the home Josiah had built before his disappearance.

Mary Elizabeth Yancy had named the place Broken Heart, because it had taken her beloved husband from her. And Broken Heart it had remained to this day.

Perhaps it was ironic that the present owner, Ty Yancy, was half Blackfoot Indian on his maternal side. And then again, maybe it was fate completing a cycle.

Lee Ann's glance slid over the dark silent house. This wasn't the original homestead, but it had been built on the exact spot where the first one had stood.

How sad the place looked. With arms folded across the steering wheel, she studied it critically. She'd never been a frequent visitor, even when Ty was welcome at her own house. But, surely, it hadn't been in such a terrible state of disrepair the last time she'd seen it.

Her eyes traveled over the structure. Its surface reminded her of a cur dog suffering from mange. It's once-white color had faded to an overall dirty gray, but in some places the paint had cracked and peeled, leaving large patches of dark rotting wood.

The front door was missing and both of the tall narrow windows on either side of the gaping maw left by its disappearance had been shattered, either by storms, or broken out by vandals. Shards of glass dotted the warped boards of the curiously angled porch.

In the last few weeks, she'd heard news reports stating that gangs from big cities like Los Angeles were slowly moving into the rural cities and towns. Even into less populated areas like this one. She shuddered at the thought of spending even one night in this place alone and unprotected.

Ty mustn't be staying here. She hadn't seen a vehicle anywhere around, but something about the air of desolation surrounding the place told her better than words that it was unoccupied.

Obviously, Nora Peebles had been mistaken. And yet she reached for the flashlight on the seat beside her. Telling herself she'd take one short look around and then she'd leave.

If vandals had been at the place, it was her duty to notify Nate Baskum, the sheriff. She knew he was determined to keep undesirable elements out of their town.

Doing her best to ignore the persistent voice inside, comparing this escapade with those of the past, when she'd followed Ty in secret to watch him practice for the rodeo, she climbed from the car. It didn't occur to her that she could very well be in physical danger, if indeed there was a gang operating in the area.

She turned on the flashlight, directed its beam toward the door and saw the red spray-painted words on the interior walls.

"Damn!" The word burst explosively from between clenched lips. Maybe he *was* getting too old for the game.

Rodeo. Just the thought of it filled his nostrils with the achingly familiar, pungent odor of horseflesh, human sweat, manure . . . and blood.

His stomach knotted in remembered anticipation of the waiting, wondering which unruly bronc or bad-tempered bull would be his by the luck of the draw. Wondering which one, this time, would give him the ride of his life.

"No, by damned," he muttered half-angrily, "I'm not too old." He might be pushing thirty, but he still had a thing or two to show them on the suicide circuit, as the cowboys called the rodeo.

Ripping open his shirt, he shrugged it off lean shoulders. Long, tanned fingers began to knead the muscles of his upper arm, working deep, where stiffness had turned to soreness.

His glance shifted toward the two lengths of chain suspended from the rafters. Light from the lanterns he'd placed on the floor careened off their shiny surfaces as they swayed lightly back and forth, a challenge waiting to be met.

And he'd meet it or be damned. A sudden curious grin breached the strained severity of his darkly handsome face. He was already damned, if most people were to be believed, so he guessed it didn't matter one way or the other.

Flexing the muscles in his upper body, feeling the quiver of raw flesh, he flinched and glared around at the dilapidated barn. How in the hell had he ended up back here? He'd never intended it.

He didn't even know why he'd kept up the taxes on the place. He supposed that at the back of his mind had been the idea of selling it somewhere down the line and using the money to further his career in rodeo. But he'd certainly never intended living here again.

His glance shifted toward the rear of the barn where he'd rigged a barrel to practice staying on the bulls, then slid toward the bale of hay in the far corner where he worked on his spurring. He shook his head almost in derision. He'd thought his days of using those two props were long past.

It seemed he'd been wrong on both counts. That was nothing new, he'd been wrong about a lot of things in his life. Like the fact that after years of spending too many nights on the road sleeping out in the open or in barns in worse shape than this one, because he couldn't afford the price of a bed, he'd finally made it to the big time.

The motel rooms had gradually gotten finer and the beds softer. He made lots of money, learned what the good life was all about and kept right on going down the road—as rodeo cowboy's referred to traveling from one rodeo to another—with the best of them.

And now he'd come full circle. His uncle had been a firm believer that everything moved in circles; sooner or later, we all ended up where we'd started in life.

Maybe the old man had been right. His shoulders drooped as his eyes turned inward to a time not all that long ago when he'd been little more than a boy teetering on the brink of manhood.

All at once he stiffened. No, by damned, he wouldn't end up the way he'd started in life, with too little food in his belly, holes in his jeans—way before it became fashionable—and the brunt of everyone's jokes.

Now that he knew what it was to have money in his pocket, to walk down the street with his head held high, admired by some—instead of ridiculed by all—for being who he was, he'd never go back. He'd never again be the poor half-breed kid who had to take what was dished out to him, or use his fists in self-defense.

A lot of people referred to their childhood as the good old days, but there had been precious little good in the days of his youth. There was his uncle, of course. Nathan Yancy had taken him in when Ty's mother had dumped him and run off. He'd been little more than a baby at the time. And for that, he'd always be grateful to the man.

His uncle had been a good man who just couldn't seem to pull himself out of the spell of bad luck he'd fallen on. Nathan had taught him what it was to work hard for a living and what it was to be a cowboy in the finest sense of the word. Ty had taken the lesson to heart. He lived to be a cowboy, because it was the one thing he was good at.

As for the rest of it, he had no good memories . . . well, maybe one. . . .

An image of turbulent gray eyes and full, trembling lips took shape in his mind. With a twisted grin, he doubted if she'd ever thought of him as a good memory.

But all that was in the past. Nothing mattered now, except the game, and the name of the game was *rodeo*. What he wanted most from life was to be able to climb aboard another bull, another wild bronc, and still be there when the buzzer sounded eight seconds later. And then he'd do it all over again.

Rubbing his palms down the seat of his jeans, he moved toward the ladder to the hayloft. He'd been working out as hard as his healing body would allow ever since arriving here on foot, four days ago.

A lot of cowboys went to health spas if they could afford it or worked out in gyms to keep in shape. Ty had always favored the hands-on method of staying fit. There was nothing like climbing aboard an arm-jerker—a horse that bucks powerfully, causing a lot of pull on your arm—or a rank bull, and going the round with him to keep your muscles in tone and your wits sharply honed.

Trouble was, he'd had to sell everything he owned, including his rigging, a few weeks back to pay his medical bills. And until he was again ready to climb aboard and make some real money in the arena, he was flat broke.

The good thing was that it looked as though no one in Rainville knew of his presence on the ranch. If he was lucky, no one would find out until he was ready to leave. All he wanted from this place and the people in town was time enough to heal and get on with his life.

Holding on to the rough wooden rung of the ladder with his bare toes, he leaned forward, stretching toward the closest loop of chain. A muscle in his side that had been recently stitched together twitched at the strain and his jaws clamped down against the pain. He'd do it—damn it—or die trying!

One hand slipped between the circled links and he felt their coolness slide against the dry palm of his hand. He braced himself for what was coming and leaned out, letting his arm and shoulder take on the job of holding his weight, while he reached for the second loop.

The muscles knotted in his shoulder and across his upper back as white-hot pain seared the length of his torso. Ty bit down hard on his lower lip, tasting blood, the pain of stretched, half-healed tendon and muscle almost more than he could bear.

It was chilly in the barn, but beads of sweat dotted his forehead and chest as he strained toward the second loop.

He had it in his hand. A sense of triumph engulfed him as he grabbed it and hung on, kicking his legs gently back and forth, moving his body in a widening arc.

Yes! He was doing it! Just a little more and he'd be able to do some of the exercises he'd been taught in therapy—

Ty sucked in his breath and held it as a spasm of pain lashed its way from his groin to his left shoulder. Sweat ran from his scalp into his eyes. He blinked against the sting and closed them, waiting—waiting for the pain to lessen.

But it grew worse, adding stress to his wrists and shoulders. His upper body glistened wetly in the light from the lanterns as he hung suspended, ten feet above the ground, like an ancient offering to some pagan god.

All at once, the agony became intolerable. With a cry of outrage, his fingers twitched and his body plunged to the floor like a dead thing.

The pile of hay he'd gathered beneath the area somewhat cushioned the impact of his fall. Still, he had to sit a moment, letting the pain possess him, riding it to its peak, before it would release him.

When he could, he lifted his head and pushed at the damp clumps of black hair on his forehead and cheeks—and froze. A sensitive spot between his shoulder blades warned him that he was no longer alone.

Lee Ann clamped a hand over her mouth to smother a scream as she saw the body plummet from the rafters to the floor. At first, uncertain about what she'd actually seen, all kinds of improbable possibilities passed through her mind.

When the dark head slowly lifted, she caught sight of its profile and knew without a doubt the identity of the man sitting less than twenty yards away.

She saw the naked shoulders stiffen. An instant later the dark head turned and their glances meshed. Lee Ann couldn't prevent a nervous flutter in her chest at this first sight of him after so many years.

Her eyes toured his face from the stiff unshaven jaws to the pale sensuous mouth. How she had once loved to hear those lips whisper her name.

She looked beyond them to the sharp cheekbones standing out against the dark skin. He looked drawn. Was he ill?

Her glance shifted again and she saw that he still wore the silver necklace his Indian mother had left him.

All at once she became aware of the silence. It loomed between them like a high, thick wall. Why didn't he speak? Didn't he recognize her?

Her glance veered from his smooth-muscled chest to the deep hazel eyes—and floundered. He looked . . . angry.

Suddenly she knew why. He recognized her, all right. The last time she'd seen him, he'd stared at her in just such a manner, his beautiful almond-shaped eyes filled with bitter contempt as he accused her of spying on him for her father.

Did he think she was spying again? She wanted to protest her innocence, just as she'd wanted to protest it back then, but the words died in her throat. There were so many things she wanted to say to him. So many questions between them left unanswered. So much stood between them. How could she make him understand . . . ?

The clenched fingers hovering near her mouth opened and fluttered toward him, as though trying to convey some message that he might more readily understand than the spoken word.

Then she was gone, disappearing into the night. Her feet stumbled over the unfamiliar grounds. The sweet scent of hay from the barn mixed with the acrid odor of decay surrounding the whole place and filled her nostrils as she ran, her eyes blind to everything but the haunting expression of hostility on Tyler Yancy's tormented face.

Chapter 2

Lee Ann made her way across the town square with lagging feet. She shouldn't have bothered going to lunch. She hadn't been able to force down a bite. But she didn't want to go back to work, either.

Last night, after her little foray to Ty's ranch, she'd been unable to sleep. She'd tried for hours to put his image out of her mind, but every time she closed her eyes, his dark sensuous face rose before her, making her senses reel, evoking feelings that she hadn't experienced in years.

Six o'clock this morning had found her sitting at the kitchen table staring fuzzy-eyed at a plate of leftover lasagna. Unfortunately, she ate when she was upset. Thank God—maybe God was a woman and understood these things—her nervous eating hadn't yet begun to show on her hips.

All night she'd asked herself the same question. Why? Why hadn't she spoken to him, exchanged a polite greeting and asked about his reasons for coming back, how long he intended to stay—mentioned that her father was out of town, but would be returning before long?

And that was the real crux of the problem. Her father. He hated Ty with an unhealthy passion. He blamed him unquestioningly for her brother's death.

Lee Ann had loved her brother. They hadn't been close, but that didn't matter, he was still her brother. But she wasn't lashing out at everyone because he was gone.

She loved her father, too, even though he seemed to prefer almost anybody and anything over spending time with his daughter. She'd thought Les's death might bring them closer together, that in his pain, her father might turn to her for comfort and realize that he still had one child left who loved him.

It hadn't worked out quite that way. Wade Newley had buried his pain beneath layers of bitterness, because no one had been charged with his son's death. And he'd thrown himself into his work with a vengeance.

In the past, he'd gone on business trips that had lasted up to a month. Now, his trips lasted anywhere from one to three months. Lee Ann wondered if he stayed away because he couldn't face the reminders of her brother around the place.

She was honest enough with herself to admit to feeling hurt by the thought that her presence on the ranch didn't seem to matter to him. Her father had his faults. He was arrogant and opinionated and couldn't tolerate human flaws.

He'd been hard on Les, but Lee Ann had always thought it was because he loved him so much and wanted him to be as good as he could be. Yet she sensed he would have been disappointed had the younger man outshone him in anything, especially when it came to rodeo.

She tried to excuse the things that bothered her about her father by attributing them to the loss of her mother so soon in their marriage. By all accounts, her mother had been more than capable of blunting her father's rough edges with her gentle, yet firm handling of him.

Lee Ann wished she was more like her mother. Maybe then she'd know how to handle this present situation between her father and Ty.

One thing was certain, Ty mustn't be in Rainville when her father returned from his latest business trip. For both their sakes, she wanted to prevent a confrontation between the two men.

Wade Newley was no longer a young man. She didn't want to lose him before they'd had the chance to become close. She still fostered the hope that one day it would happen.

As for Ty... she was confused about her feelings toward him. Was it only sweet memories that made his presence in Rainville seem important to her now?

He'd been away for a long time. A lot could happen to change a person in twelve years.

"Afternoon, Miz Newley."

Lee Ann looked up, smiled and waved as Sheriff Baskum drove past. She wondered briefly if she ought to mention to him the graffiti she'd seen last night.

If she did, it would be all over town that she'd been at the Broken Heart Ranch with Ty... and when her father returned... Maybe it would be best to keep it to herself.

As she crossed the street, Lee Ann thought about how she and Jennifer had tiptoed around each other all morning long, going out of their way to appear cheerful and polite as though nothing had happened the day before. Someone was going to have to make the first move if their friendship was to be salvaged and Lee Ann decided it would have to be her.

After all, in all honesty, she supposed she was the one responsible for their discord in the first place—along with a little help from Nora Peebles.

Making her way around a baby blue pickup parked next to the curb, Lee Ann stepped up onto the wooden walkway and approached the door. As she went inside the building, her sense of smell was immediately gratified by the fragrance hovering in the air.

It was her custom to keep a bowl of potpourri burning during business hours. The store was as close to an old-fashioned mercantile as possible, carrying everything from yard goods to baby chicks, leather tack, barbed wire, fresh meats and can goods. And even some exotic things like special candies and perfumes.

The potpourri helped nullify the effect of the combined odors, which could become staggering on hot days. And the customers—especially tourists—seemed to like it.

Lee Ann and Jennifer were constantly in good-natured disagreement over what scent they should use. Jennifer's favorite was lilac and she insisted it was a scent that went with rich handmade lace—which they carried occasionally—and a time gone by.

Lee Ann preferred country spice.

The store didn't boast air-conditioning, but large ceiling fans kept the air flowing along the high ceilings, and most days that was enough. Only during the rare, really hot days of summer, did they occasionally have to resort to opening the double doors out front and along the side alley.

Swinging her purse off her shoulder, Lee Ann took a deep breath and grinned. It seemed Jennifer, too, was ready to make up. The unmistakable aroma of country spice wafted through the large room.

She headed down the wide central aisle, toward the deep counter that went two-thirds of the way across the back of the store, and stopped short, her eyes following the curved backside of a cowboy in faded jeans. He was leaning over the counter, engaged in conversation with Jennifer.

For a heart-stopping instant, as her eyes raced over worn leather boots to the wide-brimmed hat pushed to the back of his head, Lee Ann couldn't move. Then she took a closer look and realized it wasn't *him*.

Nervous laughter rang out and Lee Ann recognized it as Jennifer's. She made a sudden detour to the side door, and once outside, used her key to let herself into the store-room/office.

Half an hour later, Jennifer came searching for her. She found Lee Ann sitting at the desk, hunched over the store accounts ledger.

"Hi."

Lee Ann glanced up. "Hi, yourself. Have things quieted down out there?"

Jennifer grinned wryly. "The sudden influx of patrons was due to the appearance of an earlier customer. A man showed up while you were at lunch, asking about Ty Yancy." She watched Lee Ann's face closely as she added, "He said he was a friend of his."

Lee Ann looked surprised. In the past, Ty hadn't had any friends. But then, as she'd noted earlier, people change.

Jennifer continued, "I didn't know what to tell him. I don't know where the Yancy place is located. And you were gone. So I sent him down the street to the garage." A glint of mischief entered her green eyes. "I figured if anyone would know how to give directions to the Yancy place, it would be Nora Peebles's brother, Wylie."

Taking a seat in the chair across from Lee Ann, Jennifer studied her hands, her eyes serious now. "About yester-day—"

"It was a bad day—definitely a Monday," Lee Ann interrupted with a quick smile.

Jennifer glanced up, caught the smile and flashed one of her own. "Yes," she agreed, darting a side glance at the calendar on the wall, which clearly stated that it had been Thursday. "Definitely a Monday."

"I stopped by the Yancy ranch on the way home last night," Lee Ann said abruptly.

"Alone? At night?"

Lee Ann threw down the pencil she'd been using and got to her feet. "I'm not afraid of Ty Yancy, if that's what you mean," she said impatiently.

"That's not what I meant. Well, not exactly, anyway. It's bad enough your staying out there on the ranch alone with your father gone and the ranch crew off in the mountains somewhere—"

"No one around here would hurt me," Lee Ann interrupted. "I've known these people all my life."

The memory of a white truck flashed through her mind, along with a fragment of thought concerning gangs moving into the area, but she thrust it aside. "Look, there's something I should have told you yesterday. When I was younger, Ty worked for my father. I—we knew each other rather well...."

Jennifer caught her breath. "You don't mean..."

Lee Ann glanced up with a frown, then, catching her friend's drift, straightened in affront. "No—not that, you idiot! I mean we spent a lot of time together on the ranch."

Outlining one oval-shaped nail with a thumb, she admitted, "I was lonely. Dad was busy with the ranch, and Les didn't have time for a kid sister."

She shrugged. "I guess Ty was lonely, too. We were pretty much in the same boat. His father was dead, his mother had left him and his uncle worked too hard to have much free time to spend with him.

"He didn't have any friends around town, so when he came to work for Dad—" Lee Ann shrugged again "—we just sort of gravitated toward each other."

"Why didn't he have any friends?"

"What?"

"I said, why didn't he have any friends in town?"

"I don't know."

But she did. Her brother had been only too glad to tell her that no self-respecting *white* woman—or girl—would be caught dead with the likes of Ty Yancy. And it seemed the men and boys all agreed. Prejudice was alive and well in Rainville, Montana, Lee Ann thought with disgust, remembering Nora Peebles's words of the day before.

"So what happened?" Jennifer asked. "If your father hired him to work on the ranch, then he must have liked him. So, how come he thinks he had something to do with your brother's death?"

Lee Ann dropped onto her chair and propped her arms on the heavy desk. "I'm not really certain," she admitted slowly. "When he first came to work for us, Dad couldn't say enough good things about him and his work. Ty was even treated like a member of the family. He took some of his meals with us. It's all so confusing," she said in exasperation. "And I'm not even certain I know why I'm worrying about it.

"All I know," Lee Ann continued, "is that one day I caught my brother and Ty fighting out back, near the branding pens. They stopped when they realized I was there.

"Les jumped on his horse and took off at a gallop. Ty's face was cut and bleeding. I offered him my bandanna, but he shoved it back at me and took off after Les.

"I guess I was kind of hurt," Lee Ann admitted reluctantly. "He'd never been so…hostile to me. I followed him back to the ranch, but real slow. I knew he'd gone after my brother, and I didn't want to see them fight anymore. They were always fighting," she added sadly, "if not with their fists, then with words.

"When I got back to the house, Ty was leaving it. He walked right past me, without looking to the left or the right." She frowned in memory. "There was a strange look on his face. I don't think he was at all aware of his surroundings.

"I don't know what happened between him and Dad and Les that day, but he left the ranch and never stepped foot on it again."

"Your brother didn't like him, I take it," Jennifer said.

Lee Ann shook her head. "I guess they never got along. Sometimes it's like that with people—instant antagonism. It had been going on since they started first grade."

She looked at Jennifer with puzzled eyes. "That's one of the reasons why Dad's hiring Ty surprised me. I know I was young at the time, and after I met Ty I didn't look too closely for a reason, but..."

"What?"

Lee Ann hesitated. This part was still hard to understand. "A few days after he left Dad's employment, I heard a rumor circulating around town about Ty. I went to Dad to ask if it was true. And he confirmed it. He said he'd had to fire Ty, because he'd caught him mistreating one of the horses."

"But—"

"I know." Lee Ann met her friend's puzzled stare. "I told you about Ty's strange affinity with animals. He would no more have mistreated an animal than he'd have horse-whipped me," she said solemnly.

"So your father lied," Jennifer commented slowly. "Why? And why did he fire him?"

"I don't know. But after that, no one in the valley would hire Ty to work for them. And he and his uncle needed the money. They lived on some pension his uncle had coming to him from the military, I think. Anyway, they needed the money Ty made to get by."

"What did he do?"

"He had to leave home to find work. He even quit school for a while, so he could make more money. His uncle had come down with pneumonia that year and Ty needed the extra cash to pay the hospital bills."

"That's when he left town?"

"No. His uncle got better and Ty went back to school. He graduated the next spring and that's when he left town." A note of bitterness crept into her voice as she said, "To go on the rodeo circuit."

"And that's how he and your brother managed to catch up to each other again," Jennifer concluded.

"Yes. Ty never came back to town. His uncle died ten years ago and left the ranch to him. I thought he'd at least come back for the man's funeral. But he didn't. After that, we just got on with our lives and forgot all about Ty Yancy."

That wasn't quite true, but Lee Ann couldn't confess, even to Jennifer, how his memory had followed her around all these years.

"And then your brother died."

"Yes. And Daddy blamed Ty."

"Does he have any proof that Ty was involved?" Jennifer asked logically.

"If he did," Lee Ann assured her, "he'd have given it to the authorities a long time ago. No," she shook her head, "it's all in Dad's mind."

"Why does your father hate him so much? Even if he did mistreat one of your dad's animals, that's not reason enough for a lifelong vendetta." Jennifer hesitated before asking, "Could it have anything to do with the fact that you and he were... fond of each other?"

Lee Ann laughed without humor. "Where did you get the idea that *he* was fond of *me?*"

"You said..."

"I know what I said. I followed him around like a puppy. He simply tolerated me a lot better than my brother did. In the end, he lumped my father and brother and me all together in one heap.

"Believe me," Lee Ann added with a snort, "when he left town, he was hoping never to see *any* of the Newley clan ever again."

"But you went to see him last night," Jennifer protested.

Lee Ann covered her face with unsteady hands and pressed a finger against each eyelid to ease the tension she could feel building behind them. It was growing harder to maintain the control over her emotions that she'd developed these last few years. Why was she letting all this talk of the past affect her so adversely?

Lowering her hands, she compressed her lips, then shook her head before confessing, "I guess I wanted to see him again. I didn't realize that's why I went…until I actually saw him. I guess I wanted to tell him… I don't know." She shook her head again. "I guess I just wanted to say I was sorry for the past."

Tears burned Lee Ann's eyes, making them shine like gray-blue glass. Jennifer made a move as though to go to her, but Lee Ann sat up straighter, regaining her control, and motioned for her friend to stay seated.

"God! What's the matter with me? I haven't seen or heard from the man in twelve years. You'd think that by now—"

You almost gave yourself away, a voice inside chided softly. But that was ridiculous, there was nothing to give away.

"You haven't forgotten him," Jennifer said gently. "Even if you'd like to."

Lee Ann shrugged without looking at her. She felt unbelievably foolish.

"What did you say to him last night?" Jennifer asked curiously.

Lee Ann stared at her friend for a long time without answering. And then she smiled a crooked smile. "You're going to love this. I didn't say a word."

Jennifer frowned. "I don't understand."

Lee Ann's voice grew brittle. "I didn't say a word," she repeated. "I simply stood and gaped at him like some—some *idiot*—and then I just ran away."

"You what?"

"I shot out of there like a scalded cat," Lee Ann admitted ruefully.

The two women gazed at each other blankly and then all at once they were laughing, each with a picture in her mind of Lee Ann running through bushes and weeds as though the very devil were on her heels. After a moment, they got themselves under control and the laughter died.

"It was crazy, Jen. He still makes me feel like a giddy teenager. I took one look into his eyes and my toes curled. All coherent thought flew right out of my head."

Lee Ann gave a nervous titter. A sound as foreign to her as the tears that had glazed her eyes a moment ago.

When she thought about it later, it really wasn't all that funny, but the laughter had helped to relieve the tension. The rest of the day passed smoothly.

After closing that evening, the two women shared dinner in one of the two restaurants in town. They were at the dessert stage of dinner—debating on whether to have peach cobbler and ice cream, or be kind to their waistlines and stick with an extra cup of black coffee—when the restaurant door opened and all conversation came to an abrupt halt.

Jennifer was the first to notice the stranger standing just inside the door. He tipped his hat to her and she smiled, then blushed and looked away in confusion.

Lee Ann caught sight of her friend's pink cheeks and turned to find out what had caused them. Ty Yancy met her glance head-on as he stepped around his taller companion. Keeping his eyes locked with hers, he led the way to a table, one away from where she sat in stunned silence.

Only the room wasn't really silent. Every sound within the four walls suddenly became magnified to Lee Ann's ears: the rasping breath of the man to the right of her; the hiss and rattle from the kitchen as Polk Johnston put another steak on the grill and poured himself a cup of coffee in the old tin cup he always used; the abrupt scraping of a chair against the floor as Ty pulled it away from the table and sat down.

A moment later, her other senses seemed to sharpen. The smell of barbecue sauce, frying onions and fresh-brewed coffee hung thick in the air, assaulting her nostrils.

The rough wooden walls adorned with old harnesses, spurs and horseshoes suddenly appeared shoddy to her eyes. The decor looked like what it was, a cheap attempt at reproducing a Western atmosphere without going to the expense of redecoration.

Lee Ann was seeing it as Ty must be seeing it for the first time. The Horseshoe Restaurant hadn't been in existence when he'd lived in Rainville, but the building had been here, housing a feed store.

Was he remembering the day she had ridden into town with him to pick up feed?

She'd never forget the humiliation she'd felt that day on his behalf, when he'd been ignored by the owner, Ed Flint. The man had waited on customers who'd come in after him and left Ty standing until the store was once again empty. But Ty had politely given the man the note and money her father had sent and stood silently while the order was filled. And on the way home, when she tried to apologize to him for the man's behavior, he'd pretended it didn't matter.

All at once something warm touched Lee Ann's cold hands, gripping each other on her lap beneath the table, and Jennifer whispered, "Do you want to leave?"

Lee Ann ripped her glance from Ty's face and transferred it to her empty coffee cup. "It would look like I didn't want to be in the same room with him," she answered softly.

"Well, then, we could always go over and join him and his friend," Jennifer suggested facetiously.

"Jennifer!"

"We've got to do something," she warned quietly. "Look."

Chester Kittridge, a longtime friend of her father's, had gotten to his feet. At six and one-half feet tall, he towered over most people, and Ty, like most bull riders, was compact and slender and not much above average height.

"This restaurant is full," Chester announced sternly, coming to a halt beside the men.

Ty's friend looked at the table before them, raised a sandy eyebrow and said, "I guess your eyesight must be failing, friend, 'cause this table sure looked empty to me."

Chester took a step closer. "It will be," he said through clenched teeth, "just as soon as you leave. Find someplace else to eat. As a matter of fact," he added, "find yourself someplace else to stay. We don't want your kind in this town."

"Just a minute, mister, this isn't the Old West. I'm not a gunfighter and you sure as hell ain't the sheriff—are you?" he asked quickly.

"I don't have to wear a badge to know we don't want any low-down murdering cowards in our town. Take him," Chester gestured toward Ty, "and get out."

"Now, look here, you—"

Ty laid a restraining hand on his friend's arm. "It's okay, Cody, let's go."

"What? But—"

"Let's go," Ty interrupted firmly.

Lee Ann watched with mixed emotions as Cody slammed his chair back and vaulted to his feet, causing Chester to take an involuntary step back. A moment later, the two men left the restaurant without a backward glance.

Lee Ann was glad Ty had elected to go instead of making trouble, but she was amazed by his self-control. Twelve years ago, in similar circumstances, he'd have let fly with both fists.

"Are you ready to go?" Jennifer asked almost as soon as the door had closed behind the two men.

"Yes, let's get out of here."

Lee Ann caught a movement out of the corner of her eye and realized everyone had turned to look at her, apparently waiting to see what her reaction would be.

"Your father doesn't have to worry, as long as I'm around," Chester said at Lee Ann's elbow. "I'll see you aren't bothered by the likes of him."

Lee Ann knew it would be best if she ignored the man's words and left as Ty and his friend had done. But she couldn't. After years of restraint, keeping her own opinion to herself in the face of everyone's bigotry, she just couldn't keep her mouth shut anymore.

Turning toward the burly man, she met his glance dauntlessly. "I do not now—" she spoke in carrying tones that reached every ear in the restaurant "—nor have I ever, needed your services as watchdog, Chester. If someone's company is disagreeable to me, I am perfectly capable of making it known to them."

With her eyes locked unflinchingly with his, she touched the napkin to her lips as though wiping something distasteful from them. Dropping it to the table, she picked up her purse and said, "Let's go, Jen, suddenly I feel nauseated."

Everyone's eyes followed the two women as they left the restaurant. And by the time she had stepped into the night air, Lee Ann really did feel sick, because she knew she hadn't begun to hear the end of this night's events.

Chapter 3

An hour later, Jennifer lay in a lounger beside the pool in Lee Ann's backyard, staring up at the night sky. After the scene in the restaurant, Lee Ann hadn't wanted to be alone and had asked Jennifer to spend the weekend.

"Did you call Mary and tell her I wouldn't be coming in in the morning?" she suddenly asked Lee Ann.

"Yes," Lee Ann answered, watching the water shimmer in the underwater lights like wind-rippled silk. "She said to tell you to relax and enjoy yourself."

Getting to her feet, she crossed the patio in long graceful strides, stopping at the small refrigerator behind the chrome-and-glass bar her father had recently had installed. He was drinking more and more of late and it was beginning to worry her.

"Want one?" she asked Jennifer, indicating the cold can in her hand.

The other woman looked back over her shoulder. "No, thanks... Have you decided what to do about your friend?"

Lee Ann shrugged. "I wish I had some idea why he's come back." She wasn't fooling herself that it had anything to do with seeing her again.

"What did you think of his friend?" Jennifer asked abruptly.

Lee Ann crossed the patio to her chair. "Who?"

"Ty's friend. His name is Cody Fargo. He's a rodeo clown."

"Well," Lee Ann gibed softly, lifting one shapely leg over the edge of the lounger and lowering herself onto it, "obviously you didn't have time this afternoon to find out much about him."

"Look, it's been a long time, okay?"

"I was only teasing," Lee Ann said, raising herself on one shoulder to stare at her friend's solemn profile. "And I think your Cody Fargo has a cute backside."

"When did you see his backside?" Jennifer asked, clearly surprised.

"I came back from lunch while he had you engaged in conversation. I didn't want to interrupt, so I went in the back way."

"You didn't have to do that."

Lee Ann shrugged again and settled back, lifting the can to her lips, then lowering it without taking a drink. Running one finger around the outer rim, she asked, "Jen, do you think Ty could have had anything to do with my brother's death?"

Jennifer glanced at her sharply. "I think you're asking the wrong person. And I thought you believed he was innocent."

"I do."

"Then I don't understand the question."

"It's just . . . my father—"

"I know what your father thinks. Look, do you think Ty would lie to you?" Jennifer asked.

Lee Ann thought for a moment, then said, "No."

"Then why don't you ask him?" Jennifer got to her feet and picked up her towel, apparently prepared to go inside. "And while you're at it, ask him why he's come back."

"I can't do that."

"Why not?"

Lee Ann hesitated. "I don't know."

"Well, you think about it. I'm going in to bed—" She hesitated, casting an inquiring look over her shoulder in her friend's direction. "Unless you want me to stay up with you."

"No, go ahead. I think I'll sit up a little while, maybe have another swim."

"Aren't you getting chilly?"

"No. I'm fine."

"Well, don't stay out here too long. Good night."

"Good night."

After Jennifer had gone, Lee Ann plunged into the pool and raced from one end to the other, until she was exhausted. Breathing heavily, she climbed from the water, picked up the thick beach towel and began to dry herself off.

The exercise had been just what she needed. For a short time, it had pushed everything from her mind.

But, now, sitting beneath the stars with the balmy night air whispering over her moist skin, her mind drifted back through the years to another night, much like this one, a few months after her fourteenth birthday.

She'd been late coming in from her ride. Her father didn't like tardiness at mealtime, so there hadn't been time for a shower. She'd wiped off, dusted herself with bath powder and quickly changed into a dress.

In the hallway, outside the dining room door, she'd stopped to smooth her hair. Her father and brother were already at dinner. But as she started to enter the room, her ears picked up the sound of her brother's voice and the mention of Ty's name.

It had been more than a year since her father had fired Ty Yancy. Ty had left the area, working in another county, but he'd recently returned to finish high school.

She hesitated, listening. Les was telling her father that he'd heard Ty was leaving town and this time it was for good.

Lee Ann couldn't hear her father's murmured reply over the uneven beating of her own heart. He couldn't be leaving!

All at once she became aware of Francine standing behind her. Lee Ann didn't know how long she'd been standing there, but apparently it had been long enough for the woman to wonder why Lee Ann was hesitating outside the door.

Lee Ann knew she had to go in to dinner and make a pretence of eating, or the housekeeper would be suggesting to Wade that something was wrong with his daughter. It seemed to her that of late Francine had taken an undue interest in everything Lee Ann did.

So she had entered the room, apologized for being late and choked down her food, answering politely when spoken to, and keeping her anxiety to herself. Later, after everyone had gone to bed, she knew what she had to do.

It hadn't taken her long to dress. She sneaked out of the house to the barn, where she saddled her horse in record time, and headed in search of Ty. Though her father had banned him from the ranch and refused to have his name spoken in his presence, Lee Ann still managed to see him. But, no one, not even Ty himself, knew about it.

Early on in their friendship, Lee Ann had learned that Ty was crazy to get into professional rodeo. She also knew that at night he practiced his roping and riding in the arena near the edge of town. It was less than ten miles across country to the arena, and she'd made a habit of sneaking out to watch the young man perform.

But tonight there was an urgency in her need to see him. She had to find out if it was true—if Ty was leaving town— because she was going to ask him to take her with him.

She knew there was no reason for him to, he'd never pretended she was anything special to him; he'd treated her as little more than a kid sister. But she hoped to appeal to him on the basis of the similarities in their backgrounds. They were both virtually without a family. Her father and brother certainly didn't notice, or care whether she was around. In her eyes, that made them kindred spirits.

Lee Ann's mind was on the journey's end and not the manner by which she'd achieve it, and that's why she didn't see the tree branch until it was almost too late. She managed to duck, thereby preventing any serious injury, but she was still knocked from her horse to the ground.

It was a long moment before she could get her thoughts together and take stock of her condition. She was pretty certain nothing was broken, and with the help of her horse, Pal, who had stayed by her side, she managed to get to her feet. A little dizzy at first, she climbed into the saddle and continued on her way.

A short time later, she caught sight of him. He was sitting astride his horse, Gray Sock, in the glow of one of the security lamps edging the arena. How handsome he looked, just like a cowboy from the Old West with his boots, cowboy hat and colorful bandanna.

From a hiding place behind the barrels at one end of the arena, she watched him place his pigging string—the short rope he'd use to tie the feet of a calf if he were actually going to lasso a live animal—between his teeth, holding his lariat in one hand and the horse's reins in the other. All at once, he put the spurs to his horse and thundered across the arena.

In the center of it, he'd placed a couple of wooden horses, one turned upside down atop the other. And as he drew near them, the hand holding the lariat lifted above his head. With a quick flick of his wrist, the rope sailed through the air, landing dead center around one of the wooden legs sticking up.

Jumping from Gray Sock almost before he'd come to a dead halt, Ty threw the wooden horse to the ground, flipped it over, jerked the pigging rope from between his lips and looped the rope around three of the wooden legs, then jumped up and stood back with his hands in the air and nodded to an imaginary crowd in the stands.

It was done so quickly that if she had blinked, she'd have missed the whole thing.

He was good—damn!—he was good.

Lee Ann watched as he rode, spurred, roped and tied his way through the next half hour. She couldn't help but admire his talent, but the thought of where that talent would lead him made her heart heavy.

Finally, it seemed he'd had enough. With the sweat sticking his shirt to his back, the black hair to his forehead and cheeks, he gathered his gear and mounted his horse, ready to leave. And still Lee Ann hadn't gotten up the courage to step from her hiding place and let him know she was there.

Dropping back to the ground, wondering how to keep him from leaving, while getting up the courage to say what she'd come to say, she was startled to hear his voice growl from the other side of the barrels, "All right, whoever you are, come on out. I know you're there."

Reluctantly, Lee Ann climbed to her feet and sidled into view.

"You! What the hell are you doing sneaking around after dark—and so far from home?"

Lee Ann swallowed, surprised at the concern in his voice. She wanted to speak, but the words were stuck at the back of her throat.

"Well," he demanded, "are you going to answer me?"

"I—I came to . . . I came—"

"Does your father know you're here?" he asked abruptly.

The guilt on her face gave her away. If her father found out she was here . . .

But Ty took that look of guilt to mean something altogether different. Muttering, "That bastard," he grabbed her by the shoulders and shook her roughly. "So, he sent you to spy on me. What are you thinking, out here alone at night, where anything could happen—"

As Lee Ann's thin form crumpled toward him, his tirade halted in midsentence. If he hadn't caught her in his arms, she'd have fallen to the ground.

Picking her up, he carried her toward one of the security lamps, knelt beneath it and laid her across one knee. Smoothing the thick brown curls back from her pale forehead, he saw the bruise and small stain of blood near her right temple.

Anger turned to concern as he assumed the blow to her head had been made by a human hand. Knowing what he knew of her father, he wouldn't put physical violence toward his own daughter past the man.

Clicking his tongue, he called to his horse and the beast moved toward him. Still holding Lee Ann in the crook of one arm, Ty removed the bandanna from around his neck and reached for the canteen looped over the pommel of the saddle.

A moment later, Lee Ann opened her eyes to the gentle touch of a damp cloth against her aching head.

"Are you okay?" Ty asked softly.

She'd never been this close to him before and her young heart cried with joy. He smelled like leather, horseflesh and sunshine. Closing her eyes abruptly, she drank it all in.

"Are you in pain?" the boy holding her asked quickly, noting a slight quiver at the corner of her full lips.

"Not now," she whispered hoarsely.

"Can you tell me what happened? How you got that bump on your head?"

"It was an accident," she whispered shakily, feeling his fingers probe gently at her hairline.

"I'll bet," he muttered beneath his breath. "Look, would you like me to take you someplace?"

Lee Ann's eyes popped open, filled with unbridled hope. "Where?" she breathed.

"I don't know." He shrugged. "Wherever you want to go."

"Do you mean it?" Lee Ann asked, grabbing his hand and placing it alongside her cheek. "Oh, thank you! I didn't think—I didn't dare to ask."

Ty looked surprised and a little embarrassed. Clearing his throat, he said, "Well, it isn't all that much. I just thought you might want me to take you someplace—maybe to a friend's house for tonight."

"Friend's house?" Lee Ann repeated in uncertainty. "Not with you?"

Ty stared into the soft gray eyes and felt something in his chest grow tight. He swallowed. Lee Ann's hand pressed his callused fingers tighter against her warm cheek and Ty's heart bumped against his ribs.

He'd never held a girl in his arms and it was causing a confusing reaction inside him. This was Lee Ann, the kid who had followed him around when he worked for her old man. She was little more than a child—

His eyes took in the gentle curves beneath the plaid shirt and he revised his thinking. But she was still too young for what his body was beginning to crave. His jaw hardened in determination. He couldn't do this.

Lee Ann didn't know what was running through his mind, but she sensed his sudden withdrawal. And she couldn't let that happen. Lifting herself toward him, she caught the side of his face with one hand and forced it toward hers.

"Please," she whispered, her warm breath flowing over his lips.

Ty wanted to pull back—he really wanted to for her sake—but not as badly as he longed for the touch of those soft lips. Just one touch.

They came together hesitantly, gently searching for something neither one was experienced enough to fully understand. Suddenly, he pulled back, his fingers twined in her silky hair, cupping her face to the light so he could see her expression.

She was so beautiful, his heart ached. No one in his whole life had ever been this close to him, so close he could feel her breast flattened against his chest. And if the bemused expression on her face was anything to go by, she was as caught up in what was happening between them as he was.

"Open your eyes," he whispered.

"Why?"

"Because I want you to know who's holding you like this."

"Silly," she said, giggling, opening her eyes as he'd asked. "Of course I know who it is."

"And you don't mind?" he asked hesitantly. "You don't mind who I am?"

Lee Ann's arms reached clear around him so that she could gather him against her, holding him now, too. "I . . . like who you are," she said shyly.

The word *love* hovered in the air between them, and though she was too afraid to say it, her eyes glowed with its warmth.

And then he was clasping her to him, their lips melded together. Hearts pounding riotously in their chests, they tried with hands and lips to convey to each other the depth of their awakening feelings.

When they drew apart to gaze at each other in silent wonder, eyes glowing, both had grown a little older in experience.

"I heard you were leaving town," Lee Ann gasped unsteadily, her fingers clutching at his young shoulders. And then, before he could make a reply, she urged, "Take me with you!"

A shutter slammed down over the almond-shaped eyes. The arms holding her grew tense. "I can't," he murmured without looking at her.

Lee Ann couldn't believe her ears. He had to! Hadn't he just—hadn't they just...?

"Why not?" she asked with dry lips.

"We're both underage. You're just a kid. Your father—"

Lee Ann pushed her way out of his arms and jumped to her feet. "My father! What has my father got to do with this...with us?"

Ty was confused by her quick change of emotion and couldn't keep up with her. "He'd have me put in jail," he answered quickly, getting to his feet to face her squarely.

"Not if he didn't find us—"

"But he would," Ty interrupted. "And I'd go to jail—if he didn't kill me first. Besides," he added after a slight hesitation, "like I said, you're just a kid."

That galled Lee Ann to the quick. "I'm not a kid! And you're not so old yourself," she added childishly.

"Old enough to know we wouldn't make it. You belong here with your family. And I—" He shrugged. "I don't know where I belong, but it ain't here."

She could see by the dogged expression moving over his face that nothing she said was going to change his mind. He was leaving and he was leaving alone.

"I'll tell my father," she blurted out rashly.

Ty stiffened. "You'll tell your father *what?*"

"I'll tell him you—we—I'll say you—" She couldn't go on. What she had in mind to say was a lie and she knew it. She'd never tell her father anything about tonight. Just as certainly as she'd never do anything to hurt the boy standing before her.

But it seemed he didn't realize that. The icy look creeping into his eyes made her suddenly feel sick to her stomach.

"So that's what this is all about." Face filled with contempt, he said, "I thought you were different from your father and brother—from the whole town. I guess I was wrong."

Moving toward his horse, he mounted in one deft motion. "Go on home to your father, tell him anything you want about me. I'm through with this place... Oh, and while you're at it, tell him his little scheme would *never* have worked. I'm not into molesting children!"

His shape was already disappearing in the darkness when Lee Ann finally moved. She ran after him, calling, "I didn't mean it! Ty, I didn't mean it! I would never tell him anything that would get you into trouble!"

She didn't know if he heard her. The next day he was gone.

After he'd left, at every opportunity, she listened avidly to the gossip around town, hoping to catch some news about him. But it wasn't long before the people of Rainville seemed to have forgotten him.

Finally, she'd taken her courage in hand and gone to see his uncle. There she'd heard all about how he'd joined the rodeo circuit and was on the road all the time.

And when her father found out about her visits to the Yancy ranch, he'd exploded in fury. That was the first and only time she could ever remember him striking her.

Time passed and Ty's letters to his uncle became fewer and fewer. Lee Ann knew, because she liked the old man and had refused to let her father's anger keep her from seeing him.

When Nathan Yancy took sick, she'd written to Ty at the old man's request to tell him the ranch was his. Before she could mail the letter, the old man had died and she'd added a postscript telling Ty the time and place of the funeral. But

Ty hadn't shown up and the old man was buried with no one in attendance but herself, the undertaker and the minister.

After that, for a while, she'd come close to hating Ty. It seemed he'd shaken the dust of the town off his feet and nothing, not even the death of the man who'd given him a home, was going to bring him back.

Anger turned to hurt and the hurt to bitterness. She convinced herself that what she'd felt for him had been nothing more than a childish crush and she'd gotten on with her life.

Twelve years ago he'd run from her. But this time it had been she who'd done the running. She knew that whatever was between them would never be over, until there was peace between them.

Jennifer was right. She needed to see him and talk to him. She needed to tell him what she'd tried to tell him that night so long ago. She would never side with her father against him.

As much as she craved her father's love, Lee Ann could never agree with him that Ty was a cold-blooded killer. She'd seen blood in his eye many times when they were younger and he'd been in a temper. But to kill in cold blood? Again, no, she had *never* believed in Ty's guilt.

Maybe they could put the past aside and become friends. They'd once had the makings of a pretty good friendship.

How that friendship would develop, with her father's potent hostility a strong force between them, and her own leftover adolescent feelings to contend with, she didn't know.

In any case, Ty needed to know her father's anger hadn't faded since her brother's death. She had to tell him it wouldn't be prudent for him to be around when the man returned home.

Chapter 4

"What the hell was that all about back there?" Cody broke the silence that had lasted for most of the ride.

Ty shrugged and kept staring out the window on his side of the truck. Neither man had mentioned the scene until now.

They'd left the Horseshoe Restaurant and driven fifty miles to Bozeman before finding another place to eat. And though Ty's appetite had left him, Cody had put away a hefty meal.

"Fletch Reid took the Allentown rodeo last month," Cody said. "He shaved one-tenth of a second off his calf roping and beat Red Hodges for the prize money in that one. Everyone was sure Curley Sanchez had him on the bull riding, but Curley got thrown before the buzzer sounded."

His hands tightened on the steering wheel and when he spoke again, a note of sadness had crept into his voice. "Tom Pope bought it in Texas last week."

Ty's head swiveled toward the other man. "What happened?"

"Sweetwater threw him out the back door and he landed on his head. Broken neck."

Sweetwater was a bronc known in rodeo circles for his unpredictable behavior. No one ever knew what he was going to do. One time he'd come straight out of the chute and run you around the arena, while trying to brush you off against the fence. Another time he'd jump straight up in the air and come down stiff-legged, again and again, until the rider felt as if he were on a pogo stick, and the next time it would be something different.

In the case of Tom Pope, Sweetwater had reared up onto his hind legs and thrown the cowboy over his rump. Ty had had his turn on Sweetwater a couple of years ago and he'd ended up in the hospital with three fractured ribs and a broken collarbone.

Tom had been one of the few men Ty was able to call friend and know it meant something. "Sorry to hear about Tom," he said gruffly. "Where's his wife?"

"She took the kids and went back to Arkansas to her folks. She's taking it real hard. She was never really a part of the game."

Ty understood what Cody meant. The men and women who followed the rodeo circuit were one big family. And if you were a part of it, whatever you needed was yours for the asking.

If you needed to be staked to pay entrance fees, someone would stake you, knowing he might never see that money again, but knowing, too, that if you made it big, not only would he get his money back, but if he was ever down on his luck, you'd be there with a helping hand.

"Sorry to hear about Tom," Ty repeated softly, returning his glance to the window and the black night outside.

"Well, that's not why I'm here. I came to give you something."

Ty stiffened. While it was true others borrowed from their friends, he'd made it a rule to accept nothing from anyone.

He'd given to others, but he didn't take. And that's one of the reasons *he'd* never quite fit in with the crowd. The other cowboys were uncomfortable about asking something from someone who never asked in return.

"Don't get your dander up," Cody continued as they bumped down the lane to Ty's ranch and stopped near the abandoned house. "I didn't come here to offer you money."

Reaching behind, Cody lifted something from the back and set it on the seat between them. He switched on the overhead light and waited for the man beside him to say something.

Ty stared down at the familiar canvas bag. After a long moment, he opened it and looked inside. It held the rigging he'd used on his last ride, the ride that had almost cost him his life.

"Where did you get this?"

"I got it from Shorty Sims. And if you look in the bottom, you'll find something mighty interesting."

Ty dug deep and pulled out the length of double-braided half-inch manila-grass rope. Most cowboys used the newer synthetic ropes made of nylon. But Ty had learned his roping and riding from his uncle, and Nathan Yancy had preferred the old-style ropes. So that's what Ty used. And every time he climbed aboard a horse or bull, the feel of it reminded him of the man who'd raised him.

He pulled all twelve feet of the rope from the bag, letting it slide through his fingers, feeling the rough braid taper to a narrow three-eighths of an inch thickness. But something was missing. The bell normally attached to the bull rope by an adjustable bowline knot, put there to make the bull buck harder and to provide enough weight to pull the rope from the bull after the rider had let go of it, was missing.

Cody took hold of the ends of the rope and held them up for his friend's inspection. "What do you think?" he asked musingly. "Cut with a knife?"

Ty examined the ends closely. It was obvious the rope had been cut nearly all the way through, so that the weight and friction of the ride would snap it in two. Someone had wanted him to take a fall.

"Where did you get this?"

Cody rubbed his left ear between his index finger and thumb, a habit he had whenever he was thinking things over. "It's kind of a complicated story."

"I'm listening."

"Well, I heard something that day, just a little while before your ride, that stuck in my mind. And later, after you were thrown, it came back to me."

"What did you hear?"

"I heard a man telling someone on the telephone outside the rest rooms that he'd taken care of things. His actual words were, 'The meat is on the hoof and it won't be long until it's ground beef.' And then he said something about not worrying about that, he'd stash the grass in the trash."

"And you understood that?" Ty asked skeptically.

"Not at the time. Obviously, it was a code. But later, after your fall, it came back to me while I was asking around about your rope. Not too many cowboys use the grass ropes anymore, so yours was easy to spot. But no one seemed to know what had happened to it.

"A few days later, while you were in the hospital, I talked to Shorty Sims to see if your rope had ever turned up. You know Shorty, he always seems to know where things have gotten to. He gave me your bag. And then, before I could leave, he told me a strange story.

"He said that after the rodeo had ended, he'd been behind the stock pens looking for his young nephew, when he spotted someone stuffing something into one of the trash cans. He said he wouldn't have thought too much about it, but the guy was acting so suspicious that he decided to see what he was getting rid of.

"He waited around until the guy left and then he searched through the can—" Cody nodded toward the rope in Ty's hands. "That's what he found. He said he didn't know what to do with it. So he just hung on to it.

"He said there were only two cowboys he knew right off-hand that used that kind of rope, and one of them was dead."

"Les Newley," Ty said slowly.

Cody nodded. "And you."

"Seems to me it would have been smarter for the man who put it in the trash can to have taken it with him," Ty commented.

"Yeah, well, maybe he isn't too bright. Or maybe he figured he had no reason to worry about it. Who'd suspect someone of cutting your rope?"

Ty gave him a sharp glance. "What you really mean is, who'd care?"

"No, that isn't what I meant."

"Didn't Shorty look at the damned rope and see that it had been cut?"

Cody rubbed his ear. "Shorty is getting on in years. You know how he likes to steer clear of anything controversial."

A few years back, Shorty had been in a lot of trouble because he took the wrong side in an argument. It had cost him some stiff fines from the Professional Rodeo Cowboy's Association, but most importantly it had cost him his wife.

Ty stuffed the rope back inside the bag and climbed out of the truck. Well, at least this explained the feeling he'd had that day that something had suddenly let go.

"What the hell!" Cody followed him from the truck. "Is that all—you're just going to walk away?"

Ty kept on walking, heading to the barn. Cody wasn't far behind. As Ty entered the building and dropped the bag to the ground, his friend caught up with him.

Ty faced him slowly. "What do you want me to do? Go to the cops? They think I snuffed Les. They're going to take one look at this rope and laugh in my face. How are they supposed to know I didn't cut the damned thing myself?''

"I'll tell them what I heard. I'll tell them to talk to Shorty.''

Ty snorted. "What you heard is a lot of gibberish. So *you* think it had something to do with my fall—what makes you think anyone else will?

"Can you prove the telephone conversation even took place? Did anyone else hear it? Do you know who the man was talking to?'' Ty fired the questions at him in much the same manner a police detective might do and Cody looked just as confused as if Ty were the real thing.

"No to all three questions,'' Cody answered reluctantly.

"You don't even know if the man who put the rope in the can was the same one on the telephone.''

"Yes, I do. Shorty described him to me. It was the same man, I'd stake my life on it.''

"And as far as Shorty Sims goes . . .'' Ty continued as though the other man hadn't spoken, letting his words trail off. They both knew that if the older man had been willing to do something about what he'd found, he'd have done it at the time.

Ty stuffed his hands into his back pockets. "Look, I appreciate what you're trying to do. But I think it's too late. We don't know who cut the rope and we don't know why. Maybe he just wanted to see that I got a little roughed up—''

"Roughed up! Man, you almost died.''

Ty shrugged. "Maybe it was just meant to scare me. If it was meant to kill me, it failed. I'm still walking around, ain't I, so just let it be.''

"It failed that time,'' Cody said heatedly, watching Ty turn to take a lantern from a nail on the wall. "But what about the next time?''

"How do you know there's going to be a next time?''

"Do you know there won't?''

Ty lit the lantern and placed it on the floor. Lowering himself to his knees, he began to spread his bedroll over the hay.

"You think it was one of Les's friends, don't you?" Cody asked abruptly. "Someone just wanting to get even because they think you had something to do with his death."

Ty froze, his eyes on the bedding. "Leave it alone," he muttered softly, a hint of warning in his voice.

"I won't, damn it! Haven't you yet realized that this is how Les died? It's because his rope was cut the same way, that they accused you of his murder."

Ty looked up at him. "So?"

"So what if there's some crazy out there with a hate on for cowboys? Maybe you and Les were just the first in a long list."

Ty's glance hardened. "What makes you so sure I didn't kill Les? Everyone else thinks I did."

"Did you?" Cody asked without expression, his blue eyes locked with the hazel.

"No." Ty sat back on his haunches and shook his head. "No, I didn't kill him. Not that there weren't many times, when we were growing up, that I would have liked to," he said half-seriously.

Cody grinned. "That doesn't count. There were more than a few times, when my kid sister and I were growing up, that I wanted to strangle her, but I managed to restrain myself."

A shadow passed over Ty's face, gone in an instant. Once upon a time, he had wanted to strangle a girl who'd been like a kid sister to him. "Let's get some sleep. I'm beat."

"Hello?" Lee Ann held the phone to her ear without opening her eyes.

"That you, chicken?"

Her father's gruff voice rumbled in her ear. She gave a start and her eyes opened wide. He'd started calling her chicken a few months after Les had died, referring to her being the lone chick in the nest. Before that, when she was growing up, he'd mostly referred to her as girl. A time or two, she'd wondered if it was because he simply couldn't remember her name.

"Y-yes," she answered hesitantly, "it's me. Where are you?"

"I'm still in Mexico City. How are things on the ranch?"

"Fine."

Surprised at the unexpectedness of the call, she didn't know what to say. Her father came and went as he pleased. Mostly, he left her notes telling her of his comings and goings, but he rarely phoned.

"The men are all out on the range," she offered, "but Smokey sends word about once a week that things are going fine."

"Good, good. And what about the store, having any trouble there?"

"The store is fine."

"Good. No problems at all—not afraid to stay on the ranch by yourself?" he asked mockingly.

"I'm not alone. Jennifer is staying the weekend with me."

"That's good." He laughed. "Tell her I said hello and that I'm glad she's there to keep you safe till I return."

"I'll do that." Lee Ann murmured dryly. "Was there something else?" she asked when he didn't immediately hang up.

"No," he answered after a short pause. "Nothing else. Just don't do anything I wouldn't do," he said softly and the line went suddenly dead.

"Goodbye," Lee Ann murmured into dead space.

Replacing the receiver with a frown, she lay back against her pillow and stared up at the ceiling. What had all that been about?

A sudden chill moved through her. She'd seen her father angry and it wasn't a sight she cared for. He could be both callous and cruel at the best of times, but when angry, he was deadly. The whole town had been rocked by his fury a year ago, when he'd learned Ty had been released from custody after his son's death.

Did he know Ty was back? If so, why hadn't he mentioned it?

Lee Ann knew with a certainty that if Ty were still around when her father returned, there would be hell to pay. The half-formed plan she'd made last night to visit his ranch again, solidified. She had to warn him that her father's anger over Ty's guilt had become an obsession.

Ty wasn't a fool and she couldn't believe that he'd deliberately seek trouble with her father. If the past were anything to go by, he'd do just the opposite and run.

Later that morning, after breakfast with Jennifer on the patio, Lee Ann left her friend happily writing letters home, to load some things into the store's delivery truck. One of her customers living in the mountains outside of town was laid up with a broken leg. Lee Ann had promised to deliver some craft supplies the woman needed.

After the delivery, Lee Ann headed toward Broken Heart Ranch. She was apprehensive about seeing Ty again after last night's fiasco at the restaurant. What must he have thought of her for sitting there and letting Chester Kittridge speak to him the way he'd done?

Probably no more than he'd thought about her running from him, like a scared rabbit, the evening she'd found him in the barn. But, maybe this visit would clear things up between them. The more she thought about it, the more she decided they could be friends.

Her father wouldn't like it, but then, it was time she stood up for the things she wanted and believed in. Maybe it had been a mistake to return home after college. She wasn't that far from being thirty years old, maybe it was simply time she lived on her own.

Even though she thought it best for Ty to leave town before her father returned home, that didn't mean she wouldn't be willing to continue with their friendship. She'd just let her father learn about it gradually, once he'd put aside his prejudice about Ty.

It seemed that all her life she had either given in to what her father wanted, or simply kept her opinions to herself, letting him assume what he wanted about how she felt. And it had made precious little difference to their relationship. Maybe what he needed was something to shake him up and make him see her as a person in her own right.

At the crossroads to town, a blue king-cab pickup crossed the road in front of her and turned toward town. She recognized it as the truck she'd seen parked out front of the store the day Ty's friend had come asking about him. She was relieved to know he wouldn't be around when she faced Ty.

The house looked even worse in daylight than she remembered. She took a quick look inside, careful not to fall through any of the holes in the porch, and then turned toward the barn.

Everything there looked as it had on her last visit, except for the two bedrolls stowed in a corner near the door. Ty was nowhere in sight.

Lee Ann moved behind the barn, heading down a path that had once been well-worn and still showed traces of the passage of many feet, despite its being overrun with buckbrush and serviceberry. She felt the sun on her bare shoulders and glanced up at the sky. It was a beautiful day. A few puffy white clouds floated in the blue sky and the scent of ponderosa pine hung thick in the air.

She wished things were already different. That she was on her way to see Ty because they were friends.

Picking her way through a yellow-and-orange field of woolly sunflowers and devil's paintbrush, she climbed a rocky hill, dodging trees and tall leafy ferns, then stood

staring at the stream down below. It formed a deep pool
where it spilled out of the mountains in a huge waterfall,
before narrowing again and making its way across the valley to disappear in the mountains on the other side.

Shading her eyes with one hand, she scanned the vicinity, seeing only water, rocks and trees. She was about to give
up and head toward the house and barn when something
drew her eyes to the falls.

He was there, partially hidden from view by the cascad-
ing water, and he appeared to be bathing. Transfixed by the
glimmer of dusky skin glimpsed though the sun-sparkled
water, she stood riveted to the spot. Her eyes following every
movement he made as he lathered his face, neck and shoulders, with a large bar of white soap.

All at once he ducked beneath the water. And when he
bobbed to the surface, he blew the water off his face and
shook back his black hair. And then he lathered it, scrub-
bing his head hard with his fingernails before ducking beneath the water again.

Lee Ann panicked for an instant when he didn't immediately come to the surface, but she caught sight of him a
moment later standing beneath the falls. That's when she
realized he was ready to get out of the water.

Whirling suddenly, feeling like a voyeur, she stumbled
back the way she'd come. Except she couldn't remember
exactly which path she'd taken to the waterfall, and she
couldn't see the barn or house from where she stood. Before she could get her bearings, she heard the familiar sound
of a whistle and Ty stepped onto the path directly in front
of her.

It's hard to say which one was more surprised. Lee Ann
was so flustered at the sight of him, standing in the middle
of the trail with a wet towel draped around his middle, that
she couldn't speak. Did he suspect that she'd seen him
bathing?

Giving her a slight nod of greeting, Ty murmured, "It's been a long time." Apparently, he'd chosen to discount her first visit and the scene in the restaurant last night.

Lee Ann straightened her shoulders and lifted her head. If he could be so generous, then it would make what she'd come to say a lot easier.

"Why did you never write me?" She found her mouth forming words she hadn't meant to say. "I thought we were friends."

The pleasant expression on his face turned guarded. "Did you?"

"Weren't we?"

He shrugged.

Stung by his careless manner, Lee Ann demanded, "Why have you come back?"

Narrowing his tawny eyes, he asked insolently, "Why not?"

Her irritation grew. "As you may have guessed, you aren't a very popular person around these parts."

Ty grinned without humor. "So what else is new?"

"You always encouraged dislike, didn't you?" she challenged. "Why? Was it easier to use your fists than your wits?"

The grin on his face disappeared. "I didn't have to encourage it. It grew out of the very ground I walked upon."

"You picked fights with my brother—I saw you."

A cold light silvered the hazel eyes. "I didn't have to pick fights with your brother. He hated my guts from the moment he laid eyes on me." Taking a threatening step closer, he asked, "Is that what this visit is all about? Did you come to accuse me of murdering your brother?"

Intimidated by his nearness, she took a halting step backward. "I came to tell you, you have to leave here—"

"You're too late," he interrupted. "I already got that message last night...remember?"

"My father—"

Again he interrupted her. "I don't care about your father. If he has anything to say to me, let him say it to my face." He looked her up and down insolently. "Instead of sending his—little girl—to do his dirty work for him."

The implication was clear. He still thought her father had sent her to him that night at the arena so many years ago.

"Look, let's put the past behind us." Lee Ann tried to speak reasonably. It would defeat her purpose in being there if she were to fight with him. "There were certain... misunderstandings between us back then. But we were a lot younger. We're both adults now, so let's act like adults.

"I came here to tell you it isn't safe for you to be here. The townspeople hold you responsible for my brother's death— whether you had anything to do with it or not," she added quickly. "And my father—"

"Damn your father! Damn being reasonable! And damn you!" Ty growled, grabbing her bare shoulders.

"Take your hands off me!" She jerked against his hold, suddenly frightened of his anger. "I came here out of consideration—"

"Ha!" Ty mocked. "When did a Newley ever know the meaning of the word? Oh, no, wait, I suppose it was *consideration* that made you take pity on the poor dirty half-breed who worked for your father, and that's why you befriended him.

"Or was it so you could keep an eye on him for your old man? Was he afraid I'd steal the family silver?"

His grip tightened as he leaned closer. "I'm sure it was *consideration* on your father's part," he taunted, "when he hired me so he could try to steal my uncle's ranch out from under him—"

"That's a lie!" Lee Ann shouted. Her father was a hard man, but he wasn't a thief. "My father didn't have to steal anything from you. He could have bought and sold you any day of the week."

Pulling her close, so their noses were almost touching, Ty muttered through clenched teeth, "Your father is a liar and a cheat. He thinks he can buy anything! Well, you can tell him I'm not for sale!"

"Yes, you are," Lee Ann contradicted scornfully. "You sold your soul to rodeo and nothing else means anything to you. Not even your uncle—"

"My uncle's dead!"

"I know that! And you didn't even think enough of him to attend his funeral. You don't give a damn about anybody or anything—except yourself—and your *damned rodeo!*"

Ty pushed her away from him, wanting her out of his sight.

Lee Ann stumbled, lost her footing and started to go down.

At the last possible instant, Ty came to her rescue. Catching her beneath the arms, he hauled her upright. In the process, his towel became loosened. And though Lee Ann was now in no danger of falling—the towel did.

Lee Ann caught the flutter of blue out of the corner of her eyes and it proved beyond her control to halt the spontaneous downward slant of her glance. But it progressed only as far as the puckered scars crisscrossing the tight muscles of Ty's abdomen.

Her eyes widened in horror. And then she was running. Again, she was running away from him as fast as her legs would carry her.

"Is that the usual reaction you get when you take your clothes off in front of a woman?"

Ty jerked his head to the left and met Cody's sardonic expression. "What are you doing here? I thought you went to town to make a few calls."

"I did." Bending forward, he picked up the towel and handed it to Ty. "I struck out."

"With everyone?" Ty asked as he wrenched the towel around his lean hips and cinched it at his waist.

"Your friend, Wade Newley, is a very powerful man."

"Don't call him that!" Ty growled, leading the way down the path.

Cody gave him a sidelong glance. "What—powerful?"

"My friend—he was *never* my friend."

"Look, you can always use my horses," Cody offered.

"Your horses are saddle horses. What good are they going to do me, when it comes to bronc riding or bull riding? I'm way past the barrel and hay stage of the game," he said, referring to the makeshift items he'd been using for practice since his return.

"I need some real muscle and bone between my legs to help me get these muscles toughened up." He slammed an impatient fist against his chest and lengthened his stride, putting distance between himself and the other man.

Chapter 5

Jennifer glanced up from the book she was reading as Lee Ann strode into the sun room and flopped down on a chair. "What's wrong?"

Lee Ann lifted her feet onto the padded footrest matching the fan-backed chair and brushed a stray curl off her forehead. "I blew it," she muttered angrily.

"Blew what?"

"I went to see Ty, like you suggested last night. I was going to warn him about Dad's obsession with his guilt—Dad called early this morning." She inserted without taking a breath. "I was going to tell Ty it would be better if he wasn't here when Dad returned—he's coming back before long. He never stays away more than three months at a time and he's been gone nine weeks."

"Yes, so what happened? How did you blow it?"

"I couldn't find Ty at the house or barn, so I went looking for him on the ranch. God, what a fool I made of myself." She tried to explain, "It's just that he wasn't wearing anything—"

"What?" Jennifer asked in surprise.

"He was wearing a towel," Lee Ann said hastily. "But I couldn't remember which way I'd come—and then he was just there!" She gestured with both hands to the space in front of her.

"I didn't know what to say and I said something stupid. Then he got mad and lost his towel and I saw those awful scars—"

"Whoa! Wait a minute." Jennifer sat up and dropped her feet to the floor. "What scars? And what do you mean, he lost his towel?"

Lee Ann jumped up and paced the floor, stopping to remove a dead leaf from one of the many hanging plants adorning the glass-enclosed side of the room.

"I don't think I want to talk about this right now," she answered in a quieter voice. Moving toward the door, she stopped abruptly and said, "Jen, call Mary and see if she can work next week. I need some time off."

"But, I can take over."

"No. I want you to come with me. If you want to, that is."

"Where are we going?"

"To the mountains. I need to think things through."

"So, again I'm the bad guy," Ty muttered, sipping from a steaming cup of black coffee as he leaned against the wall of the barn.

"What do you mean?" Cody asked.

"Out there. She came onto my property," he emphasized, "to tell me I had to leave before her father gets back, and she made out as though she was doing me a favor."

"I take it that was Les's sister."

"Yeah. That's her, all right."

"Maybe she really thought she was doing you a good turn. Her father appears to hate your guts."

"That he does, but the feeling is mutual."

"Want to talk about it?"

"No." Ty got to his feet and threw the coffee on the ground outside the barn door. "Your offer to use your horses still good?"

"Sure."

"Good. Let's go get them saddled."

"Where are we going?"

"When I was growing up, there was a herd of wild horses living in the mountains. I figured we'd take a ride up there and see if we could round up a few to practice on."

An hour later, they were saddled up and heading toward the mountains. They'd been riding single file, Cody behind, but as the trail widened, he moved up to join his friend.

"You given any more thought to what I suggested a while ago?" he asked.

Ty shot him a look from beneath the rim of his black felt hat, but didn't answer.

"None of this is going to go away. You can't walk away from this one, my friend. You're going to have to find the culprit responsible for Les's death and the attempt on your own life and hand him over to the law, if you want it to end."

"What the hell do you know about it?" Ty asked dangerously.

"I know there's something between you and Les Newley's sister," Cody challenged the other man. "And I know you won't do a damned thing about it, 'cause you're too busy running away from the real things in life and chasing after the myth."

"The myth being?"

"The World Championship Rodeo. It's the only thing that really matters to you."

His friend's words came too close to mirroring what Lee Ann had said earlier. Anger raced through him. "You're full of it! Just because you weren't good enough and gave up riding to paint yourself up like some fool and mop up after the real cowboys, don't come down on me.''

Cody stared at him unblinkingly. Without a word, he dropped back to ride single file.

Ty bit down hard on his inner jaw to keep from saying any more. He'd said enough. He'd probably just killed their friendship with his runaway mouth.

And Cody had been the one close friend he'd ever made. No, that wasn't quite true. He was the *second* real friend he'd ever made. Lee Ann Newley had been his first—before he'd run her off, too.

''Are we there yet?'' Jennifer asked, bringing her mount up alongside Lee Ann's. They'd been riding since six that morning, only stopping for a quick meal at lunchtime. Whatever was eating at Lee Ann had its teeth firmly planted.

''Just a little farther,'' Lee Ann answered, nudging her horse into a gentle gallop. ''We're almost there.''

Two hours later, they dismounted and looked around at the box canyon enclosing them on three sides. Trees rimmed the canyon walls. The floor was a colorful patchwork quilt of wildflowers. A slight overhang at the back gave them plenty of shade from the hot summer sun. They had all the fresh water they needed from the narrow stream meandering through the entrance, curving toward the sheer rock walls before widening into a small clear pool at their feet. It was the perfect place for a camp.

''It's beautiful,'' Jennifer breathed. ''How in the world did you ever find this place?''

Lee Ann smiled. She hadn't found it, Ty had. The canyon was on Yancy land. Technically, she supposed they were trespassing. But in these parts, unless it involved strangers, or stealing, there was no such thing as trespassing. One man's property flowed into another's, and though the boundaries were clearly marked on paper, no one—not even her father—enforced them against his neighbor.

"Let's set up camp," Lee Ann suggested, "and then we can go exploring."

They spent the afternoon checking out the area. By the time they returned to camp, they'd spotted a bighorn sheep, a white doe and a fawn, a small herd of wild horses, and had gathered an armload of colorful wildflowers.

"Phew!" Jennifer removed her wide-brimmed straw hat and wiped the back of her hand across her gritty forehead. "What I wouldn't give for a dip in your pool."

All afternoon long, Lee Ann had been keeping an eye on the sky to the west. Removing her own hat and swinging it by the chin strap, she headed toward the tent.

"If those clouds are any indication, you won't need the pool to get wet."

"What do you mean?"

"I'd say from the looks of that sky, we're in for some rain."

Her words proved to be prophetic. By ten o'clock that night, the ground was soaked and the small clear stream had widened by a good three feet.

"Are we safe here?" Jennifer asked nervously from her side of the tent, hearing the crack of thunder and the pistol-shot sound of the rain.

"Don't worry, we're safe," Lee Ann assured her. "If we have to, we can always move to higher ground."

The rain became an even patter that lulled them to sleep. Lee Ann was lying on her stomach, dead to the world, when all at once she gave a jerk and opened blurry eyes. Raising her head, she cocked an ear and listened intently. She'd thought—there it was again—a sound that didn't belong!

Sliding from the blanket, she reached for her jeans and pulled them on. What she'd heard had sounded like someone calling for help.

Because of Jennifer's nervousness, Lee Ann had left the lantern on. And though it seemed unlikely that someone could have seen the light from the entrance to the canyon—it appeared someone was out there.

Lee Ann picked up the lantern and bent to tap Jennifer on the shoulder, before moving toward the entrance to the tent.

"What is it?" Jennifer asked, sitting up and rubbing her hands over her eyes.

"There's someone out there. They may be in trouble."

Lee Ann dashed from the tent, leaving Jennifer to fumble in the dark for her own jeans.

Holding the lantern aloft, Lee Ann peered through the darkness and could just make out a form moving toward her. Jennifer joined her a moment later, holding a jacket over both their heads to protect them from the steady downpour.

"It looks like one person on foot," she commented, raising her voice above the rain to be heard.

"No," Lee Ann contradicted, squinting through darkness and rain. "Two people—one carrying the other. Come on, it looks like someone might be hurt."

The two women made their way toward the stream, where the man had halted with his burden. "Help me," he shouted. "He's got a bad lump on his head."

"Bring him up here," Lee Ann directed, "and get him in the tent out of the rain."

A few minutes later, Ty straightened away from Cody's silent figure and looked up at Lee Ann. "What do you think?" he asked, a note of anxiety creeping into his voice. "Is it serious?"

Jennifer was busily wiping the blood from a cut near the crown of the unconscious man's head. The water in the small metal basin was already stained a dark red.

Lee Ann motioned for Ty to follow her. "He may be able to hear us," she cautioned in a soft voice. "I read somewhere that unconscious people are able to hear what's said in their presence."

Once outside, she said, "I don't know how bad it is. I do know that head wounds bleed an awful lot, 'cause I've seen plenty around the ranch. I think we should get him to a doctor as quickly as possible."

"So do I. Damn it!" he muttered, slapping the side of his leg with a doubled fist, staring into the rain.

"I don't think we should try to move him in the dark," Lee Ann murmured, conscious of his nearness and trying to act as though it had no effect on her. "With all the rain we've had tonight, it will be hard to determine which streams are swollen and where they're impassable."

"I agree," Ty concurred. "We have to wait until daylight."

"What happened?" Lee Ann wanted to keep the conversation going, because she didn't think she'd be able to go on standing this close to him in the dark if they weren't talking.

"I'm not sure," Ty said. "We were looking for a place to make camp. The storm blew up—I should have spotted it before it hit, but I didn't. The thunder made the horses skittish. And when lightning struck a tree near Cody's horse, the animal reared up and threw him.

"I dismounted to try to get hold of the horse's reins and make sure Cody was all right. The lightning was flashing all around us by then and my horse pulled away. The next thing I knew, both horses had taken off."

He shook his head in exasperation. "Everything we had with us was on the animals. Cody was unconscious and bleeding like a stuck pig, so I tied a makeshift bandage around his head and headed back toward the ranch."

For the first time since he'd begun speaking, he glanced down at the woman at his side. "I was surprised to see a light way out here. At first I thought it was my imagination."

Something in his voice made her lift her chin and say, "I know we're trespassing—"

"I didn't mean it that way," he interrupted, his voice an octave lower. "I'm glad you were here."

Lee Ann shifted uncomfortably. "I think I'd better go take a look at the horses."

Ty stuck his head into the tent to ask if there was any change in Cody's condition and Jennifer shook her head. "Don't worry," she told him, meeting his worried glance, "if there is, I'll let you know."

At the base of the mountain, a stone overhang provided shelter from the storm. It was there that Lee Ann had secured the horses for the night.

"Why did you come to the ranch the other night?"

Lee Ann stiffened. She should have guessed that he'd follow her.

"It was a spur-of-the-moment decision," she answered honestly, rubbing a gentling hand over her mount.

"For what purpose?" he asked, moving up behind her.

"I wanted to talk to you," she admitted softly.

"About what?"

Lee Ann tried to shrug, but the small space was crowded with the horses, herself and the man standing too close behind her. Stepping away from him, she pressed her back against the damp rock.

The rain had ceased and the moon chose this moment to make an appearance. Still, in the shadow of the rock, Lee Ann could barely make out her companion's stern features.

She wondered if he remembered the last time they'd stood on this spot, both their backs pressed against the cool rock, hiding from her brother. It had started out as a lark, but when her brother had found them, it had ended in one of the many fights Les and Ty were always getting into. She'd never understood their animosity toward each other.

Thrusting the memory aside, Lee Ann edged toward the opening.

"Ask me," Ty said abruptly.

Lee Ann jumped. "W-what?"

"Ask me what you came to ask the other night, and didn't."

"Ah, no, it doesn't matter." Propelling herself away from the wall, she tried to scoot past him.

Ty caught her wrist and held her. "Doesn't matter? Or are you afraid to ask it—" his voice grew softer, sending chills down her spine *"—alone in the dark with a murderer?"*

Lee Ann gasped and tried to wrench her arm from his grip, but he held on, drawing her closer.

"That *is* what you came to ask, isn't it, if I killed your brother?"

"Let me go."

"No, not until I get an answer. Why are you so eager to get away? Are you afraid of me?" he taunted.

"Don't be ridiculous," Lee Ann sputtered, searching for a logical reason for them to get back to camp. "I just think we should get back and see how your friend is doing."

Twisting her toward him, her arm now behind her back, making her helpless against him, he brushed a strand of her hair from one damp cheek. "I think he's in capable hands for the time being. Did you tell your father?"

Lee Ann froze. "Tell him what?" she asked, pretending she didn't understand.

"Did you tell him I took advantage of you that night? Is that why he's so determined to make me a murderer in everyone's eyes?"

So that's what he thought! "No," she denied hotly. "I didn't tell him anything."

"I don't believe you." But he did. And maybe that was only because suddenly he wanted to. "Do you think I'm a murderer?" he asked softly.

They were so close, they breathed the same air. "Well," he asked, "do you?"

The fingers of Lee Ann's free hand touched his jeans, and as though they had a will of their own, they crawled slowly up his side to his waist. Her insides were churning. The heat from his body was burning her. Lifting her lips toward his, she whispered, "Do I what?"

Ty let go of her wrist to cup her face with both hands. "Do you want me to kiss you?" he said hoarsely.

She'd waited so long. "Yes . . ."

Ty's mouth took the word from her lips. Dragging her against him, he pressed her back against the mountain, his hips grinding into hers. Fingers threaded into the damp curls at the sides of her face, he deepened the kiss, moving his lips back and forth over hers, the blood pounding through his veins.

Something was happening to him that he didn't understand. He'd only meant to get things straight between them and maybe tease her a little as payment for what she'd said the last time he'd seen her. But at the touch of her soft skin beneath his callused fingers, his insides had started to feel tight and fluttery.

"Lee Ann—Ty—hurry! He's regaining consciousness!"

Ty released her abruptly. What in the hell was he thinking, hadn't he had enough trouble without this complication?

"Ty—"

"Cody's awake," he interrupted, whirling away from her without a backward glance.

Cody looked like death warmed over, but he managed a slight smile when Ty ducked into the tent a moment later, followed by Lee Ann.

"How are you feeling, buddy?"

"I've got the mammoth of all headaches," Cody whispered unevenly, "but I think I'll make it."

"We're taking you out of here in the morning. I lost both horses," he admitted tersely. "But I was lucky enough to stumble across the women's camp. They're offering us shelter for the night and a way back home in the morning. They managed to hang on to their mounts," he added derisively.

Cody's blue eyes shifted toward Lee Ann. "Thanks. By the way, my name is Cody Fargo."

Lee Ann nodded and whispered her own name before his glance moved to Jennifer's face and lingered.

"You're welcome," Jennifer replied, snatching a quick glance at Lee Ann's immobile face. "And now I think we all need to get some sleep."

They divided up the blankets. Ty and Cody were installed on one side of the tent and the women on the other.

Jennifer turned the lantern down low, so they could monitor Cody's condition during the night and then turned toward her friend. Lee Ann heaved a sigh of relief when Jennifer finally fell asleep. She'd caught the probing looks the other woman had thrown her way after she and Ty had entered the tent, but she couldn't deal with questions just now.

She was still reeling from Ty's kiss. It had come as a shock, because though it sounded unbelievable even to her own mind, it had made her realize that she was in love with him.

When he'd left her that night all those years ago, after refusing to take her with him, she'd been hurt beyond words. But she'd gotten over it, even understanding later that he'd been far wiser than she. He'd been right when he'd suggested that they were too young to run away together.

As she'd matured into womanhood, she'd told herself that he stayed so firmly fixed in her memory because he'd been her first love. Wasn't that the one you were never supposed to forget?

Like any normal teenager, she'd dated in high school. And in her sophomore year in college, she'd gotten engaged to a perfectly nice young man who was studying to be a lawyer. But they'd broken it off, at his request, a month before the wedding.

Paul had told her as gently as possible that she didn't love him. He knew she *wanted* to love him, but he felt sure there was someone else between them. He said he'd realized it from the start of their relationship, but he'd been arrogant enough to think he might be able to replace the man—whoever he was—in her life. He'd finally realized it wasn't any good. The spark between them just wasn't there.

At first, Lee Ann had denied it hotly, but in the end she'd agreed that they weren't right for each other. She'd dated other men over the years, but there had been no other engagements.

Only in the hours of darkness had she even allowed herself to think about Ty Yancy. If she was honest with herself, she'd admit that the only reason she had returned to Rainville after college was the hope that one day Ty would come back to claim his inheritance—and her.

It was time she faced the truth. The only man she had ever loved was Ty Yancy. And if the past fourteen years was anything to go by, it looked as if she was never going to love anyone else.

But what was she going to do about the situation? Her father hated Ty and he hated her father. She wasn't certain where that left her.

She'd been willing to settle for friendship a few hours ago, but that had changed with Ty's kiss. Now she wanted it all, his love, a life together, a home and his children.

The trip back to the ranch was slow, with Ty on one horse, holding Cody before him, and Jennifer and Lee Ann riding double on the other. They headed for Lee Ann's house, because there wasn't a phone at Ty's place.

Ty had hesitated a long moment when they'd come to the fork in the path that would take them to the Newley ranch or his own property, depending which turn they took. And if it hadn't been for the urgency of the situation and the guilt he felt for the things he'd said to Cody the day before, he wouldn't have considered stepping a foot on Wade Newley's property.

Lee Ann held her breath, waiting to see what he'd do and heaved an inaudible sigh of relief when he turned the horse to the right and headed toward her house.

For the next couple of hours, she watched his shoulders become tense as they drew near the house. When both horses paused at the paddock gate, Lee Ann jumped down and opened the gate.

At the barn, she instructed Jennifer to call Dr. Finley and ask him to come to the ranch. She needed a moment alone with Ty. Cody had fallen into another one of the deep sleeps he'd been drifting in and out of all morning.

Touching Ty on the knee before he had a chance to dismount, she looked up at him and explained, "I think it might be better to get Dr. Finley to come out here, rather than take Cody into town to the doctor's office."

Ty nodded without comment, letting her steady the other man, while he dismounted.

"Would you like me to help you carry him?" she asked softly.

Ty hesitated, really looking at her for the first time that day. "No. I can take him." He followed as she led the way to the house.

"I don't think there's any doubt about it," Dr. Finley said a little while later. "He needs to go to the hospital. He's probably suffering from a concussion and that head wound needs stitching."

"He's going to be all right, ain't he?" Ty asked quickly.

"I don't see why not, but we need to monitor him closely for the next couple of days."

"Then I guess you'd better make the arrangements," Ty said.

Dr. Finley nodded, then turned to Lee Ann. "May I use your phone?"

Jennifer spoke up. "Follow me and I'll show you where it is."

"And what about you?" Lee Ann asked softly.

"What about me?" Ty asked.

"Are you going to be all right?"

"I'm fine. I'm always fine. It's the people around me who seem to get hurt," he muttered with a warning glance in her direction as he left the room.

Dr. Finley elected to take Cody in his own car. Jennifer was to follow and do the paperwork once they had arrived. Ty had turned over Cody's wallet to her, along with the sketchy bit of information he knew about the man's medical background.

Taking a few minutes alone with his friend, Ty explained why he wasn't going to the hospital with him. He intended to go back to the mountains to round up his friend's horses.

"It's okay." Cody grinned weakly. "I know the real reason you aren't coming. It's because you're afraid of doctors and nurses."

Ty grinned obligingly, then sobered. "Listen," he said, not quite meeting Cody's eyes. "About what I said yesterday... that was just me shooting my big mouth off. I didn't mean—"

"Don't worry about it," Cody interrupted. "It's forgotten."

"Yeah?" Ty eyed him searchingly.

"Yeah. Now go find my horses, before one of them breaks a leg."

Lee Ann saw the trio off, then went in search of Ty. He was behind the barn headed back the way they'd come a little while ago.

"Where are you going?"

Ty stopped reluctantly and turned to face her. "I'm going after Cody's horses."

"On foot?"

"Looks like," he nodded and started to turn away.

"You can borrow a horse," she offered.

"No, thanks," he muttered. The last thing he wanted was to borrow anything that belonged to Wade Newley. It was bad enough that he'd had to make use of his daughter last night and this morning.

"The bay you rode here belongs to me. I bought him on a trip to New Mexico a couple of years ago."

Ty hesitated. He could travel the distance on foot, but it would be easier to chase the mounts down if he was on horseback.

"No strings attached," Lee Ann added.

He nodded and strode past her toward the barn. He was lifting the saddle onto the chestnut gelding when she followed him into the barn and stood watching.

"Wouldn't it be easier if you had help finding the horses?"

He should have known this was coming. "I know the area like the back of my hand, I'll find them a lot quicker alone."

"I'm coming with you," she said abruptly.

Ty stopped and turned toward her. "No."

"Yes," she said stubbornly.

"I thought there were no strings attached," he said tersely.

"No strings. I want to help you."

"I don't need your help."

"You can't stop me," she said fiercely.

"I prefer my own company."

"That's my horse and saddle," she quickly retorted.

The almond-shaped eyes narrowed on her face. It was on the tip of his tongue to tell her what she could do with her horse and saddle. And then, suddenly, he gave in.

"Suit yourself." He shrugged, turning away to tighten the cinch and adjust the stirrups. He was mounted and heading out the barn door before Lee Ann had saddled her own horse.

Running into the house, she scribbled a note to Jennifer, telling her where she was going, and made a quick change of clothes. Grabbing a couple of dry blankets, she hurried outside.

"You might think you're leaving me behind," she muttered tightly, catching a glimpse of his back disappearing over the hill, "but you've got another think coming. You might not realize it yet, but you've left me behind for the last time, Tyler Yancy!"

Chapter 6

Lee Ann rode hard, the sun's heat burning through her shirt, the trill of a bird following her as she spurred her mount toward the peaks in the distance and the man whose return had suddenly given new purpose to her life.

She soon caught up with him, but he ignored her and they rode in chilly silence. Undaunted, she was determined to change his attitude.

Was his hostility only a veneer masking his true feelings? She had no basis for thinking that; a stolen kiss was hardly a declaration of love, but she hadn't realized the depth of her own feelings until now.

Lee Ann darted a glance toward his lean face, but it was impossible to see his expression beneath the low brim of his black felt hat. Her eyes traveled up over the beaded hat-band and she was reminded of his Indian heritage.

The expression 'stoic Indian' flitted through her mind and she almost laughed out loud. There had been nothing stoic about him when she'd first gotten to know him; he'd been as impassioned about things as she'd been, once she'd found someone to share her passion with.

"Do you remember the time we put burrs under Benny Jones's blankets because he was always bragging how he could sleep on a bed of cactus and it wouldn't bother him?"

"I remember."

"Remember the cake Smokey ordered from Mrs. Shelton for your seventeenth birthday? It was supposed to be a cowboy on a bucking bronc, and when he opened it up that night in the bunkhouse, it was all pink and white, with a little girl on a merry-go-round?"

Ty's lips twitched. "I remember."

"You thought he was having you on, but it was an honest mistake on Mrs. Shelton's part. You got the merry-go-round and Becky Walters got your cake. You were so mad, I thought you were going to murder him—" Wrong choice of words.

Ty stiffened and brought his horse to an abrupt halt. "What are you trying to do, remind me about what a chip I had on my shoulder back then?"

"No, I was just trying to make conversation."

"Well, I don't like to talk while I ride. So, if you don't mind..." He let the words trail off and jerked on his reins, spurring his horse ahead of her.

Lee Ann wanted to kick herself for her verbal blunder. She'd only wanted him to recall some of the good times they'd shared, and instead she'd made him think she was castigating him.

She didn't know how long they'd been riding when Lee Ann began to notice that Ty was favoring his left side. Remembering the scars she'd seen the day she'd caught him in the waterfall, she wondered if he was in a lot of pain. She moved closer and saw evidence of his suffering in the taut lines edging the corners of his full mouth.

Figuring he would rather die than admit to needing a rest, Lee Ann cleared her throat and said, "Can we stop for a few minutes? I need a break."

Ty glanced her way coolly, noting that her hat had fallen to her back, held in place by the chin strap, leaving her head bare. He started to mention what the sun could do to her skin, but quickly changed his mind. It was nothing to him. Besides, even though he wouldn't admit it, he liked the sight of the long dark curls gathered at the back of her neck and tied with the bright blue-and-green scarf.

His glance flickered over the short sweat-dampened curls framing her heart-shaped face, the twin spots of deep color dotting each cheek and the tired smudges rimming her gray eyes. No one had gotten much sleep last night, he remembered, because of Cody.

With a short nod of agreement, he turned his horse toward the stream and dismounted, his movements slow and awkward. He'd been making progress until last night. Carrying Cody in the rain had put a lot of strain on muscles not yet healed.

Easing down on his haunches beside the water's edge, he removed his hat and laid it on the ground beside him. Pulling a red-and-black bandanna from his back pocket, he dipped it in the clear mountain water and wiped his forehead and the back of his neck.

Lee Ann sat astride her own mount and watched, feeling a sudden burning desire to be the one bathing his forehead. Dismounting, she joined him, sitting cross-legged on the ground, her elbows resting on her knees as she studied his face. He looked like hell, but he wouldn't thank her for mentioning it.

Ty felt her eyes on him and glanced in her direction. "Who's taking care of the store, while you're off gallivanting around the countryside?"

Lee Ann stiffened. She didn't like what the remark implied. It sounded as though he thought she didn't take her work seriously. And she did.

"A woman in town comes in on the weekends," she informed him tightly. "And if I need a few days off during the week, she works for me then, as well. And of course there's Jen, she helps run the place."

Ty leaned over to submerge his bandanna. "I just can't picture you as a businesswoman." But he could picture her on the paint she used to ride with her hair blowing wildly behind her as she challenged him to a race.

"What's wrong with my being a businesswoman?"

"I didn't say there was anything wrong with it."

"But that's what you meant," she insisted testily.

"No, it isn't. You used to spend every waking minute out of doors. How can you stand being cooped up inside for hours at a time?"

"You get used to it."

"Not me. I'd rather be dead."

"Are you going to be a rodeo cowboy all your life? What about when you get too old? What are you going to do then?"

"I'll never get too old. I know men who are in their seventies and still riding."

"What if you get hurt real bad and can't ride anymore?"

"That hasn't happened. I'll worry about that when—if—it ever happens."

Lee Ann glanced at his side. It looked to her as though he'd already been hurt real bad.

"What happened to your engagement?" It was none of his business, but he was tired of questions about himself.

"How did you know about that?" Lee Ann asked.

Without looking at her, he picked up his hat and wiped the inside brim with the damp bandanna. And then he couldn't keep his eyes to himself. "Les made sure I heard about it. I guess he wanted to let me know your reputation hadn't been tainted by your involvement with a half-breed.''

"Paul was a nice man, we just didn't suit each other.''

"I imagine he felt a bit... overpowered by the men already in your life," he said dryly.

"How did you come to be friends with such a *nice* man like Cody?" she asked sarcastically.

Ty hid a slight grin by pulling his hat low on his forehead before replying, "Surely you've heard that opposites attract.''

Lee Ann got to her feet and stood staring at him. What did he mean by that?

Grabbing his horse's loose reins, Ty threw himself into the saddle. "Have you rested enough?"

Lee Ann nodded.

"Good. We need to get some more distance behind us before we lose the light." Without waiting for a reply, he clicked his tongue at his mount and took off at a steady gallop.

Lee Ann got up on her own horse and galloped after him. Even though he'd probably meant to anger her so she'd leave him alone, he'd given her an opening to apologize for the misunderstanding that had been between them for so many years. Now all she had to do was come up with the right words. It seemed that every time she opened her mouth, she put a little more distance between them.

The winding curve of the stream led them steadily upward into the Gallatin Mountains. This was the kind of country that aroused a man's senses and made his heart beat faster. Ty had been to a lot of places and seen a lot of sights, but none stirred him like his home state of Montana.

Twisting in the saddle, he looked back and saw that Lee Ann had fallen way behind. Settling back against the cantle, he cursed silently at the sudden stab of emotional pain robbing him of breath.

He'd endured a lot worse than this. Most times, all it took was a little concentration to ignore it, but since he'd looked up to find Lee Ann standing in his barn, he hadn't been able to focus on anything but the past. And remembered pain was just as bad—sometimes worse—than anything the present could throw his way.

The sun was slipping behind the tops of the mountains when Ty pulled his horse to a halt and wearily dismounted. They'd reached the spot where he and Cody had lost the horses the night before.

"Find something?" Lee Ann rode up beside him and stopped.

"Maybe," he murmured from a squatting position, his eyes on the ground.

Lee Ann leaned over her horse's neck trying to see what he saw. The art of tracking had always fascinated her, but she'd never gotten the hang of it, even when Smokey had tried to teach her what to look for. And when Ty sat back on his haunches and pushed his hat to the back of his head without elaborating, she couldn't contain her curiosity.

"Well—what is it?"

"It looks like a grizzly," he said after a moment.

"Grizzly!"

"That's right. I've been seeing signs for some time now, but those tracks were old. These are fresh and they're following Splinter and Bumper."

"Splinter and Bumper?"

"Cody's horses."

Lee Ann felt her blood run cold. A grizzly could kill a full-grown horse with very little trouble… "Jen and I didn't see any sign of a grizzly when we were here, yesterday."

"It's a good thing you didn't. You know what a grizzly is capable of doing."

"Yes, and we were so excited about seeing the wild mustangs, we didn't spare a thought for danger."

"Mustangs—" He gave her a quick glance. "You saw them? Where?"

"Up near the box canyon where we were camped."

"I knew it! Damn it," he cursed.

"What's wrong?" Lee Ann asked, watching him mount up.

"We were looking for that herd when the storm blew up."

"So that's what you were doing out here."

"That's right." He shot her an impatient look. "I wasn't trespassing," he mimicked.

Lee Ann let that go. "Why were you looking for the wild horses?"

Ty folded his arms across his thighs and eyed her. "Well, it's like this, I can't seem to get within a mile of anyone's stock. But, of course, you wouldn't know anything about that," he added mockingly. "Anyway, I figured I would round up a few wild head and use them for practice."

"That could be dangerous—what about your side?" Lee Ann asked without thinking.

Ty straightened abruptly. "What about it?"

"Should you be riding?"

"I don't have a daddy to buy me a business," he said, whipping his horse to a gallop, "so I have to *earn* my money."

Lee Ann caught up with him and kept pace. "My father didn't buy me a business. The store belonged to my mother's family. And if it was money you wanted," she shouted at his back as he prodded his horse into a gallop, obviously intent on leaving her behind, "why didn't you claim your inheritance?"

Ty jerked his horse to a stop. "Money?" He shook his head at her ignorance. "My uncle never had two cents to rub together. And this *inheritance* has done nothing but *cost* me money. Is that what's biting you," he asked, "the fact that I didn't come back?"

"Is that what you want to believe?"

Without answering, Ty spurred his horse forward, leaving her behind.

Again they rode in silence, the track getting steeper, making it necessary to ride single file. After a while, he mumbled, "My uncle understood."

"I beg your pardon?" Lee Ann said.

Ty shot her a glance over his shoulder. "I said, he understood. My uncle understood my not coming back."

"I wish I did," Lee Ann whispered as they moved on.

As the sun began to sink in the western sky, Ty picked a place near the stream for their camp. He built a fire, and Lee Ann fixed a meal. They ate in silence.

They were drinking the last of the coffee when Lee Ann spoke, knowing she couldn't abide the silence a moment longer.

"About money," she said, as though taking up their earlier conversation. "I have some—some I can lend you—if you need it."

Her companion sipped his coffee as though he hadn't heard her.

"Ty?"

"I'd rather starve than accept money from your father," he said bitingly, throwing the rest of his coffee into the flames and getting to his feet.

"The money wouldn't be from my father," she explained quickly. "I have money of my own, left to me by my mother."

"No!" Dropping his cup, he stomped off into the trees.

Lee Ann watched him go. It seemed that in some respects he hadn't changed. He might not be so quick to use his fists, but he was just as proud and stubborn as she remembered.

She cleaned up the last of their meal and decided to make a trip to the stream for a wash before the sunlight was completely gone. Remembering the bear tracks, she crept down to the water's edge with one eye directed over her shoulder, watching the path behind.

The water was icy cold, so she didn't stay in it for long, but it felt good to wash away the dust from the trail. Wrapping her long wet hair in a towel, she dressed in the soft sweats she'd brought along to sleep in and headed back to camp.

She was wondering what had happened to Ty when she spotted him standing at the water's edge, wearing only his jeans. She thought he was in the process of undressing, then she realized his hair was wet and that he must have already bathed.

Standing back in the trees, she watched him withdraw the bandanna he'd used earlier and wet it in the stream. The sun's dying rays bathed his upper body in a golden hue. He turned and Lee Ann saw him press the wet cloth against his exposed abdomen.

He flinched and a slight groan escaped the clenched lips as the cloth touched damaged flesh. Lee Ann bit her lip in sympathy. She should have turned around right then and left him to his privacy, but her feet moved and she found herself standing behind him.

"Does it hurt very much?" she whispered with a catch in her voice.

Ty stiffened, but not because her presence surprised him, he'd felt her out there somewhere behind him. He turned slowly to face her. It would be ridiculous to pretend otherwise, so he admitted to the pain. "Yes, it hurts like hell."

Her eyes were on his long fingers, pressing the cloth against his flesh. "How did it happen?"

"I took a fall from a bull."

"God! Why do you do it?" she exclaimed, her eyes jerking to his face. But the anger that had been with her since Nora had mentioned his return—anger against him for leaving her and not returning sooner—suddenly died. She reached toward him, thrust his hands aside and removed the cloth to press gentle fingertips against the throbbing scars.

Ty sucked in his breath, a white-hot tide of desire rushing through him. "What are you doing?" he said through clenched teeth, stepping back.

Lee Ann raised puzzled eyes to his face. "Why do you do it?" she repeated. "I never understood my brother's fascination with rodeo and I don't understand yours. Surely it isn't for the money—there are easier ways to earn money."

A muscle twitched in his lean jaw. "It isn't the money," he answered in a strained voice. "At least, that's not all of it." It was hard to think, hard to speak, with her touching him. He wanted to cover her hand with both of his and press it lower.

"No?"

"No. I guess it's different for every man," he hedged. He knew what drove him, but he couldn't tell her that. "I don't know what drove your brother." His voice roughened. "I didn't kill him."

His hand tightened over hers. Suddenly, he realized that as he'd been speaking, his hand had moved to press Lee Ann's small hand flat against him, holding it there.

"I never thought you did."

He should let her go. The thoughts inside his head would scare her if she could read them.

"Go back to camp," he said hoarsely. "I'll be along soon."

"Yes, I will," she agreed without moving.

He knew what he should do. He was in enough trouble at the moment without adding to it. But Lee Ann's fragrance mixed with the scent of the night and swirled around him. God, how he ached for her.

"It's late," he murmured tautly. "You need to get some sleep." The hand covering hers pressed tighter. "We have a long ride ahead of us in the morning."

"I'm not sleepy," Lee Ann whispered, edging a little closer.

"It's late," he reminded her again, trembling with a need he could barely hold in check. He'd dreamed of being with her like this.

"Yes," she agreed, raising her lips toward his.

"Lee Ann," he warned, his hands at her shoulders, holding her away. "We aren't kids anymore." He'd been wanting her all day—hell, he'd been wanting her all his life.

"I know."

Reaching up, he pulled the towel from her head, dropped it to the ground and pushed his fingers through her damp hair, spreading it over her shoulders. It was almost dry and it felt like silk between his fingers. He wanted to bury his face in it, feel it against his lips, feel it draped across his chest.

"I'm going to—"

"Hush," she murmured, touching his lips with an unsteady fingertip. "Don't tell me, just do it."

He crushed her in his arms, his mouth slanting hard over hers. God, she was sweet. In all his life, nothing had ever tasted as sweet as this.

His lips clung to hers, and while he held her and caressed her soft body, at the back of his mind was the fear that someone—her father—would suddenly appear and stop them.

In desperation, his hands slipped down over her shoulders and around to her hips, his fingertips recording the softness of her. Pulling her tight, he cradled her against him, his hands cupping her derriere, his loins on fire for her.

Lee Ann had never felt such passion. It made her feel light-headed. Twisting her head to the side, she buried her hot face against his neck to try to catch her breath.

"What's wrong?" Ty whispered unsteadily. "Did I hurt you?"

"N-no. I just..." She shook her head, unable to explain the tumultuous feelings raging inside her.

"Have you changed your mind?" It took every ounce of courage to ask and wait for her reply.

"No!" Lee Ann pulled back to look into his face. "No, I haven't changed my mind." Laying a gentle hand against his rough cheek, she stroked a finger across one dark eyebrow. "Kiss me." Raising herself on tiptoe, she pressed her lips to his.

Ty held himself back. He wasn't a virgin, but no one had ever come close to arousing him to such a fever pitch. "Are you sure?" he said against her lips. His hands cupped her face and held it inches from his.

Lee Ann hesitated. Was there some reason *he* was holding back?

Before she could answer, Ty was covering her mouth with his, taking her lips with a hunger born of desperation. He didn't want to know if she had doubts—*he just wanted her!*

He couldn't believe that she wanted him, him with his holes in his boots and jeans and not a penny to his name. Him with his mixed heritage. He knew what her brother had thought of him, the things he must have said to her about him.

One day, he'd heard Les tell Lee Ann that no decent white woman would want her name associated with Ty's. He hadn't hung around to hear her reply, but now she was here in his arms and he felt as though he'd just been handed a prize.

Lee Ann's knees began to quiver as Ty's mouth moved down the side of her neck. One hand moved beneath the sweatshirt and she felt his fingers tremble against her.

She clung to him, head back, eyes closed, letting the sensations sweep through her body. Her knees buckled and Ty lowered her gently to the ground and came down beside her.

Lifting the shirt over her head, Ty leaned back to gaze at the melting softness of her body. Leaning forward, he pressed a long kiss against one bare shoulder.

"You're beautiful," he breathed.

Lee Ann lifted herself to his kiss and then his lips were sliding down her chest, his hot lips kissing her through the lace of her bra. His tongue dampened the material and Lee Ann's stomach turned a flip-flop as he drew her nipple inside his mouth.

Ty pulled one of her hands from his hair and slid it down his chest to his belt and lower. Her hand moved on its own and his head jerked back, releasing her nipple in a deep groan.

Lee Ann froze. "Did I hurt you?"

"N-no," he gasped. "Don't stop."

His mouth was on hers as his hands unfastened her bra. He planned to kiss every bare inch of her sweet flesh. The memory of this night would burn in his mind long after they parted.

Lee Ann felt her shirt and bra slip away; a sudden chill raced over her exposed skin. A vision of her father's stern face popped into her mind and for a moment she couldn't move. Then Ty's tongue dipped into the hollow of her navel and all coherent thought slipped from her mind.

Ty helped her unfasten his belt. They stripped the clothes from each other's body and used the garments to lie upon.

Lee Ann leaned over him, her hair tickling him as she traced the pattern of old scars on his smooth chest. His fantasy was coming true, Ty realized as he gathered her long hair in his hands and rubbed its silk against his chest.

Drawing her face down to his, he covered her mouth with his, making the kiss last. And as it deepened, his passion grew. He needed her now. His fingers touched her and he knew she was ready for him, too.

Lifting her to lie atop him, he fit her to the cradle of his hips. One hand smoothed its way from her shoulders to the back of her thighs in a gentling motion as he entered her.

Lee Ann gasped at the suddenness of it and held perfectly still. This was better than any fantasy she'd ever had about him. He was here, the flesh-and-blood man and she wanted to give him everything. Her fingers slid through the long hair at his forehead and temples as she moved forward and then back in a gentle rocking motion.

Ty gasped and lifted his hands to her breasts, rubbing his palms against her pebble-hard nipples. Their bodies moved in unison, each filling with a growing need for the other. The pace became stronger, as sensation after new sensation exploded inside them.

Suddenly, Ty was twisting their bodies so that now she lay beneath him. His hands braced on either side of her, he drove into her harder and harder, the corded muscles in shoulders and back rigid with strain. The pain in his abdomen was overshadowed by the pain of his need to satisfy them both.

Lee Ann pushed back the long damp hair from his forehead and strained up to kiss his closed eyes. Her hands moved down his sweat-slickened shoulders and up across his heaving chest. And then she was arching back, her eyes closed as Ty's cries filled her ears.

Ty pulled her up tight against him and they clung together, riding each new wave of ecstasy until the night sky burst into a million bright stars. Then they simply held each other, shuddering in the aftermath of a passion neither had expected.

After a moment of lying side by side, Ty took her hand and drew her to her feet. Leading her to the water's edge, he knelt before her and moistened his bandanna. While Lee Ann stood with heart pounding at the unbelievable tenderness of the act, Ty bathed her tender thighs. When he'd finished, he patted her dry with her towel.

Lee Ann stared down at the top of his dark head in the moonlight and sudden tears came to her eyes. She could never remember anyone being this gentle with her. Going down on her knees, she took his face between her hands and directed his eyes to hers.

On the brink of speech, she saw him give a slight shake of his head and closed her mouth on what she'd wanted to say. He leaned forward and touched her lips with his in a kiss that made her heart ache.

"Go on back to camp. I'll be along in a few minutes."

She understood. One hand was pressed tightly against his abdomen. He was in pain and needed a few minutes alone.

Nodding, she moved away, stopping to slip on her sweat suit. After a moment, with her lantern in hand, she headed for camp.

The next morning, Lee Ann sat up in her bedroll and looked around. Where was Ty?

Then she remembered last night and her whole body flushed a deep pink. She must have fallen asleep waiting for him; she didn't remember his return to camp.

Her eyes darted toward his bedroll. It didn't look as though it had been used. Her eyes shot to the fire. It had gone out.

A lick of fear darted through her. Where was he? And then she remembered the grizzly tracks. Oh, God—no!

Getting to her feet, she grabbed her jeans and shirt and hurriedly began to change. She slanted a glance toward the sky and realized she'd slept half the morning away—while Ty could be lying somewhere torn and bleeding. . . .

In the act of pulling on a boot, she heard something and froze. Cocking an ear, she listened. There it was again! It sounded like—

"Well, I see I returned in the nick of time."

Lee Ann sat with one foot raised and her boot half on, staring up at Ty on horseback. "Are you all right?" she finally managed to ask.

"Sure. Why wouldn't I be?" His glance grazed her figure and a flash of pale pink skin darted through his mind.

"Where have you been?"

"I couldn't sleep—" He shifted in the saddle. "I remembered your saying you'd spotted the wild horses near the box canyon, so I played a hunch and headed there. Sure enough, I found Splinter and Bumper."

Lee Ann pulled hard on the boot and her foot slid inside. It took only a moment to get the second one on and then she was on her feet, her hands on her slender hips.

"Are you telling me, you took off last night, right after—you took off and left me here alone?"

"You were safe."

"Was I?" she asked angrily. "Well, not safe enough. I sure as hell wasn't safe from you!"

"You would have been," Ty replied coldly, "if you had wanted to be."

"Like hell!"

"Are you implying I *forced* you?" he asked, his eyes blazing amber fire.

"You left me alone with a grizzly out there on the prowl!"

His eyes held hers. "There was no grizzly."

"What?"

"There was no grizzly."

"But you said—"

"I only said that hoping you'd go back and I could go on alone."

She didn't know which hurt more, knowing he'd lied to her about the bear to try to get her to leave, or realizing that what they'd shared a few hours ago hadn't meant a bloody thing to him. Either way, she wanted to curl up and die. She was the one who had forced things between them last night.

Lee Ann twisted away from him. She didn't want him to see the hurt on her face. She felt like such a fool. She rolled up her bedroll and tied it in a quick knot.

Throwing her saddle on her horse, she began to fasten it in place, ignoring the man who sat watching her. When she was finished, she mounted and moved away from him.

"Where are you going?"

"Home."

"Alone?"

"Yes."

"Lee Ann..."

Lashing her horse with the reins, she spurred him in the sides and galloped away. She didn't want to hear anything he had to say. She just wanted to get away and never have to look at him again.

Chapter 7

Ty parallel-parked Cody's truck in front of the Rainville National Bank, turned off the engine and sat with his hands on the steering wheel, staring at the smoked-glass door. He knew Vint Patterson, the bank's president, was a friend of Wade Newley's. What he didn't know was whether or not the man would lend him money on the ranch.

He knew his uncle had borrowed money from the bank once or twice while Ty was growing up, but his uncle had been liked and respected in the town. At least he had been until Wade Newley had put the word out that Nathan Yancy's nephew was not to be trusted with the care of other people's animals.

After that, everyone had pretty much stayed away from the ranch, and Ty's desire to leave the valley grew. It wasn't only because of the way everyone treated him, but also because he knew that with him gone, his uncle's life would be a whole lot easier.

Only it hadn't worked out that way. After he left, Nathan's health had quickly deteriorated. Instead of spending the money Ty regularly sent him on a doctor, he put it all back into the land. There hadn't been that much money to begin with, and by the time Ty had begun winning larger purses, his uncle was gone.

He'd received Lee Ann's letter telling him about Nathan's death, but he couldn't get back in time for the funeral. Afterward, he'd had no reason to return.

He didn't care about the land the way his uncle had. But it wasn't until he found his mother living with her people on the reservation that he understood his own thinking. Her people believed that no one could own the land, the land belonged to everyone. When you looked at it like that, it changed the significance of a piece of paper called a deed.

It was then that he began to realize that he couldn't hide his heritage from himself, any more than he could hide it from the rest of the world. In his youth, the Indian in him had constantly been at war with the white man in him. But his mother's father, a wise man among his people, had taught him there were good points to being both.

Which didn't mean a damned thing when it came to his borrowing money on the ranch, because the people of Rainville still saw him as the savage youth Wade Newley and his son had done their damnedest to make him out to be.

Ty's grip tightened until the knuckles showed white. It did no good to live in the past. Hadn't the trip into the mountains yesterday with Lee Ann Newley taught him that? He'd made a real mess out of that.

Jerking the door open, he climbed out of the truck. Instead of moving across the sidewalk to the bank, he delayed what would probably only be another lesson in humiliation and stood looking up and down the street. The old stone courthouse looked much the same as when he'd lived in the area.

The unfamiliar sign on a nearby window caught his eye and he realized that though a few new businesses dotted the town square, overall, the place had remained unchanged. It was still a quiet little town in the mountains holding out against chain stores and fast-food restaurants.

Pivoting on his heel, deciding he'd put off the inevitable long enough, he turned and bumped into someone on the sidewalk behind him.

"*Excuse* me," the woman said haughtily.

Ty stared in surprise at the tall rawboned woman barring his way. He removed his hat and gave her a polite nod as he stepped back to let her by.

With a snort, the woman lifted her long nose in the air and swept past him, holding herself away from him as though she were wearing long skirts instead of bibbed overalls, work boots and a sunbonnet. Ty's eyes followed her gaunt figure as it clumped down the street. Something about that long neck and those skinny legs looked familiar.

She disappeared inside the feed store and Ty shrugged. With his hat in his hand, he turned toward the bank. He might as well get this over with.

In a remarkably short time, Ty exited the building, a thoughtful expression on his face. One hand reached behind to pat the bulge in his back pocket, just to reassure himself that the last hour hadn't been his imagination.

He now had the money to do what he wanted, get back into rodeo competition, and he wasn't quite certain how he'd managed it. Vint Patterson had agreed to loan him ten thousand dollars for one year, using Ty's land as collateral. He had twelve months to pay it back in one lump sum. And all he had to do in the meantime was pay the interest on the loan in quarterly installments.

Ty climbed in the truck and pulled away from the curb. He wasn't stupid, nor was he gullible, and he wasn't sure he trusted the man. But he couldn't see how Vint Patterson could use this situation to take advantage of him. Unless he was betting on Ty's being unable to get back into competition. And nothing was going to stop him from doing that.

When he spotted the Hanly General Store, his spirits took a nosedive. His foot touched the brake and the truck slowed.

Lee Ann. What was he going to do about her? Would she read more into his making love to her than was good for either one of them?

He should have resisted her—he'd meant to. But when she'd touched him...

She'd made him feel just like that cocky kid who'd been suspicious of her childish adoration when he'd first gone to work for her father—and then humbled by it. She was the only one, besides his uncle, who could make him feel that he was worth something, that his feelings and thoughts were important.

The boy had grown to love her, but he hadn't realized it until the night she'd tried to use him to get away from her father. And he was tired of being used by the Newleys.

He'd known rumors had been flying around town that he was leaving. Up until then, he'd only been thinking about leaving the ranch to try his skill on the rodeo circuit. It was what he wanted more than anything, but there had been his uncle to consider... and Lee Ann.

But then she'd uttered her threat and the half-formed feelings inside him had been swept away on a tide of fury. She was no different than her father and brother, she was just better at disguising her real motives.

The next day he'd told his uncle that he was leaving. The old man hadn't tried to stop him, he'd simply told him to take care of himself and write.

Rodeo became his way of life. Except for his uncle, it was the only thing he truly loved.

He caught sight of Lee Ann through the store window and the sudden pain burning his gut had nothing to do with his injuries. He stomped on the gas pedal and the truck picked up speed.

She hated rodeo, she'd made that perfectly clear. And rodeo was still his way of life.

* * *

Lee Ann waved goodbye to Mary Tompkins and left the store. She hadn't planned a trip to town that day, but she hadn't been able to stand being by herself at the ranch. All she thought about was the mess she'd made of things with Ty.

She was no longer angry with him about the grizzly, she was hurt. How could he make love to her with such tenderness and then act as though nothing had happened between them?

Yesterday, when he'd held her and kissed her, she'd been reminded of their first kiss. There had been that same innocent passion in his touch. Not that she thought he was inexperienced, just not practiced. And because of that, she'd felt certain that Ty loved her, too.

There was no question about how she felt. She loved him and wanted him. The only things standing between them was her father and Ty's love for rodeo.

The problem of her father was one that she felt could be worked out with patience and time. But rodeo?

She had never been a real fan, not even when she'd worked alongside the ranch hands on her father's ranch. She'd never understood their thrill in riding the bulls and wild horses for sport.

When Ty first came to work on the ranch, she'd been amazed at his skill in handling animals and applauded his ability to break horses to saddle for her father. It was later, when he began to ride the bulls, that she learned about his desire to become a professional rodeo cowboy someday.

To her young mind, the future had seemed a world away. She and Ty became friends. He understood her on a level no one else did. He treated her as though she was important, and she never wanted to lose his friendship.

But one day she did. Ty was banished from the ranch and her whole world fell apart. Then he left town and that was when she grew to hate rodeo. Not only had it taken up all her father's interest and time, it had taken the one person to whom she could relate.

And now, years later, nothing had changed, except she had a longer list of reasons for disliking the sport.

No, that wasn't true, a lot had changed and very little of it good. Her brother was dead and her father hated Ty even more than before. And in all that had happened since his return, Lee Ann still hadn't made it clear to Ty just how angry her father would be to know he was here.

Yet she didn't want him to leave. She was so confused. If only there was someone she could talk to. . . .

Cody Fargo. A picture of the man darted through Lee Ann's mind. He was Ty's friend. Maybe he could give her some insight into the man.

An hour later, Lee Ann slipped into Cody's hospital room to find Jennifer sitting beside his bed.

"I hate to intrude," she said with a smile, "but I understood there was an injured man in this room who needed cheering up."

Jennifer got to her feet. "I was just leaving. I came by to see if there was anything Cody needed."

Lee Ann's grin faded. "Hey, don't run off."

"No, it's all right," Jennifer said. "I've got to go. Mary called with some questions about a missing back order and I promised I'd go in and straighten it out."

"Hey," Cody called softly. "You will come back and see me—won't you?"

Jennifer paused at the door. "Yes," she answered hesitantly, "if you want me to." And then she was gone.

"She's a very nice lady," Cody murmured with his eyes on the closed door.

"Yes," Lee Ann agreed. "The very best."

"Well, ma'am," he said, turning his attention to his new visitor, "as you can see, I'm doing fine. How's Ty?"

Lee Ann took the chair Jennifer had recently vacated and sat with her hands on her lap. "That's what I came by to talk to you about."

Cody slanted her a quick look. "Is he all right? I know he was determined to go after the horses. It's really my fault they got away. Darned silly thing for a man to do—get thrown from his horse in a storm."

"Ty is all right," Lee Ann assured him hastily. "I didn't mean to upset you. And he found your horses," she added.

"He did?" Cody looked up and grinned, shaking his head. "Oh—" He frowned and grabbed his head with both hands. "I've got to quit doing that," he groaned.

"Are you all right? Is there anything I can get you? A nurse?" Lee Ann asked, half rising from the chair.

"No, no, I'm fine."

Lee Ann sat back, but continued to eye him uncertainly.

"That man's a wonder when it comes to animals," Cody said, taking up their conversation. "I think he could charm the hide right off one of them if he wanted to."

"He's had that gift for as long as I've known him." Lee Ann smiled. "He calls it 'talking' to them. I tried it a couple of times when I was trying to break a horse." Lee Ann shook her head ruefully. "All I got for my pains was a quick trip to the ground on the seat of my pants and a couple of matching bruises."

Cody smiled and rested against the pillows, studying Lee Ann's face. "Excuse me for being blunt, but if you want to ask me about Ty, go ahead."

"I—" She hesitated, looking down at the bag on her lap. "Can you tell me what he's been up to these past few years? We knew each other when we were younger, but we lost touch a long time ago."

"Ty's a hard man to get to know." Cody rubbed at his ear. "He's got a hair-trigger temper—which you may or may not already know—and he likes privacy."

"Yes," Lee Ann agreed. "That's what I remember about him."

"He's darn good at what he does," Cody continued. "If it hadn't been for all the trouble he's had since Les died, he'd be close to winning the world championship." And then he seemed to realize to whom he was talking and stammered, "Sorry, ma'am. I forgot he was your brother."

Lee Ann leaned forward. "Were you there that day—the day Les died?"

"Yes, ma'am."

"Can you tell me what happened?"

"Well—" Cody shifted in the bed. "You probably already know anything I can tell you."

Lee Ann's hands gripped each other tightly. "Please, tell me, again."

"I saw your brother in the chute. He lowered himself onto Dynamite and I saw the chute gate open. They sort of exploded into the arena—that's how the bull got his name.

"Anyway, it was all over in the blink of an eye. Your brother came off that bull in a couple of seconds. But it wasn't a clean fall," he explained. "His hand got hung up in the rope, and Dynamite dragged him."

"Your brother's hand finally worked loose and he fell between the bull's legs. By then, Ty was off the chute and out in the arena—"

"Ty! Ty went into the arena?"

"Yes, ma'am. I don't know how much you know about rodeo, but there's usually a clown in there to help distract the bulls. There was one that day, too, but some kids had climbed through the fence on the far side of the arena and one of the clowns was over there trying to get them out of danger.

"Another clown ran into the arena, but by that time Ty was at your brother's side...Les was already gone."

Lee Ann swallowed tightly. She'd never really known how the accident had happened. In a way, she wished she still didn't. Now it was all too vivid a picture in her mind.

"Are you all right?" Cody asked softly.

Lee Ann nodded. "W-what happened afterward?"

"I guess you mean about Ty."

Lee Ann nodded.

"Well, your brother was taken away in an ambulance. It wasn't until later, after they found your brother's rope had been tampered with, that the talk started.

"It was no secret that Ty and your brother didn't get along. But the thing that focused people's suspicions on Ty was the fight he and your brother had the night before Les's death."

"They were always fighting when they were younger, but this—" She looked at him helplessly. "Les had a temper, too. Surely Ty wasn't the only one he ever fought with, so why was the finger of suspicion pointed at him?"

"Ty was one of the men on the chute that day, helping your brother get seated on the bull." Cody's lips tightened. "A couple of the men who had also been there, suggested that it wouldn't have been hard for Ty to palm a knife and cut the rope while it was being slipped around the bull."

"But why would he do that?" Lee Ann asked softly. "Because of the fight, he had to know that he'd be one of the first people they'd suspect."

"Rodeo is a very competitive sport," Cody explained. "And the prize money can be very tempting."

"Are you saying they think he did it, just so he could win the damned rodeo?"

Cody shrugged. "The men siding against Ty think he did it because your brother was the only thing standing between him and the gold buckle." He hesitated. "They've also suggested that Ty hurried into the arena after the accident so he could make sure your brother was dead before anyone else got to him."

"And what do you think?"

"Ty isn't a killer. I think your brother knew the chance he was taking when he climbed aboard that bull."

"Does that mean you think his death was an accident?" That didn't explain the knife cuts found on the rope.

"I don't know. Ty would like to think it was. Course, he'd like to think his own fall was an accident, too."

"His own fall?"

"Yes, ma'am. But I found evidence—" Cody shifted uncomfortably in the bed.

"Go on," Lee Ann prodded.

"Well, maybe I shouldn't. Ty will tell you about it, if he wants you to know."

Lee Ann scooted her chair closer to the bed. "Cody..." She felt uncomfortable about what she was getting ready to say. "I'm not just anyone. I care very much about Ty. If you think he's in danger, please, tell me."

Cody studied her face pensively. He could see she was serious about Ty, but there was still Ty's feelings to consider. As he'd said, Ty wasn't a man who discussed his private life with anyone. And Cody knew Ty wouldn't thank him for discussing it behind his back with this woman.

"I think someone tried to kill Ty a few weeks ago," Cody said after a few minutes of silence. "And maybe," he added, "it was the same man who killed your brother."

"My God!" Lee Ann sat back in her chair, a chill hand gripping her heart. "Do you have any proof?"

"Yes, ma'am. There's Ty's rope, cut just like the one your brother used. And there's the conversation I heard—and what Shorty Sims saw."

"Shorty Sims?"

"Yes." Cody explained what the man had seen and found.

"Can you identify the man you saw at the telephone?" she asked when he'd finished.

"Yes, ma'am."

"But you don't know him. Before that day you never saw him at any of the rodeos?"

"No, ma'am," Cody admitted reluctantly. Then, his jaw hardened and he said, "But I know I'd recognize him if I ever saw him again."

"Have you been to the police with this information?"

"No. Ty refuses to believe someone wants him dead—or at least that's what he pretends to believe."

Lee Ann swallowed dryly. "Why do you think someone would want to kill Ty? Do you think it has anything to do with my brother's death?"

"Well, that's hard to say, emotions run high with the rodeo crowd. A few years back, we were reputed to be real hell-raisers." The corners of his mouth lifted. "We're trying awfully hard to live down that reputation . . . but rodeo is a rough sport, and it attracts a certain type of individual."

"I think I understand," Lee Ann said. Men who lived on the edge—who played a hard and dangerous sport for money—needed release.

"As I said before, Ty isn't one to make friends easily. Sometimes that makes others uncomfortable around him. And when people feel uncomfortable . . . well, they just have to have a reason for it. And sometimes they have to have someone to blame it on."

"I understand that." It was only too easy to remember how the people in town, and her brother, had reacted to Ty's go-to-hell attitude when he was a teenager. Sometimes, because they expected the worse from him, they got it.

"But that isn't a reason to kill someone," she murmured out loud.

"No, not for you or me. But there's always the possibility that someone holds a grudge against him for something we don't know anything about."

"Against Les, too?"

"They were a lot alike."

Lee Ann started to protest and then she realized that what he had said was true. There were many similarities between the two men. Why hadn't she seen that before? Maybe that's why they hadn't gotten along with each other.

"You said Ty didn't believe he was in any danger." Lee Ann went back to the part of the conversation most important to her. "What can we do to convince him otherwise?"

"I don't know. I tried, but I didn't get very far... Maybe you can convince him."

It was on the tip of her tongue to say that she was probably the last person on earth who'd be able to get him to do something he didn't want to do, but then she said, "Maybe I can. If so, have you got a plan?"

Cody scratched his head, winced and patted the white square of bandage. "If we only had a picture of the man on the telephone."

Lee Ann laughed without humor. "If we had a picture, we could give it to the police."

"Wait a minute! That's not a bad idea."

"Really?" She frowned.

"I used to do a little sketching when I was in school. I could sketch the man."

Lee Ann's eyes lit up. "Yes, and we could make copies of it and—"

"Circulate them at the rodeos," Cody finished for her.

"Do you think it would work?"

"It's better than doing nothing."

"There are a lot of rodeos," Lee Ann warned. "How would we ever make it to all of them?"

"We couldn't. But if we split up, we could cover quite a few."

"All right." Lee Ann got to her feet and held out her hand. "We've got a deal. I'll talk to Ty and you do a sketch. Shall I bring you pencil and paper?"

"No, ma'am. I'll get some from one of the nurses."

Lee Ann was halfway to the door when he stopped her. "There's something maybe you ought to tell Ty."

She turned back. "Yes?"

"I made a few calls for him the other day and I heard something he won't be pleased to hear. Remember what I said about that hell-raiser image?"

Lee Ann gave a puzzled nod.

"Well, they don't want it back."

"They?"

"The governing board of the PRCA. There's a rumor that Ty is real close to suspension. That would mean he couldn't ride in any board-sanctioned rodeos. All it will take is a vote, and he's out—maybe permanently."

Lee Ann felt her heart skip a beat, and for a moment all other sound was drowned by a voice inside shouting, *No more rodeos, no more rodeos!*

Cody continued. "That's where the big money is and Ty needs money. After this last accident, he had to sell everything he owned to pay his medical bills. Besides, Ty lives for the sport. If we can prove someone killed your brother and tried to kill him, he'd be absolved from any guilt and the PRCA would have to rethink their decision."

"I thought you said they hadn't voted yet."

"They haven't, but it's only a matter of time."

"Why didn't you tell him about the suspension?"

Cody looked at her without answering and Lee Ann understood.

Outside in the hallway, she paused, going over all she'd just learned. One thing stuck out in her mind. She'd almost bet that her father's fine hand was behind the rumored suspension. He was on several boards that dealt with rodeo and providing stock for them, but she wasn't certain if the PRCA was one of them.

She ought to be ecstatic about the idea of Ty's being banned from rodeo. So, why wasn't she?

Having him quit was one thing, but having him forced out was altogether different. That isn't how she wanted them to get together.

And wasn't she jumping the gun? There hadn't been any indication in Ty's behavior toward her to suggest that he had any lasting plans for the two of them. On the contrary, he'd almost convinced her of the exact opposite.

Sweeping her hair behind her shoulder, she marched down the hall. "Oh, excuse me."

"My fault." The tall man who'd taken her arm, until she could regain her balance, smiled. "Lee Ann, I was just trying to call you." Vint Patterson led her over to a spot near the water fountain.

"Call me?"

"Yes. I need to talk to your father—it's urgent."

"He's out of the country and I'm not certain when he'll be back. Is it something I can handle?"

"Ah, no. This is something your father will want to take care of himself." He glanced down at the gold watch on his wrist and made a face. "I have to run. My wife's mother is going to surgery in a little while and I promised I'd be there before they take her. What I have to tell your father will have to wait. Just tell him to give me a call if he happens to get in touch with you any time soon. Okay?"

Lee Ann nodded and watched the distinguished-looking man, dressed in an impeccable blue suit, hurry down the hall. That was strange. What could be so urgent that he needed to speak to her father before Wade got back from Mexico City?

Out on the street, she hesitated. She could go to Ty's ranch immediately and try to convince him to listen to Cody, or she could take a little time to think about it and decide the best way to approach him.

Jennifer had said she was going to the store to clear up a missing back order. Her friend always favored the direct

approach, so maybe she'd have some ideas about how Lee
Ann could make Cody's plan sound plausible to Ty.

But Jennifer was nowhere in sight when Lee Ann entered
the store a short time later. Mary stood at the front counter.

Lee Ann's nose curled at the sweet scent of strawberry
potpourri forced her way by the overhead fans. It was Mar-
y's favorite. Waving at the woman, she headed toward the
office. Spotting the back of the customer responsible for
the desperate look on Mary's face, she veered silently in the
other direction.

"Good day, Mrs. Peebles." Lee Ann almost smiled as the
older woman jumped and whirled around.

"Well, I didn't think you worked here anymore," Nora
said snidely. "Haven't seen you around the place lately."

"I've been taking a few days off." She absolutely would
not let this crabby old woman upset her.

"Really?" Nora snorted. "I thought maybe you were
busy helping *him* fix up his place."

"And who is that?" Lee Ann asked pleasantly, catching
a glimpse of Mary's repressed smile out of the corner of her
eye.

"You know who I mean all right, missy," Nora de-
clared, peering at her through cramped eyes. "I shouldn't
be surprised you're in town today. I saw your—I saw *him* a
little while ago, coming out of the bank."

"You saw Ty at the bank?" Lee Ann asked quickly.

"I saw him," Nora croaked. "Wonder what he'd be doing at the bank?"

Trying to maintain her composure, Lee Ann answered
brightly, "I'm sure I wouldn't know. But if you're curious,
why don't you go ask him?"

Mary gasped.

Nora set her jaw, gave Lee Ann an up-and-down glance
of disdain and clumped out of the store.

"Wait!" Mary called, starting after the woman, but Lee Ann stopped her with a quick shake of the head. "She didn't pay for the chocolates," Mary protested.

"Let her have them," Lee Ann muttered. "I hope the old biddy chokes on them."

"Lee Ann!"

"Oh, I didn't mean it. They're probably for her husband, anyway. I don't think she eats anything but vinegar and nails."

Mary eyed her in amazement.

"I'm sorry, but she really gets my goat sometimes."

"It's okay, I've wanted to tell her where to get off more than once."

Now Lee Ann was surprised. Mary was normally so soft-spoken. "Where's Jennifer?" she asked.

"In the back, doing paperwork."

"Need any help?"

"No, thanks, everything is fine."

"Okay, see you later, then, I'm going to talk to Jennifer before I leave."

Lee Ann moved toward the back of the building, a picture of Nora's spiteful face still in her mind.

Jennifer was bent over the desk doing paperwork, but she looked up as Lee Ann entered the room and said, "Hi."

"Hi, yourself."

Jennifer nodded toward the door. "I heard that just now and I am truly shocked by your behavior," she admonished jokingly.

Just then, Mary entered the room.

"Is she gone?" Jennifer asked apprehensively.

"Yes," Mary answered.

"And good riddance," Lee Ann muttered. "It's after one," she said, glancing at the clock on the wall. "Let's take a late lunch break," she suggested, knowing it would give Mary a chance to regain her composure.

"I wonder," Mary asked hesitantly, "if you'd mind my going home for lunch today? The triplets have colds and Mrs. Brady, their baby-sitter, panics if they run a little temperature."

"No," Lee Ann replied. "Go on home, we'll stay till you get back. Do you need to take the rest of today off?"

"No," Mary said, looking for her purse. "They're not that ill, but thanks anyway."

After she'd gone, Jennifer hung the out-to-lunch sign on the door and she and Lee Ann retired to the back room for sandwiches and cold drinks. Lee Ann toyed with her food, thinking about her recent conversation with Cody.

"Jennifer, how would you like to attend some of those rodeos you're always talking about?"

"Are you kidding?"

"No."

"What about the store?"

"What about it? Mary's doing okay. Any questions she has will keep until we return, and she won't have to do any ordering while we're gone—"

"*We?*" the other woman asked quickly. "I thought you didn't like rodeo."

"I don't. But after you left the hospital this morning, Cody told me some upsetting news." She hesitated, wondering how best to explain what they'd be doing at the rodeos without scaring her off. "It could be dangerous," she said, realizing there was no easier way to put it.

Jennifer's green eyes widened. "Dangerous?"

"Yes," Lee Ann answered solemnly. "We're going to be tracking a killer." Leaning forward, she quickly explained what Cody had related to her.

A little while later, after she had agreed to help in any way she could, Jennifer went out to take the sign out of the window and reopen the store to customers.

Lee Ann sat back in her chair, a puzzled frown creasing her forehead. Though she'd told Jennifer what Cody had aid, she hadn't mentioned her conversation with Vint Paterson. She'd been curious about what he'd wanted with her ather, but after Nora's comment about seeing Ty outside he bank, Lee Ann was afraid she knew why he'd been there. And if her suspicions were correct . . .

Damn him! She slapped both hands flat against the desk. Why hadn't he accepted her offer? She'd have lent him money and her father need never have known.

Now, it appeared as though Ty may have played right into her father's hands. How could she eliminate the bad feeling between the two men, if her father insisted on playing he bad guy in this?

Damn it, what was happening to her life?

Gone to hell in a hand basket, Smokey would have replied with a hoot of laughter.

An hour later, Lee Ann was on her way to Ty's ranch. She didn't know whether to congratulate herself for obtaining Jennifer's agreement to help, or kick herself for involving her friend in something that could be very dangerous.

Either way, if her father found out what they were up to, here would be hell to pay. She had to keep telling herself hat she was doing this for him, too. She was determined to prove to him that Ty hadn't been responsible for her brother's death, and Cody and given her the means to do it.

Whether or not that would make any difference to the way Ty felt about her, Lee Ann didn't know. But it would eliminate the bitterness and anger between the two men she cared most about and that's what counted.

Sensing that Ty wouldn't appreciate her efforts in that direction any more than her father would, she decided to keep that aspect of clearing his name to herself for the time being. But she couldn't suppress a smile at the thought of how badly Nora Peebles's nose would be out of joint, and

how greatly the old woman's reservoir of gossip would be
depleted, when the time came.

Now, all she had to do was convince Ty that Cody's plan
was legitimate.

Chapter 8

Ty kneeled beside the stream, cupped water into his hand and splashed it onto his hot face. It had been slow work, but he was nearly finished. Twisting around, he looked at the small structure, studying it critically, then nodded. It would do.

He'd modeled the sweat lodge after the one his grandfather had made when Ty had visited with him and his mother. He'd worked all morning, cutting willow branches and sticking them into the ground, bending and interlocking them to create an oval-shaped structure with an opening at the top toward the rising sun. Then he'd covered the entire structure with an old tarpaulin he'd found in the barn.

A short distance from the small flap near the ground where he would enter the lodge, he'd built a fire, gathered several large stones and placed them in the flames to heat. Nearby stood a small shovel which he would use to lift the heated stones and carry them to the small pit he'd dug in the center of the structure.

The sweat lodge had been used in the past by the men of his mother's tribe for all kinds of ceremonies, to secure dreams, and for pleasure. It was also used to help get them through rough emotional ordeals, like anger or deep depression. Some used it with prayer as a means of increasing their spiritual power, some to promote physical healing.

Ty was using it to expedite his own physical healing. And at the back of his mind was the hope that it might help him forget about Lee Ann. Now that he'd secured the money he needed, he was ready to return to rodeo.

Climbing to his feet, he picked up the small shovel and began to carefully transfer the stones, one by one, into the lodge. When he finished, he moved toward the stream, lifted the bucket he had filled with water and set it beside the entrance.

Then, seating himself beside the stream, he removed his boots and socks, stood and ripped open his shirt, preparing for the cleansing bath he must first take before entering the lodge.

"Ty—I've been looking for you everywhere."

He froze, the sides of his shirt in both hands and away from his body. *Not now.* He wasn't ready to deal with her yet.

"I wasn't expecting visitors." The words sounded stiff and unwelcoming, but there was nothing he could do about it. At this moment, she was the last person he wanted to see.

"I'm sorry." Lee Ann's throat tightened. Obviously, she wasn't welcome. "I didn't mean to intrude, but I went to see Cody at the hospital a little while ago and—"

"How is he?" Ty asked abruptly, his back still turned toward her.

"Better." What was wrong with him? He acted as though he was angry. If anyone had a right to be angry, it was her.

"Did he send you?" Ty asked tautly.

"No... well, not exactly," she hedged.

Releasing his breath, he turned to face her. "He told you about the accident. About the man he heard on the phone and the rope Shorty found."

Lee Ann stared at his impassive expression and knew things weren't going as she'd planned. Every defense he'd ever built against her was firmly in place and she realized that nothing she said was going to get through to him.

"He told me," she admitted. Ignoring the sudden tightening of his jaw, she continued, "And I think you're a fool if you don't do something about it. Do you *want* to die?"

"No," he answered tersely, "I do not want to die. But I'm not going to go chasing after shadows, either."

"Then what are you going to do—just pretend it never happened?"

"It was an accident. Just like your brother's death was an accident. So let's just leave it at that."

"It wasn't an accident," Lee Ann insisted. "Cody said the rope had been cut, just like my brother's had been cut."

"What are you saying? Do you really think there's some serial killer on the rodeo circuit, killing cowboys—because he doesn't like the clothes they wear, or because his mother was frightened by a horse before he was born?" he asked scathingly.

He shifted as though to move around her and Lee Ann grabbed his forearm. "Don't make fun of me, this isn't a matter for levity."

"You're damned right it isn't," he agreed, staring her down.

But Lee Ann wasn't daunted for long. "Why did you go to the bank?" she asked abruptly, feeling the muscles in his arm grow rigid.

"How did you know about that?"

"The whole town probably knows about it by now." She didn't mention Vint Patterson's urgent desire to speak with her father. At this point, that would only make things worse.

"But that's not what's at issue. Someone wants to kill you and if they tried once, they'll try again."

Ty wrenched his arm from her grasp and moved toward the sweat lodge. "I guess now is as good a time as any to tell you that I'm leaving, just as soon as Cody can travel."

She should have known he'd run away, that's what he'd done the last time things had gotten too complicated. "You're good at running, aren't you?"

"What am I running from? I came back, and now I'm leaving." He shrugged.

"Why did you come back?"

"I had no place else to go," he said bluntly.

"And what about . . . us?" She hadn't meant to ask that question, but she hadn't expected him to say he was leaving, either.

Ty closed his eyes against the pain in her voice. "Us?" he asked softly, knowing he was being brutal, but unable to say what she wanted to hear.

Lee Ann bit her lip and swallowed hard. "You're planning to go back to rodeo."

"It's what I do."

"It almost killed you!"

He shrugged again and she wanted to grab him and shake him until he made sense. How could he do this? How could he simply walk away?

Taking a deep breath, swallowing the terrible anger that wanted to lash out at him, she lifted her head and said, "What if you can't go back to rodeo?"

Ty swung slowly to face her. "What's stopping me?"

"Nothing . . . yet."

The hazel eyes narrowed on her pale face. "Yet?"

"The other day, Cody talked to someone who told him about a rumor circulating through the PRCA. They're talking about suspending you."

"They can't do that!"

"Cody says they can. He said they worry a lot about image."

"It sounds to me like Cody had too damned much to say."

Lee Ann ignored his sarcasm and continued. "And right now, with my brother's death still in question, your image isn't very good."

"Damn you!" Twisting away from her, shirt flapping, he strode toward the trees.

Lee Ann took a few hurried steps after him, then halted, anger getting the better of her. "Don't take your rage out on me!" she shouted. "I didn't have anything to do with your being an arrogant, self-centered, pigheaded fool!"

Ty skidded to a halt, fury in every line of his body as he turned slowly to face her. "What you need is someone to take you in hand," he growled, his long strides taking him to within a foot of her. "If your father hadn't been so busy all his life, perfecting the art of being a bastard, he might have found time to do it."

God, he made her so mad! She wanted to... Her eyes fell on his chest, on the silver necklace lying so lovingly in the hollow of his throat. "You think I need taking in hand?" she asked faintly.

"Yes" was his quick response.

Her glance moved over his smooth hairless chest, down past his navel to the hint of black hair at the open waistband of his loose jeans. "The job's open," she whispered, her eyes darting to his face. "Want to apply?"

For an instant, the hazel eyes locked with hers grew dark and turbulent with emotion, then shifted abruptly to a spot past her shoulder. "I wouldn't be any good at it."

"How do you know?"

He pulled his brown shirt open and said, "Look at me. Look at the scars. Is this what you want?"

Lee Ann stared at the faint lines crisscrossing his chest and side. In the near dark, the other day in the mountains, they hadn't been so evident.

"You want to know why I didn't attend my uncle's funeral? I was laid up in the hospital with a fractured collarbone and a couple of busted ribs."

Lee Ann pressed her lips together, blinked and looked away.

Ty took hold of her chin and pulled her face up to his, forcing her to meet his eyes. "You don't like it, but it's what I do—I take chances."

"Why?" she asked, trying to mask the tears in her voice.

Ty let her go and stepped back. He shrugged. She wouldn't understand. "The money is good."

"You can make good money doing something else, something that doesn't require you to take chances with your life," she insisted.

"What? What can I do? I finished high school by the seat of my pants. And I spent most of my time while I was there in detention. This is what I'm good at—it's the only thing I'm good at."

"I don't believe you. You're an intelligent man, I know you could do something else if you tried," she said earnestly.

"Sure, maybe I could be a banker," he said derisively. "Oh, no, that wouldn't work—no one would trust someone like me with their money. I'm not white. I've got it—" he snapped his fingers "—I could work for the city, clean streets for a living, dig ditches. Is that what you want me to do?" Without waiting for her reply, he almost shouted, "No thanks! I like what I do and I don't plan to change my life to suit someone else. I'm sorry, but that's the way it is."

The expression on her face had become wounded. Ty wanted to pretend he didn't see it, but he couldn't.

"Look," he said softly, wanting to touch her, taking a step in her direction and then stepping back, "you don't like what I do and that's all right. You can't help your feelings any more than I can help mine. Anyway, you don't want someone like me—"

"Don't tell me what I want!"

"Then don't tell me what I have to do," he countered in a louder voice. And then his face softened. "Look, we can still be friends. I'll send you a postcard every now and then, and you can send me fudge at Christmas." He tried a smile.

Lee Ann gazed at him without expression. It hurt like hell, knowing she'd humbled herself to him and he'd rejected her. But she had an ace in the hole that he didn't know about.

"Who do you think is behind the possible suspension?" she asked deliberately. And when he didn't speak, she added, "Vint Patterson stopped me to tell me he has an urgent message for my father. Now, what do you suppose it could be about?"

Now she'd done it, she'd set the cat among the pigeons with that question. In order to straighten things out between Ty and her father, maybe she'd have to use their enmity against them. It would be tricky and not altogether what she'd originally had in mind, but if it worked . . .

Ty stepped away from her and moved toward the stream. The answer to all her questions was really very simple. So simple, even he could understand it. Her father wanted Broken Heart Ranch. And if Ty couldn't work and pay back the loan, he'd lose it by default. Wade Newley could then buy it at auction.

And like a fool, half-angered by Lee Ann's humiliating offer of money, Ty had played right into the man's hands. When Wade learned about the loan, he'd push even harder to get Ty suspended.

"What does Cody suggest we do?" he asked with his back to her.

"He's going to draw a picture of the man he saw talking on the phone. We'll make copies of the drawing and take it around to all the rodeos and see if anyone can identify the man."

"We?" Ty asked, pivoting slowly toward her.

Lee Ann swallowed. "Yes. Jennifer has agreed to help, and I thought—"

"No!"

"It only makes sense—"

"It makes no sense!" he shouted. "No sense at all." Running a hand through his long black hair, he added, "I don't even know why I'm discussing this with you. The whole thing is crazy. Do you have any idea how many rodeos are held in a month?"

"No," Lee Ann admitted. "Do you?"

He gave her a steely glare. "No, I don't. But I do know I won't be party to such a plan."

"Then what will you do?"

"Nothing. I'll go back to riding and make as much money as I can until the board makes a decision."

"Nothing I can say will change your mind?"

"Nothing."

"You can't stop the three of us from going ahead with the plan."

"Cody won't do it, if I tell him not to."

Lee Ann looked him up and down scornfully, knowing she was defeated. "You're such a fool—such a blind fool! But nothing I can say will change your mind, so I won't even try."

She felt as if she were dying inside, but she'd be damned if she'd let it show. "When I hear where they've sent your body," she said coldly, "I'll be sure and send flowers."

Ty watched her go, stung by that last remark, knowing he deserved it. If he'd wanted to hurt her, he couldn't have done a more thorough job. But it was better this way. He'd been serious when he'd told her she didn't want *him*. She wanted someone who was safe, someone she could count on to come home every night all in one piece.

* * *

An hour later, he shrugged out of his shirt, letting it fall to the ground. When he was completely naked, he stepped into the stream and slowly lowered himself into the water. This was part of the cleansing ritual and necessary, he told himself when his muscles knotted in protest as the icy water slid over his groin.

A few minutes later, he stepped from the water and hurried, shivering, to the sweat lodge. Bending low, he entered the small enclosure and darkness immediately surrounded him.

Stopping just inside, he reached through the flap and drew a cup of water from the bucket. Crawling toward the center of the lodge, he curled his knees beneath his chin and slowly poured the water onto the hot rocks. They made a hissing sound as the steam rose, filling the tiny space. And in a short time, he began to get the feeling back in his chilled limbs.

Folding his arms around his knees, he sat with closed eyes. It was a world of darkness and silence, and as he grew warmer a feeling of peace and security wrapped itself around him. He wondered fleetingly if this is what if felt like to rest inside a mother's womb.

He'd found his mother not long after leaving Rainville. She lived on the Blackfoot reservation in the northwestern part of Montana, east of the Glacier National Park. Though he'd been determined to find her, he'd held himself away from her when he did, resenting the fact that she'd abandoned him.

She'd explained why she'd left him with his father's brother. She had been very young when she'd met his father and they'd fallen in love. She had just learned she was pregnant when Ty's father was sent to Vietnam.

They hadn't been married, there hadn't been time. Ashamed, she'd scraped by during her pregnancy and the first year after Ty was born, barely managing to feed and clothe them both. But she became ill and admitted she wasn't taking proper care of her baby. She was afraid to go back home, because she'd run away, so she'd gone to Ty's uncle and he'd taken them both in.

But she hadn't been happy on the ranch. She longed for her family. She wanted to return to the reservation. Deciding it was best for him, she left Ty with his uncle and made her way back to her own people.

Later, when she was well, she had wanted to go after him, but her father had told her to wait. He'd said the boy should have the chance to get to know his father's people and that when the time was right, he would seek the spirit of the Indian inside him.

His mother's tired, careworn eyes had begged him to understand and he'd tried. For a time, he'd lived among her people—his people—and learned that they didn't resent him for being half-white.·

His grandfather had taken Ty under his wing and taught him some of their ways, telling stories about the old days when life among the people was good and the land clean and untainted. It was his grandfather who had taught him the healing qualities of the sweat lodge.

Ty straightened, reached outside the flap and drew another cup of water. He poured it slowly on the hot rocks. Steam hissed and rose toward the opening at the top of the lodge.

He continued the ritual, breathing deeply each time, feeling the heat sear his lungs until he felt as though they'd turned to leather and his skin might split apart from the heat.

Sweat dripped from the ends of his hair and collected in small pools before sliding down his body to be swallowed by the hard ground beneath him. He alternately prayed and chanted the ancient words his grandfather had taught him. And according to ritual, four times he left the sweat lodge to plunge into the cold mountain water. On his last return, he was staggering.

Sinking to the ground, he let his head fall forward because it was too heavy to keep upright. His senses were swimming and nothing felt quite real.

He must have passed out, because suddenly his eyes opened and he became aware of his surroundings. An instant later, his red-rimmed eyes widened in shock as images began to form in the vapor.

He was no longer alone in the lodge. Across from him sat his grandfather, and to the left of him, the man's son—his mother's brother—and on the right sat his mother's uncle. They nodded to him briefly and took up the chant.

The lodge faded around him and Ty was sitting on the chute at the last rodeo in which he'd competed, getting ready to slip his legs over the back of a bull. All at once, his head jerked up and he was staring into the narrowed eyes of a stranger. Ty's blood turned to ice. The man's eyes were empty as though there were nothing inside of him—as though he had no soul.

Ty's glance shifted to Les, perched beside him, staring coldly. And then Les's features began to shimmer and Lee Ann's face took shape.

The man with the empty eyes turned toward her and Ty saw he had a knife in his hand. Lee Ann's mouth opened in a silent scream and Ty knew she was calling his name, begging him for help, as she cringed from the man and the knife.

No! Ty tried to shout, tried to lunge at the man, but he couldn't speak or move. The knife suddenly thrust toward Lee Ann and she was falling over the side of the chute.

Released from his temporary paralysis, Ty heaved himself into the arena. But it was too late. He held Lee Ann's bleeding body in his arms. The last word on her lips was his name.

Ty looked up at the killer. And though the man's eyes were expressionless, he was laughing, his mouth gaping with mirth. The laughter swelled. Lee Ann disappeared. Ty clamped a hand over his ears to shut out the sound. An instant later, the man was gone and the whole scene disappeared in a burst of bright flames.

Ty snapped upright, shaking all over, and peered around him with wide eyes. He was alone. The images of his mother's ancestors were gone. But the echo of laughter still filled his ears.

Throwing himself toward the opening of the sweat lodge, he crawled outside and lay against the ground. For a little while, it was all he could do to breathe. But the cool earth pressing into his parched body, gave him new strength. In time, he managed to pull himself forward.

At the water's edge, he glanced down at his reflection, but it was his grandfather's face he saw. The old man was trying to tell him something. And though Ty couldn't hear with his ears, the words rang clear in his mind.

"Hello?"

"It's me."

Recognizing the sonorous timbre, Lee Ann pressed the phone against her cheek. "Yes?"

"I'm at the hospital." Ty eyed the man in the bed mockingly. "Cody has convinced me to give his idea a try."

Lee Ann's grip tightened. "What about Jennifer...and me?"

Twisting around so his words wouldn't be easily heard by the other man, Ty spoke directly into the mouthpiece, demanding, "Why is this so important to you?"

Lee Ann hesitated. She'd been rebuffed by him once already today and her pride couldn't take another such blow. "I want to prove to my father that he's wrong about you."

The hand holding the phone grew taut. "I don't need you to fight my battles for me," Ty muttered urgently, the image of her bleeding body in his mind.

It was for her sake, and her sake alone that he'd agreed to this ridiculous plan. The vision in the sweat lodge had been a warning. And he knew that if he didn't heed it, she'd go ahead and possibly get herself killed.

"I told you, I'm doing this for Dad," Lee Ann responded with just enough surprise in her voice to make it believable. "It isn't healthy for a man his age to get so emotionally worked up. He could have a heart attack or a stroke."

"I stand corrected," Ty said with irony. "Anyway, you and your friend are in. It will be like looking for a needle in a haystack." He shrugged. "But if that's what you want..."

Replacing the receiver without saying goodbye, he turned to his friend. "She's doing this for her father."

"And who are you doing it for?"

"I just don't want her to go off half-cocked and get into trouble," he answered gruffly.

Cody grinned. "Pardner, I think you've finally met your match."

Chapter 9

"Well, let's see what you've got."

Cody turned the sketch around and Ty leaned forward to look at it.

"You're good," Ty said, noting the lifelike detail in the figure and face. "If you can draw this good, why in blazes are you a rodeo bum?" His eyes cut to the other man's face. Cody shifted on the bed and shrugged.

Ty glanced back at the drawing and said, "If I had a talent like this—"

"You'd still be a rodeo bum," Cody interrupted.

Ty grinned without taking his eyes off the paper, something about it nagging at the back of his mind. He looked at Cody. "Can you do a sketch of the face by itself, with more detail?"

"Sure." Flipping to a clean piece of paper, the other man set to work.

Ty watched his friend's fingers fly over the page, noting Cody's air of intense concentration. His glance shifted to the man's face. He couldn't figure him out.

"How's that?" Cody pushed the paper toward him. "That's the best I can do with a pencil, but I think it's pretty accurate."

Ty reached for the drawing, shifting his attention slowly from his friend's face to the paper in his hand—and the breath froze solid in his chest.

"This is the man you saw?" he asked tautly.

"That's him, as best as I can recall," Cody said.

"I'll never forget his eyes," he continued. "Just for a moment, when he turned away from the phone, he looked directly at me. I was hidden in the shadows and I'm pretty certain he didn't suspect I was there, but still . . . I've never seen such expressionless eyes in a man's face—not while he was still breathing." He glanced up at Ty. "What's wrong? Do you know him?" he asked.

Ty shook his head, studying the thick lips, round face and receding hairline. He could hardly stand to look at the empty eyes.

"I think you're doing the right thing," Cody said. "I wouldn't want him after me. All you have to do is look real close to know he's ruthless. A man who'd never give up—not till you were dead, if that's the way he wanted it."

"And that's exactly why the idea of looking for him isn't a very smart one," Ty said, shooting Cody a sharp glance. "If he's willing to kill twice, what makes you think he wouldn't be just as willing to kill again? Especially if he thought somebody was on to him."

"Have you got a better idea?"

"Yes," Ty said getting to his feet, "but you wouldn't like it."

"It isn't like we're going after him with drawn guns," Cody reasoned. "We're only trying to find him."

"And then?"

Cody shrugged. "I go to the police and tell them what I heard and Shorty—" He broke off. "Shorty will tell them about what he saw. And when they go to question the man, if he makes a run for it, we'll know he's guilty."

Ty knew Shorty could be a problem. "And if Shorty won't cooperate?"

Cody stared at him without answering.

"And what if the man doesn't make a run for it?" Ty asked softly.

"You think he won't?"

"I think a man with eyes like those isn't going to be easily spooked." Ty picked up the drawing and stared at it for a long pensive moment. "I think a man like that is more likely to eliminate anyone who threatens him, not run."

"Are you saying you think we should forget the whole thing?" Cody asked.

"No," Ty answered without hesitation. "It's too late for that." Folding the sketch and shoving it into his breast pocket, he moved toward the door. "I'll take this and have copies made."

At the door he paused. "When are they letting you out of here?"

"Tomorrow about eleven."

Ty nodded. "I'll be back."

The only copying machine in town was located in the bank, and he didn't want to use it. Besides, he needed transportation of his own and Rainville didn't have a used-car lot. At the edge of town, he took a right turn instead of a left, calling himself all kinds of a fool, and drove toward Willow's Rest.

Lee Ann was an accomplished pianist and she was playing a piano concerto when Ty walked into the room. He stood listening, until she must have felt another's presence and whirled around on the bench.

"I didn't hear the doorbell."

Ty moved to the center of the room, his hat in his hands. "I didn't ring it."

"Oh..."

"I need to buy a truck," he announced, getting right to the point. "And since Cody's in the hospital, I need someone to drive his truck back to the ranch. If you aren't busy, I thought you might come along and show me the best place to get what I need. Things have changed a bit since I lived round here."

Lee Ann wasn't flattered that he'd thought of her. She was the only one in town he could ask and they both knew it.

"I'll just change—"

"You'll do," he interrupted her, giving the cranberry red tank top and black jeans a quick glance. "Let's go." Without waiting, he turned and strode from the room.

Lee Ann stood a moment in growing irritation. She'd been pleased when he'd called to say he was agreeing to Cody's plan, but now, she felt like telling him where to go. The only thing stopping her was the knowledge that he was right, he needed transportation of his own.

The idea of offering to use her car came and went. Her car was still in the garage. The brakes were fixed, but Wylie Peebles had found something wrong with the carburetor. And she could just imagine what Ty would say if she suggested using her father's.

A horn blared and Lee Ann grabbed her shoulder bag and headed for the door. Ty had the engine running and his foot off the brake before she climbed inside and slammed the door.

"Where to?" Ty asked, studying the skyline. "You navigate, I don't know what's here anymore."

"All right," Lee Ann agreed. "Take a left. We'll go to Bozeman."

Ty obliged and they drove the first few miles in silence.

"Did Cody make the sketch?"

"Yes."

"Is it a good one?"

"Remarkable."

The corners of her mouth twisted with exasperation. "When is he going to be released from the hospital?" Lee Ann asked, wondering if Ty planned to carry on a one word conversation the whole trip.

"Tomorrow."

"When are we leaving for the first rodeo?"

"Day after tomorrow."

Well, at least she'd gotten three words at one time out of him. She was making progress.

Ty cast her a brief look of inquiry. "That too soon?"

Lee Ann shook her head. "I'm ready today, if you are."

He removed a folded piece of paper from his shirt pocket and handed it to her. "That's the man we're going after."

Lee Ann glanced down at the face and a mild gasp escaped her.

"Still want to come along?" Ty asked sharply.

Lifting her head, she narrowed her eyes on his face. "You bet your life I do."

"And maybe it's your life you'll be betting," Ty murmured.

Lee Ann felt her flesh crawl, but she commented lightly, "I'm not afraid. I'll have you there to protect me." She felt for an instant as though he was on the brink of saying something, then he seemed to think better of it and concentrated his full attention on his driving.

"The other day, when I found you down at the stream, what was that tentlike thing?" she asked abruptly.

"A sweat lodge."

"Did you build it?"

"Yes. Why?"

"I've always had the idea that you resented your Indian heritage. At least, when we were younger, I thought you did, because of your mother."

"What about my mother?" he asked stiffly.

"Well—" Surprised at the defensive twist to the sensual mouth, she hesitated, wishing she'd kept her comments to herself. "I just meant because of the way she left you."

"She had her reasons."

"You found her?" Lee Ann asked in surprise.

"Yes," he answered sourly. "I found her."

"When? Where?"

"When I left town. She was living with her people."

"Is that where you learned to build a sweat lodge?"

"You ask a lot of questions," he muttered, giving her an irritated glance.

"I'm sorry," she said awkwardly, twisting her fingers together in her lap and staring out the windshield. She was only trying to learn more about him and what he'd been doing since he'd left town.

"Yes, that's where I learned about sweat lodges. I stayed with my mother and her people for about a year. I liked living with them," he answered.

"Why did you leave?"

"My mother's father died," he murmured reluctantly. "I liked him. And when he died—" He shrugged. "I didn't belong there any more than I belonged in Rainville."

"How can you say that? Your uncle loved you very much."

"I didn't say my uncle didn't love me. I said I didn't belong. And I didn't—I don't," he added firmly.

"Did you ever want to belong?" Lee Ann asked somberly. "From what I remember, you went out of your way to antagonize everyone."

"I guess we remember things differently," he said. "I remember bloody noses and black eyes, because I was different from the other kids." His voice became heated. "I remember being called names I'd never heard until I started school. And I remember being made fun of because my clothes had holes and my hair was too long.

"And I remember the teacher sending home papers for my uncle to sign so I could get free lunches. I tore them up. I didn't want their free lunches."

Lee Ann bit her lip and stared out the window. Even though she'd had no part in any of that, she felt guilt for the way he'd been treated, because she knew her brother had been one of the worst offenders.

She reached toward him. "I'm sorry."

"I don't want your pity." He shot her a stiff glance from angry green eyes. "I didn't tell you that so you'd feel sorry for me. I never wasted my time feeling sorry for myself. I told you so you'd understand that though we live on the same planet, we come from very different worlds."

Recalling her own lonely existence before he'd come on the scene, Lee Ann dropped her hand and said, "Not as different as you think."

But Ty was immersed in his own memories and either didn't hear, or chose not to. They finished the rest of the trip in an uneasy silence.

Two hours later, Ty signed his name on the bill of sale and pocketed keys to his new used Ford truck. It would be two more hours before the truck dealership would have it ready for him.

Once they'd reached the truck, Ty closed the vehicle's door after Lee Ann and moved to the other side to climb behind the wheel. But instead of inserting the key and starting the engine, he looked at the woman beside him and asked, "What would you like to do for the next couple of hours?"

"Would you like me to show you where your uncle is buried?" she asked gently. "It's back toward Rainville."

Ty nodded and Lee Ann gave him directions out of town. But just before they left the town behind, he pulled into a small shopping plaza and stopped.

"I'll be right back," he said briskly, reaching for the door handle.

When he returned, he was carrying a pot of fresh flowers. Putting it on the seat between them, he said, "Okay, where to?"

It was twenty miles north and another ten miles west of Rainville to the Shepherd's Hills Cemetery. They made it here in a little over half an hour. And they drove in silence.

Lee Ann directed him to his uncle's grave, then sat in the truck while he walked up the hill by himself. There were tears in her eyes as she watched him kneel and dig a place to plant the flowers with his bare hands.

Who was this man, she asked herself, watching as he bowed his head. One minute he was cold and mocking, hiding behind a wall so high she couldn't see over the top and then he did something like this. Would she ever understand him?

When they got back to Bozeman, they still had an hour before he could pick up his truck, and Ty suggested an ice-cream cone and a walk in the park. While they were sitting on a park bench, licking raspberry ice cream, Lee Ann asked curiously, "How did you and Cody get to be friends?"

Ty took a bite out of his cone and gave her a sideways glance. "You mean how did someone as nice as Cody get hooked up with a bastard like me?"

Lee Ann blushed, recalling her words of the day before and suddenly the ice cream tasted sour. "I was just making conversation."

Wiping his hands on a napkin and dropping it in the trash container nearby, he sat back, folded his arms across his chest, stuck his long legs out and contemplated the toes of his boots. Instead of answering her question, he said, "Life is funny, isn't it? Twelve years ago—hell, two years ago—I'd never have believed I'd be sitting on a park bench eating ice cream with you."

His glance swung slowly toward her face. "What about you, did you ever think of me, while you were away at your fancy college? Oh, I forgot," he said abruptly, straightening, "you were too busy getting engaged to think about a troublemaker you'd once known back home."

"I thought about you," Lee Ann admitted.

Ty's glance centered on her mouth. "Did you?"

"Yes. You know—" She couldn't look at him, so she kept her eyes on the cone. "I never said anything to my father about...that night."

"That night?" He studied her lips intently.

"The night you found me hiding behind the barrels."

"Oh," he said softly. "That night."

"Yes." She glanced up. The ice cream was melting in her hand, but she couldn't move. Something about the way he was studying her made her insides feel like warm jelly. Then he began to lean toward her and she couldn't breathe.

"You have a spot of ice cream right there," he said, touching the edge of her lower lip with one fingertip.

Embarrassed, Lee Ann's tongue flicked out to capture it and encountered the tip of his finger. Ty's glance shot upward and Lee Ann's heart skipped a beat.

Watching her, he pushed his finger over her bottom lip and against the edge of her teeth. Her lips parted automatically and his nail touched the tip of her tongue.

The pupils of her eyes expanded with emotion and the flush on her cheeks turned a deeper red. With his glance locked on hers, Ty removed the dripping cone from her fingers and dropped it into the trash container near his elbow. Taking her hand, he lifted it and slowly placed one finger inside his mouth.

Lee Ann quivered like a bowstring as he licked the ice cream from her fingers, one at a time. There were other people in the park, but all she could think about was how much she wanted him to kiss her, lay her down on the soft grass and slowly remove the clothes from her body, leaving a trail of kisses in their wake....

Pulling her finger slowly from between his lips, he kissed the tip, and Lee Ann realized he must have read her thoughts. Turning away in humiliation, she broke all contact between them.

"Why are you doing this?" she asked in an unsteady voice.

"You were sticky," he murmured deeply, still watching her with that concentrated stare. "And I'm all out of napkins."

"And I'm all out of patience," Lee Ann said firmly, getting to her feet. Why was he playing games with her? He'd told her that he couldn't be what she wanted. Did he enjoy torturing her?

"I think it's time we left," she said, marching stiffly toward the park entrance.

Ty followed more slowly. Once inside the truck, he appeared almost sullen. Lee Ann assumed she'd angered him because she wasn't willing to play his little games. Didn't he realize how much he could hurt her, or didn't he care?

It was almost dark when Ty stopped his truck in Lee Ann's driveway after leaving Cody's truck at Ty's ranch. He'd enjoyed her company, and he wanted to tell her that, but couldn't after the way he'd acted in the park.

He hadn't been angry with her, though he knew she'd thought she was the focus of his ill temper. He'd been angry with himself. He knew he ought to leave her alone, quit playing with her emotions, but his emotions were involved, too, and he seemed to be having difficulty keeping them under control whenever she was around.

"It's dinnertime," Lee Ann observed without making any effort to leave the truck. "I could make us something to eat," she offered tentatively.

"No, I don't think so," Ty answered quickly. "I've got a lot of things to do."

"Name one."

"Figure out what I'm going to have for dinner," he answered, his eyes suddenly crinkling at the corners.

Lee Ann caught her breath, thinking how attractive he was when the guarded expression left his face. Her eyes touched on the five-o'clock shadow covering his lower jaw and she realized that it added a sexy aura to his appearance. Her fingers itched to feel the whiskers.

One hand was half off her lap and moving toward his cheek before she was conscious of it. Dropping it quickly to her lap, the other hand grasping it tightly as though to keep it in place, she swallowed and gave him a tiny smile.

"Is the invitation still open, or have you changed your mind?" Ty suddenly asked with a sheepish grin.

"I'm not much of a cook," she warned as they climbed out of the truck. "But I can use a can opener with the best of them, and I have no trouble boiling water."

"Well," he said, hesitating as though about to change his mind, "boiled water isn't exactly what I call a meal." As she turned the key in the lock, he asked, "What made you decide to come back here after college and keep house for your father?"

"How did you know that?" Lee Ann stopped just inside the door to look at him.

Ty pushed his hands into his pockets and shrugged, glancing away.

"Les?"

"When he was drunk, he talked about you," Ty admitted, moving closer, backing her into the corner by the door, his hands moving toward her face. He just couldn't seem to stay away from her. All day long, he'd been thinking how good it would feel to hold her and bury his face in her sweet-smelling hair.

"I think he did it deliberately," he said softly.

"Why?" she asked breathlessly.

"Because..."

Lee Ann's heart skipped a beat. Was he about to admit that he cared about her? She swayed toward him—and the telephone rang.

Ty gave a nervous start, seemed to come to his senses and backed away looking at his raised hands as though he didn't recognize them.

"Go on, answer the phone," he said quickly. "Answer the phone. I've got to go, anyway."

Before she could offer a protest, he added, "We forgot to make copies of the sketch. If I hurry, I should be able to get it done tonight. I'll talk to you tomorrow. Thanks for going with me and driving Cody's truck back to the ranch."

And he was gone.

Lee Ann stared in bitter disappointment at the spot where he'd stood only moments before, the telephone ringing in the background. One of these days, she promised herself, he was going to admit that he loved her.

And when he did, nothing would separate them ever again.

Chapter 10

"Are you excited?" Lee Ann asked, watching her friend pat her short blond hair into place.

"I guess," Jennifer replied a little uncertainly.

"Come on, what's worrying you? Is it Cody? You aren't worried about traveling with him, are you?" Lee Ann asked carefully. She was traveling with Ty to a rodeo in one town, while Jennifer and Cody attended one in another miles away. The men were familiar with rodeo crowds and would know who to talk to about the man in the drawing. The women were along because two people could cover twice as much ground in half the time.

"No," Jennifer replied. "I like him. What about you?" she asked. "How do you feel about attending a rodeo?"

Lee Ann shrugged.

"I thought you didn't like them."

"I'm not actually *attending* the rodeo," Lee Ann explained, zipping her overnight bag and sitting down on the side of the bed. "It's the rodeo crowd that I'm going to see."

"You mean you aren't going to watch the competition?"

"No." That's the last thing she wanted to do.

"Can I ask you something?"

"Sure."

"Well, I understand a little about how you feel about rodeo, because of your brother's death, but—"

"But he could have been killed crossing the street." Lee Ann interrupted. "And if he'd died that way, would I never have wanted to cross another street? Is that what you mean?"

"Sorry, it's none of my business."

Lee Ann relented. "Rodeo has been little more than a curse in my life as far back as I can remember. I know I've never said much to you about my childhood," she said, "so you can't possibly understand. But I grew up playing second fiddle to my father's business, which is rodeo, and my brother's compulsive determination to best my father's past record in rodeo. Neither of them had a moment to spare for me."

She twisted the strap on the bag. "How would you feel," she asked abruptly, "if the man you loved preferred something else to you?" Glancing up into the mirror, she saw the surprise reflected in her friend's eyes. "I know, I was shocked, too, when I realized how I felt."

Jennifer turned and leaned back against the dresser. "I—I didn't know, I mean, I thought you felt something for him—it is Ty, isn't it?"

Lee Ann nodded.

Jennifer spread her hands, then let them fall to her sides. "What are you going to do?"

"What else can I do? I'm going to make him want me so much, he won't be able to think about anything else—especially rodeo."

Jennifer smiled. Then a worried look dimmed the green eyes. "What about your father?"

Momentarily abashed, Lee Ann jumped off the bed and moved across the room. These past few days, she'd felt as though the world had turned upside down and she was hanging on to it by her toes. She was tired of feeling that way.

"You worry too much. When we prove Ty had nothing to do with Les's death, Dad will come around."

"I hope so," Jennifer said, sounding dubious.

Lee Ann paused, picked up a brush and began to drag it through her dark curls. "Jen, you do think we're doing the right thing, don't you?" She eyed the other woman through the mirror.

"It's a little late to be worrying about that."

"I guess you're right."

"What makes you think Ty cares more about rodeo than you?" Jennifer asked abruptly.

Lee Ann ran a thumb over the bristles of the brush before answering. "Sometimes, I think he hates me."

"That wasn't the impression I got the other night in the restaurant."

"No?" Lee Ann looked up.

"No. It looked more like . . . yearning."

"Yearning?"

"Yes, like he was looking at something he wanted very badly, but was afraid to reach out to take."

Lee Ann dropped the brush to the dresser. "I doubt that," she said softly. "There's so much you don't know." She was remembering last night and the aborted kiss and Ty's subsequent swift retreat.

She hung her head. "But I know Ty isn't a killer," she whispered strongly. "And we've got to find the person responsible for my brother's death so I can prove it to my father."

"Do you think your father will believe you, even then?" Jennifer asked.

"He'd have to."

Jennifer shrugged. "What about Ty? Do you think he'll simply forget the way your father has treated him?"

Lee Ann's eyes darkened. "That's too much to ask, isn't it?"

Jennifer took her by the shoulders and gave her a gentle shake. "How much do you love him?"

"What do you mean?"

"I mean, you're asking a great deal of him. You're asking him to forget what you've intimated has been a long history of abuse at the hands of your father and brother. But, what about you? What are you willing to forget?"

"I still don't see what you're getting at." But she did.

"Do you love *him* enough to follow him from one rodeo to another?"

Lee Ann stiffened. "That isn't the same thing."

"No?"

"No," Lee Ann insisted. "Don't you understand? He's risking his life every time he rides. I don't want him dead!"

"What attracted you to him in the first place?"

Lee Ann glanced at her sharply and slid out of her reach.

"Didn't you once tell me that he was an amazing rider?" Jennifer demanded. "Didn't you tell me you used to sneak out at night to watch him ride?"

"This isn't the same thing," Lee Ann said stubbornly. "We were kids. He was only playing at it, but this is for real. This is his life we're talking about."

"Exactly," Jennifer said with meaning. "It's *his* life." And when Lee Ann made no immediate comment, she continued, "Why did you never believe Ty guilty of your brother's death?"

"Because he isn't a killer."

"Neither is he a doctor, nor a banker, nor a lawyer."

Lee Ann frowned. "I don't get it."

"You can accept that murder is beyond his character— but you can't accept what makes up the rest of it? You're asking him to change his whole way of life for you. What are you willing to change for him?"

"You don't understand."

"No, perhaps you're right...but maybe *you* don't understand, either."

Lee Ann stood in the middle of the motel room and stared at the furnishings. The color scheme was orange and brown. She had a fairly good idea why the carpet was that color—so it wouldn't show the marks of heavy traffic.

The bed was one of those built with a solid wooden frame, the mattresses laid on a piece of hard flat wood, the headboard bolted to the wall. A square wooden table, two padded chairs, a dresser with a mirror and a color television also bolted to the wall comprised the furniture.

Placing her overnight bag on the end of the bed, she marched into the bathroom and flipped on the light. A sink, a stool and a tub and shower all a sparkling white. Well, at least that was acceptable.

She and Ty had arrived in Helena a little while ago. He'd made the reservations a couple of days ago and this was all that was available at such short notice, he'd explained, handing her a room key. He'd refused her offer to pay for her own room and disappeared.

Glancing down at her watch, she decided to take a shower. The water would be warm and there were plenty of towels.

A little later, she sat in one of the chairs and flipped through the television channels. The motel boasted cable TV, because of the mountains, but there were only local stations to choose from. She wasn't much of a television fan, anyway. But she was bored and beginning to feel apprehensive.

Switching off the set, she threw the remote onto the bed and got to her feet. Her eyes fell on the drawing lying on the dresser. She wished it were all over with and the man in custody.

A knock sounded at the door. She gave a nervous start and moved toward it cautiously. Stopping within a foot of it, she called, "Who is it?"

"It's me."

Relieved to hear Ty's voice, she grabbed the doorknob and twisted the dead bolt. "Where have you been?" she was asking as the door swung open.

He stepped into the room. "I went to the arena and took a look around. I thought maybe I might spot our man right away and all this wouldn't be necessary."

"Did you?" she asked quickly.

"No such luck." Crossing the room, he dropped onto a chair and folded his hands across the silver-and-bronze championship buckle at his middle.

"You're a bundle of nerves," he commented, watching her. "This isn't exactly your scene, is it?" He gestured toward the room's shabby interior.

"It's fine." Lee Ann darted a swift glance around the room. "It's clean," she offered with a shrug.

Ty studied her a moment longer before getting to his feet and grabbing her bag off the bed. "Come on, get your things together."

"What are you doing?" She hurried toward him, reaching for her bag.

He evaded her hands. "I'm taking you home."

"You're doing no such thing," she insisted angrily. "I'm not going anywhere until this rodeo is over."

"You have no business here," he snapped. "You don't belong here. I was a damned fool for ever letting you talk me into this."

"You don't belong here, either," Lee Ann said, referring to more than the motel room.

"That's where you're wrong," he said tautly. Whipping around, he strode toward her, stopped within a few inches of her and peered into her face. "You just can't get it through your head that this is *exactly* where I belong."

Throwing her bag onto the bed, he shook his head sadly. "I've got to go."

"Ty—"

Sidestepping her outstretched hand, he jerked open the door and slammed it behind him.

Lee Ann plopped down onto the bed and stared at the threadbare carpet. Now he was really angry with her. Would he be angry enough to go without her tomorrow when they were supposed to circulate with the drawings?

She thought about calling his room and apologizing, but couldn't bring herself to do it. She wasn't sorry for the way she felt. She just wished someone could understand her feelings. Not even Jennifer understood.

Lying back on the bed, she stared at the ceiling. What was she doing here? He was right. This wasn't her kind of place and rodeo certainly wasn't her kind of sport.

She tried convincing herself that she was here to help her father and Ty. In truth, she knew it was fear on her own behalf that drove her. The fear that Ty might disappear from her life just as suddenly as he had twelve years ago.

What would her life be like in ten years? She'd be almost forty—and a spinster. An old maid. If she didn't marry Ty she'd never marry anyone.

Pride made her ask herself if she was this desperate for a man—so desperate that she'd follow him, even when it was obvious that he didn't want her around? The answer, of course, was no—not just any man—but *the* man, yes. The man she loved. Ty.

That night, sleep was an elusive thing. Every sound in the hall outside her door disturbed her. And when a group of drunk cowboys bumped their way along the wall, trying their key in every lock, because they couldn't remember which room was theirs, Lee Ann got up to prop a chair beneath the door handle and sat up in bed staring at it for most of the night.

Ty came for her at eleven the next morning. They drove to the fairgrounds, where the Last Chance Rodeo was being held as a part of the Lewis and Clark County Fair.

In silence, he handed her a couple of drawings and took a couple for himself. Still in silence, they left the truck and walked side by side to the fairgrounds.

"You circulate around that way." He gestured with one hand, speaking for the first time since knocking on her door this morning and identifying himself. "I'll go this way. Don't bother asking the fair-goers if they've seen him. Show the drawing to the people running the booths. But don't leave it," he cautioned. "We don't want the man to accidentally come across one and find out we're looking for him. And keep your eyes peeled for him, yourself."

Lee Ann nodded and walked away. She moved through the throngs of people for over two hours, showing the drawing and asking if anyone recognized the man. Everyone's response was the same. No one knew him and no one remembered seeing anyone who looked like him.

The sun disappeared behind a cloud and the humidity level rose. Lee Ann's jeans began to chafe her legs, and even the denim shirt she wore, fringed across the yoke and down each sleeve, felt hot and constrictive.

With her mouth feeling as though it were stuffed with cotton, she halted abruptly near a food tent, watching a man take a long sip from a cup filled with soda and ice. Stomach growling, she succumbed to temptation.

A few minutes later, with a corn dog in one hand and a corn on the cob and soft drink in the other, she made her way to an empty seat at one of the tables beneath a shaded canopy.

"So, this is how you work."

Lee Ann had just taken a bite from her corn dog. Her head jerked at the sound of the familiar voice near her elbow, and mustard ran down her chin. She was reaching for a napkin when Ty dropped onto the metal chair beside her and took the napkin from her hand.

"I didn't realize you were such a messy eater. What other secrets have you been keeping from me?"

Lee Ann's surprised eyes clung to his face as he dabbed at her chin. Was he joking with her?

The hazel eyes drifted upward and his eyes locked with hers. "You have the most unusual eyes I've ever seen," he said softly. "Sometimes they're like pieces of summer sky, snatched right out of the air and set in your face. And sometimes they're the color of the clouds just before it rains... When we were kids, I always knew whether you were happy or sad by the color of your eyes."

Lee Ann chewed slowly. She tried to swallow, coughed and choked.

Ty watched as she took a swift sip of soda, then climbed to his feet. He was on the point of turning away, when he paused and glanced at her motionless figure, staring up at him over the rim of the cup.

"When you've finished," he said without a trace of the tenderness in his voice a moment ago, "we need to get a move on. We've got a lot of ground to cover before the rodeo starts."

The afternoon passed into evening. The weather was a mixture of light rain showers and cloudy sunshine. It was getting late, and Lee Ann was exhausted by the time Ty found her and indicated they were finished for the day. Leading her to a row of bleachers, he told her to have a seat and wait for him.

Lee Ann sat on the hard wooden seat, crossed one leg over the other and tried to rub her instep through her boots. Her feet felt as though they were swelled to twice their normal size.

She put a hand against her stomach and swallowed thickly. After smelling hot dogs, cotton candy and popcorn all day, their scent now made her feel ill.

She would have given just about anything for a long hot bath, a foot massage and about twelve hours of uninterrupted sleep. She must have walked miles while she spoke to every barker at the fair, and for all the good it had done, she might as well have stayed in her room. No one recognized the man in the drawing.

Lee Ann closed her ears to the sound of the country music blaring over the speakers and wondered what was taking Ty so long. He'd gone to circulate the drawing one last time behind the arena in case he'd missed any latecomers.

Lee Ann eyed the arena with a jaundiced eye. There was a lot of activity taking place behind the chutes. Where was Ty? She had no intention of staying for the competition.

All at once, the country music was interrupted by a voice welcoming everyone to the Last Chance Rodeo. There was a momentary pause while the people in the stands applauded. Then the announcer thanked those who had made the rodeo possible and went on to introduce the cowboys participating in the evening's events.

As he went through the list, Lee Ann turned nervously to study the crowd behind the bleachers, looking for a cowboy in a blue-and-red shirt with a purple bandanna tied around his neck. Where was he? she asked herself for the third time.

She wanted to get away from here before the rodeo began. Damn it! She should have paid more attention to where they had parked, but she'd been on tenterhooks during the ride here and unaware of little else but the man at her side.

She could leave, but there were so many people. If she missed him, they could be hunting for each other for hours in this crowd.

Her attention was drawn to the opening ceremony. Everyone was asked to stand for the National Anthem and Lee Ann did her best to keep her attention focused on the crowd, instead of what was taking place in front of her. Her eyes darted constantly toward the people moving behind the stands. Before long, without realizing it, her attention became centered on the arena.

She laughed with everyone else as a clown blew up a watermelon. And through the team roping and barrel racing, she clapped and cheered with the best of them.

When it was time for the bronc riding, Lee Ann twisted the program, which someone had handed her earlier, into a knot. She couldn't sit through this. But she did.

Before she knew it, it was time for the last event, the bull-riding contest. Now she was on her feet, ready to leave the stands. The first rider was announced and Lee Ann froze.

"Everyone please turn your attention to chute number three. 'Cause that's where Ty Yancy, riding a ton of lean mean named Relentless is about to appear."

Lee Ann's eyes were riveted on the white-painted chute. Her knees gave way as she peered between the wooden rails and spotted a red-and-blue shirt and the distinctive purple bandanna as the man lowered himself onto the back of the snorting bull.

All at once, the chute slid open and man and beast erupted into the arena. Lee Ann's breath stopped at the back of her throat. The huge animal bucked and jerked its way to the center of the arena, kicking up clouds of dust.

Every quiver of muscle from the bull was an attempt to dislodge the man from his back. And when that didn't work, the animal made a beeline for the side of the corral and slammed him against the railings.

The crowd groaned. Lee Ann was on her feet, shredding the program in both hands. Why didn't the buzzer sound?

Ty hung on determinedly. It wasn't necessary to spur a bull the way he spurred a bronc for points, but if he managed to, it would raise his score. Legs pumping, his left hand batting at the air, he stayed with the bull and spurred for all he was worth.

The eight-second buzzer rang and Ty let go of the rope. He flew over the side of the huge beast and landed in the dirt on one knee.

A clown dressed in bibbed overalls and a red-and-white-striped shirt appeared from nowhere and danced in front of the bull, doing his best to distract the animal from the downed man. But it seemed that was no easy task.

The bull lowered his head, the long horns pointed toward Ty, and pawed the ground. Swinging his massive head back and forth between two possible targets, he hesitated as though trying to decide which one to pursue.

By now, Ty was on his feet, both arms folded across his chest as he limped toward the safety of the fence. The bull spotted the moving target and made his decision. Head lowered, he charged the limping man.

Baggy pants flying, the clown ran to a barrel lying on its side at the edge of the arena. He bent over and gave it a hefty shove in the direction of the charging animal.

It rolled across the bull's path. The animal pulled up short, dirt flying in all directions.

The massive head swung toward the clown. The crowd held its collective breath as the bull paused, lowered his head and lunged in Ty's direction.

Lee Ann gasped, putting an unsteady hand to her lips, her eyes darting between Ty's slow-moving figure and that of the fast-moving bull. Why didn't somebody do something? The animal was determined to get Ty at all costs.

Movement on the fence drew Lee Ann's gaze. A second clown had dropped into the arena. He was holding a red cape and he began running toward the bull, the cape fluttering in his hands. The bull abruptly changed direction long enough to slam its horns into the cape, then sidestepped the man and continued toward the lone figure now only a short distance from the fence.

Cowboys had climbed onto the top rail and leaned forward to thrust helping hands toward Ty. Throwing a harried glance over his right shoulder, he reached for one of them. His boots had barely cleared the ground when the bull rammed the fence.

It was touch and go as Ty teetered precariously, until someone grabbed him under the arms and pulled. He landed on the opposite side of the fence, dropped to his knees and sat there for a moment taking deep breaths.

"Well, ladies and gents, now you know why that particular bull is named Relentless. Let's give Ty Yancy a real big hand for having the stamina to go the full eight seconds, give us a good ride and make it out of the arena on both feet."

The crowd went wild, clapping and yelling and stomping their feet. Lee Ann looked down at the shredded program and took a deep, quivering breath. She didn't feel like cheering.

In fact, she wished it was Ty Yancy's neck between her hands. Giving the program a final twist, she stumbled from the stands, threw it into a trash barrel and hurried away.

She moved blindly through the horde of people toward the entrance to the fairgrounds. Let Ty Yancy hunt for her and be damned!

He found her in a surprisingly short time. She watched him stride toward her, trying not to favor his right leg. Hardening her heart against him, she refused to allow the grim look of pain around the sensual mouth slip beneath her guard.

He'd tricked her and she had every right to be angry. It was his own fault he'd been injured. He'd get no sympathy from her.

As they moved away from the fairgrounds, Ty reached for Lee Ann's arm, but she evaded his touch. If he touched her, she'd do one of two things, burst into tears or slap his face.

Ty followed her rigid back until they reached the parking area. When Lee Ann stopped, uncertain where to go from there, he silently took the lead.

She tried, but couldn't keep her eyes off his broad shoulders and narrow hips. The limp had become more pronounced and she bit her lip to keep from urging him to stop and rest a moment.

Once in the truck, she sat as far from him as possible, keeping her glance out the side window. Nothing he could say would change the fact that he'd put her through a living hell just a few minutes ago.

The motel was only a few miles from the fairgrounds and within minutes they were standing outside Lee Ann's door. Ty watched in silence as she turned the key in the lock and disappeared inside, without acknowledging his presence.

He'd blown it. All he'd wanted was to prove a point—well, maybe two. Rodeo was not the gruesome sport she envisioned. And, if given half a chance, she might learn to enjoy it. On that point, he'd been wrong.

Lee Ann closed the door and snapped the dead bolt firmly into place. Flinging herself into a chair, she sat staring blankly at the wall. Then she switched on the television and stared at it for a while, paying no attention to the program.

All at once, she turned off the set. She was going home. Ty was right. This was no place for her, she simply didn't fit in.

Obviously she'd been wrong about the two of them. He didn't care about her. They were too different. He'd never give up rodeo and she couldn't be a part of it.

It was nobody's fault. Sometimes, that's the way things worked out.

She was halfway to the closet when the phone rang. Hesitating, she stared at it, then picked it up and held the receiver to her ear.

"Lee Ann?"

She couldn't speak.

"It's me. We need to talk—"

Lee Ann dropped the receiver into its cradle and continued with her packing. Her clothes were in the overnight bag and she was slipping her toothbrush into its plastic holder, when a fist pounded on the door.

She didn't need to hear the voice calling her name to know the identity of her visitor. At first she ignored him, but when the noise escalated to the point where she could hear it above the sound of the faucet she'd turned on full force to try to blot it out, she gave in.

Pulling open the door, she stood facing him, a resolute expression on her face. She was leaving and he wasn't going to stop her.

Somewhere in the back of her mind, his appearance registered. He looked terrible. The chin-length black hair covered one eye and a bruise on his jawbone, which she hadn't noticed earlier, had turned a deep ugly purple.

"We need to talk," he repeated.

Lee Ann wrinkled her nose and stepped back into the room. He'd been drinking. Les had once told her with a derisive sneer that Ty didn't drink because he wasn't man enough.

"We have nothing to talk about," she said coolly, watching him move to the center of the room before turning to face her.

"We have plenty to talk about," he contradicted, weaving back and forth on his feet.

"Are you drunk?" she asked bluntly.

Ty straightened. "I may have had a drink or two," he said very distinctly, as though choosing his words carefully, "but I am not drunk."

"I think we should leave this discussion until another time."

"No—I want to know why you won't talk to me."

Lee Ann's lips compressed. "I'm talking to you now."

"Yes, you are. But I mean before. On the way home, on the telephone a little while ago."

"All right. You want to know why I don't want to talk to you?" she said angrily. "Well, I'll tell you why. Because you are a no-good, low-down skunk, that's why."

"You're always calling me names," he complained. "Why is everyone always calling me names?"

Lee Ann bit her lip at that, but continued, "You knew I didn't want to see the rodeo. You deliberately took me there—placed me where I couldn't possibly miss seeing it and then left me—to enter the damned thing without telling me."

"No." Ty shook his head, reached for the back of a chair to steady himself and added, "I entered the rodeo weeks ago."

Lee Ann threw her hands up in the air in a gesture of exasperation. "It doesn't matter when you entered it. You didn't tell me because you knew I'd object. You—"

"Why?"

"W-what?" She looked momentarily confused.

"Why did you object?" He eyed her sharply. "What gives you the right to object?"

"You might have been killed—"

"What's that to you?"

Lee Ann raised her chin. Was he asking her if she cared about him? Hadn't she proved that by being here?

"Don't play games with me, Ty, I'm not in the mood."

"I don't play games," he said tautly. "I leave that kind of tactic to your father."

Lee Ann didn't want to get into a discussion about her father. They were both tired and out of sorts—in one way or another—and things might be said that would make things worse between them. If that were possible.

"My father is not a saint, by any means," she couldn't help saying, "but—" Ty interrupted her with a snort of disdain.

She did her best to ignore his rudeness and continued, "He isn't the complete horror you make him out to be, either. But I don't want to get into that right now. Why don't you go back to your room and get some sleep? We can continue this conversation in the morning."

Ty glanced at the bag at the end of the bed and the way she was dressed. "I'm not a fool. You won't be here in the morning."

"If I promise to stay tonight, will you go back to your room and go to bed?"

Ty shook his head, teetered precariously, then lowered himself gingerly to sit on the edge of the bed. "May I have a glass of water?"

Lee Ann went to the bathroom to get him the water. On her return, she stopped abruptly in the doorway, a deep frown marring the pure lines of her forehead. Ty was lying facedown on her bed, snoring—*snoring!*

Slamming the glass of water down on the dresser, she marched angrily toward the bed. He had no right to practically force his way into her room drunk and . . . and . . .

Ty snorted loudly, flopped over onto his back, craned his head up and lifted one eyelid, pinning her with a dark glare. "I'm not through with you, yet," he murmured sternly. And then his head dropped back to the pillow and he was asleep.

Openmouthed, Lee Ann stared at him. He lay with one arm above his head and the other folded across his chest. Her glance lingered on his face. Each time he exhaled, silvery strands of black hair blew away from his face, then drifted slowly back as he inhaled.

There was something so disarming about him like this. She wanted to climb onto the bed beside him and curl up against him. Instead, she took a seat in the chair beside the bed and watched him sleep.

She really ought to be furious.

Chapter 11

The next week seemed to drag by. Lee Ann worked at the store as usual, but her mind wasn't on business. All she could think about was Ty Yancy and wonder what he was doing while he waited for the next rodeo. They hadn't spoken since he'd dropped her at her door the evening after he'd come to her room drunk.

She hadn't heard from her father again, either, and that bothered her, too. He wasn't due back in the States for a couple of weeks, but if he'd somehow gotten word about Ty's being in town, she felt certain that he'd cut his trip short and head home.

And she prayed that wouldn't happen. She didn't want him back in town until she'd had a chance to prove Ty's innocence.

She was no longer angry with Ty. And she hadn't given up on the idea of somehow convincing him to get out of rodeo. In the motel room, as she'd watched Ty sleep, she'd realized how much she cared about him. She wasn't ready to give up on him.

The fact that he'd come to her because he'd been upset about her being angry with him, proved that he cared about her, too. And every night since then, she'd had the same dream....

Ty burst into a rodeo arena on the back of a huge black bull. The animal bucked and twitched its way around the arena, the long horns gouging the air close to Ty's face as the imposing head swung from one side to the other in fury. And as though she could read its mind, Lee Ann knew that if the animal ever managed to throw Ty, it would grind him into dust with its sharp hooves.

If Jennifer noticed the dark circles beneath Lee Ann's gray eyes growing just a little darker with each passing day, she kept it to herself. And for that Lee Ann was grateful.

She had been disappointed, though not surprised, to learn upon her return to work that Jennifer and Cody had fared no better than she and Ty in finding someone who recognized the man in Cody's drawing. Whoever he was, the man obviously wasn't a regular part of the rodeo crowd.

Lee Ann awoke from a sound sleep and squinted down at her watch. But the room was too dark to see. She switched on the lamp beside the bed and saw that it was after seven in the evening.

She was again attending a rodeo with Ty. In the week since the last one he hadn't contacted her. He'd waited until the last minute to find out whether she was going along to this one and she'd been of two minds about agreeing. But she'd said yes and he'd picked her up late Friday evening.

They hadn't spoken a dozen words to each other on the drive to Butte, where the rodeo was being held. Parting, they'd gone to their separate rooms and it wasn't until the next morning that she'd seen him again.

At noon that day, she'd returned to her room after spending four hours circulating the drawing, showing it to anyone who would look and listen to her questions about the man. She'd showered, put on a nightshirt and lain down to take a nap.

Ty was riding again, but she had stiffly declined his invitation to watch. She steadfastly refused to sit idly by in the stands and watch the man she loved attempt suicide in front of hundreds of witnesses.

Her stomach growled as she climbed from the bed, reminding her that she hadn't eaten since breakfast. She had no idea when the rodeo would be ending that evening, but knew she wouldn't sit around her room waiting for Ty to show up—if he ever did.

Changing into a brown-and-beige-striped shirt, canvas frontier pants with oil-tanned leather suspenders and lace-up boots, she made her way downstairs to the motel's restaurant-lounge. A waitress dressed in a cowgirl's outfit led her to a table in the corner of the dimly lit room.

She ordered a drink and dinner and sat back to look around. A Garth Brooks tune was playing softly in the background and a couple of waitresses were leaning on one corner of the bar laughing at something the bartender had just said.

A leather-and-metal bull sat a couple of yards from the bar in the center of the room. It reminded Lee Ann of things she didn't want to think about and she glanced hurriedly away.

There weren't many customers, just a couple at a table directly across the room from her and two men in suits at the bar. Apparently, the rodeo wasn't over yet, because the rodeo crowd was conspicuously missing. As she smiled at the waitress as she set her rum and cola on the table in front of her, three cowboys strolled into the room and stopped to look around.

Lee Ann sipped her drink and watched them from beneath partially lowered lids. The taller of the three, a thin man with a narrow face and a mustache, led the way toward her table. The second man had red hair and looked to be somewhere in his late thirties. The younger and shortest of the three was holding a bottle of beer in one hand. Blond hair hung over his forehead and stuck out from beneath his hat.

Lee Ann's stomach tightened as they drew even with her table, but she relaxed as they passed by with nothing more than a slight nod and took seats somewhere behind her. More people drifted in as her dinner arrived and she forgot all about the trio.

She had finished her salad and started on the steak when the murmur of voices behind became suddenly louder.

"I don't give a damn what you say, the man's a low-down killer," a male voice snarled.

"Now, Hank, you don't know that for sure—"

"The hell I don't!" the first voice bellowed. "We all saw him jump into the arena to make sure Les was dead."

Lee Ann stared at the piece of steak on her fork, her appetite suddenly deserting her. They were discussing Ty, and her brother's death.

"Just ask Tom here," the angry man said. "He'll tell you. He was there that night—the night before Les was killed— he heard it all."

There was a pause in the conversation and Lee Ann found herself straining to hear what "Tom" had to say.

"I heard them argue," a softer voice said, "but it was just words, Hank. People say things in the heat of anger that they don't mean."

"You going soft, boy?" the first voice demanded scornfully. "I thought you were a man. Damn it, you and Les were close friends. How can you make excuses for the man who killed him?"

"Let the boy alone, Hank," a third voice chided. "We're not all ready to believe the worst of people like you are."

"Let me tell you something, Pete," Hank said, "I seen a lot in my life and I know a killer when I see one. Ty Yancy is a killer, sure as I'm sittin' here, drinking this beer."

"Evenin', boys." Ty's deep voice, coming so unexpectedly on the tail end of that comment, caused the hair to stand up on the back of Lee Ann's neck.

"Evenin', Yancy," Pete said warmly. "That was a mighty fine ride this afternoon. It's good to know you haven't lost your edge."

Lee Ann heard the sound of a chair scraping the floor and heavy boots. From the corner of her eye, she caught sight of the taller of the three cowboys stomp his way across the room and out the door.

"Sorry if I ran your friend off," Ty said.

"Don't worry about Hank, he's always been a hothead. He'll cool down. Say, I'm havin' a little get-together in my room later on tonight. Come and join us about nine. And bring a gal if you got one," he added with a light chuckle.

Lee Ann was straining to hear Ty's reply, when he spoke at her elbow. "Mind if I join you?"

She looked up from the fork, still holding the piece of steak, and nodded toward the empty chair across from her. "Sit down."

"That any good?" he asked, motioning toward the steak.

Lee Ann shrugged, trying to appear nonchalant, despite the rapid increase in her heart rate and the warm flush she was certain now stained her cheeks. "I've had better." Placing her fork on the plate, she pushed the barely touched meal away.

Ty signaled for the waitress and Lee Ann studied him. There was a dark spot on one cheekbone and a slight puffiness around his lower lip.

"Are you going?" she asked abruptly, her eyes centered on his mouth.

"Where?"

"To the party your friend just invited you to."

He shrugged. "I'm not much on parties."

Lee Ann rose from the table and picked up her wallet. "Come by for me at nine."

Dark eyebrows arrowed over his eyes. "You leaving?"

"Yes. I have to get ready for a party. Don't be late."

Ty watched her sweep across the room. She refused to talk to him or eat a meal with him, but she wanted to attend that party with him. His eyes narrowed on her shapely figure as it slid out of sight. What did she have up her sleeve?

Lee Ann studied herself in the mirror for the fifth time in as many minutes. She was wearing a double-ruffled skirt and matching caped shirt with black suede half-boots. Lifting the colorful skirt, she turned this way and that.

Was she dressed appropriately? She'd never been to a rodeo party and she was nervous. She'd heard her brother talk about a few of them and knew the liquor flowed like water and occasionally they erupted into violence. Just the boys letting off a little steam, he'd always said laughingly.

She glanced at her watch. It was five minutes past nine. Where was Ty?

At that moment, knuckles rapped on the door and Lee Ann hurried forward to pull it open without asking her visitor to identify himself.

"That's not a very smart thing to do," Ty said shortly, "opening your door in a place like this without knowing who might be standing on the other side."

"It's past nine o'clock, I assumed it was you."

"Yes, well, you know what they say about assuming anything," he replied evenly, stepping back into the hallway and waiting for her to join him. "Are you sure you want to go to this party?" he asked abruptly. "It isn't the kind of party you're used to."

Lee Ann caught a whiff of musky after-shave and paused to look at him, noticing the special care he'd taken with his own appearance. The unruly black hair was parted on the side and slicked back from his face, making the prominent cheekbones even more pronounced. His chin and jaw were clean-shaven and she could detect evidence of the bruise on his jaw sustained at that last rodeo where she'd been an unwilling spectator.

Her glance skimmed over the black silk shirt with the red-and-yellow embroidery around the collar and yoke, and her heart skipped a beat. He looked just a little bit dangerous tonight and she loved it.

"You don't know what kind of parties I'm used to," she said as they moved down the hall.

Ty studied her profile. "I know the man you were engaged to came from a wealthy family of lawyers back East. If that's the circle you've been running in, you're in for a real letdown. We rough-and-tumble cowboys are just barely housebroken."

Was he trying to make her angry? If so, he was going about it the right way.

"I'm not a snob," she said stiffly. "I come from a family of cowboys," she reminded him. "I'll wager that I've ridden on more cattle drives than you have."

Ty shrugged, took hold of her elbow, dropped it and motioned for her to lead the way. "The party is on the next floor."

The laid-back style of Chris Ledoux filled the warm night air as he sang about rodeo life. It was obvious there was a party going on upstairs.

Lee Ann paused to glance up at the silver-and-black sky. Did her mere presence disturb the man at her side as much as his disturbed her?

All at once, she turned toward him, determined to find out, and they collided. For a long breathless moment, they stared into each other's eyes, the air around them electrified.

Lee Ann slowly became aware of his hands, one lying flat against her right hip and the other at her breast. His touch seared her. Heart fluttering, feeling almost dizzy, she leaned into him.

"The party," Ty murmured huskily.

"They won't miss us...."

Ty's mouth swooped to capture hers and the hand at her hip pulled her against him. The touch of his lips became urgent.

Lee Ann held on to him with both hands as his lips parted hers in a soul-searching kiss. His tongue sent shivers of desire racing through her as it explored the warm recesses of her mouth.

The blood pounded in Ty's veins and his senses reeled as his lips moved over hers. The feelings were so strong between them, they had to hold each other up. And still he couldn't let her go.

With a groan, he crushed her against him. And every fiber of his body made it clear to her just how much he longed for her.

The iron control he'd kept on his feelings, even when he'd made love to her that first time, was gone. He'd been fighting this thing between them since they'd both been too young to know about love and understand the meaning of words like *forever*.

Now he had to admit to himself that she was the real reason he'd come back to Rainville. He could have gone to Cody's ranch to recuperate. He could have gone to his mother.

But he hadn't. Like a wounded animal, he'd gone to the one place where he'd known pure love, to the one person who had loved him unquestioningly. He'd gone looking for Lee Ann.

He'd found her. But she'd been very different from the adoring young girl who'd unquestioningly accepted him.

His world was in shambles. His world was professional rodeo. And she wanted no part of that world.

Pulling his lips from hers, he whispered unsteadily, "We need to talk."

"No." Lee Ann tried to pull his face back to hers. "Every time we talk, we fight. Let's not talk anymore."

A door burst open upstairs, raining light on their joined figures. Ty's head jerked up and he locked eyes with Tom Purdy.

Lee Ann felt him stiffen, saw the mask close down over his face and turned to see what had disturbed him. The young cowboy from the bar threw her a brief glance, twisted around and hurried back inside, slamming the door.

"Ty?"

"Let's go," he said tautly. "Let's go join the party."

"I don't understand," she said.

"No doubt you will before the evening is over," he said. "So let's just get it over with."

A short while later, Lee Ann stood on the balcony looking into the noisy smoke-filled room. It was so crowded, the door to an adjoining room had been unlocked and the party had spilled over into it.

Ty had disappeared soon after they'd entered the room, as though he could no longer stand to be near her. It was impossible to find anyone in the crowd, so she hadn't tried to locate him.

Instead, she'd found the only place where it was possible to breathe anything resembling fresh air. Cowboys notoriously dipped snuff, but all their wives and girlfriends appeared to be chain-smokers. She wondered if that was part of loving a man who made his life on the rodeo circuit—or suicide circuit as she'd heard several women refer to it this evening.

Turning away from the room, she leaned on the wrought-iron railing and looked down into the pool. She was still feeling unbalanced by what had taken place between her and Ty before they were interrupted. What would have happened if they hadn't been interrupted?

Then another thought sprang to mind. What had he meant by that cryptic remark that she would understand everything before the evening was over?

"I can see why you left the party to come out here."

Lee Ann turned and glanced up into a pair of the saddest blue eyes she'd ever seen. "Tom, isn't it?" she asked gently. A few minutes ago, she'd been angry with the young man, but now she felt sorry for him without understanding why.

"Yes, ma'am. And you're Miss Newley, Les's sister."

"That's right." He looked a little unsteady on his feet. She wanted to take his arm and lead him to a chair, but he lurched toward her unaided and came to rest against the railing.

Waving the bottle of beer in his hand, he said, "It's beautiful, isn't it?"

"Yes." She glanced up at the sky. "It is."

"I like the night. I like the way it closes down around you—sort of protects you from things." He glanced at Lee Ann. "You know what I mean? Like there are things people can see about you in the daylight that they can't see in the dark."

Wondering what he was talking about, but pretending to understand, she nodded. Maybe he just needed someone to listen while he talked. She had always been a good listener.

Tom stared down at the half-empty bottle in his hand. "I knew your brother," he said softly.

"Were you good friends?" she asked, sensing he wanted to talk about Les and was finding it difficult.

"Yeah." He met her glance. "We were friends." He swallowed, took a swig from the bottle and looked away. When he looked back, there were tears in his eyes.

"It's all right, I understand how you feel," Lee Ann said gently.

"No." Tom shook his head and looked at her a little desperately. "You don't understand." He took an unsteady step toward her and tripped. The bottle in his hand flew over the railing. He would have fallen facedown if Lee Ann hadn't caught him.

Grasping the front of her blouse, he said quickly, "There's something I've got to tell you."

"What the hell do you think you're doing?" Ty bellowed from the doorway. "Let go of her!"

Tom's head jerked in Ty's direction. Lee Ann could feel him shudder. Pushing away from her, he made a wide berth around Ty and practically fell into the crowded room without another word.

"Are you all right?" Ty asked, coming to stand next to her.

"I'm fine," she replied, her eyes on the room, searching for Tom's slight figure. "He wasn't trying anything. He stumbled and I simply kept him from falling."

"That isn't what it looked like to me."

Lee Ann withdrew her gaze from the party and directed it on Ty's inflexible jaw. My God! He was jealous!

Before she could open her mouth to reply, another figure moved onto the balcony. It seemed to her that the balcony had suddenly become a very popular place.

"Doesn't it bother you, just a little bit, knowing what he's done?" Hank, the tall cowboy from the bar, sneered at Lee Ann. "What kind of a sister are you, to be taking up with your brother's murderer?"

"That's enough, McCarthy." With narrowed eyes, Ty faced the man. "Whatever you've got to say, say it to me. This has nothing to do with her."

"That's where you're wrong," the bigger man answered. "I think she ought to know just what kind of a cowardly bastard you really are."

"You want me?" Ty asked. "Well, let's take this downstairs and you can have a piece of me."

"Ty—no." Lee Ann touched his arm in protest. The other man was bigger and he looked tougher. She hadn't forgotten—if the man beside her had—about the serious injuries from which he was still recovering.

"Well, isn't that sweet. She's worried about you." Hank cut her a fierce look from dark deep-set eyes. "Too bad she didn't worry more about her brother."

The muscles in the arm beneath Lee Ann's fingers tightened. There was going to be a fight if she didn't do something to stop it and she didn't know what to do.

"Well, hell, what's happening to my party?" Pete Saddler pushed past Hank's stationary figure and stepped between the two men. "Come to think of it, maybe you three got the right idea. It sure is cooler out here. By the way, Hank, that little lady of yours is looking for you. She said something about the baby making a ruckus and she needed to go lie down."

Hank gave Ty one last look before turning away. Ty jerked his arm from beneath Lee Ann's hand and twisted to face the night.

"His wife is expecting," Pete explained to Lee Ann. "She isn't having an easy time of it. Hank has been a might on edge these past few weeks."

"Are you ready to go?" Ty asked abruptly, ignoring the other man.

Embarrassed, Lee Ann shot a look of apology toward Pete, then nodded in answer to Ty's question. "Thank you for inviting us," she said as they passed the man.

"Hey, we enjoyed having you." He smiled at Lee Ann, but his expression was sober when he looked at Ty. "Don't let Hank get to you, man. He was pretty tight with Les, you know that. He'll get over it."

Ty didn't acknowledge Pete's words by so much as a blink of an eye. He took Lee Ann's arm and led her silently from the balcony and the motel room.

The silence continued between them all the way to her door. She used the key to unlock it, but before she could reach for the handle, Ty's hand was there shoving hers aside.

He jerked open the door, almost pushed her inside, followed her quickly and slammed the door.

"Ty?"

"Don't talk—" He propelled her into his arms. "Kiss me!"

And she did. Throwing herself against him, feeling him fall back against the door, she wound her arms around his neck and her legs around his middle in a shameless, wanton manner and reached for his lips.

Cupping her bottom with both hands, he lifted her against him, ducking his head to hers. The rim of his hat hit her in the eye and he drew back.

"Ouch," Lee Ann muttered, grabbing Ty's hat and sending it sailing across the room. Grasping the black hair with both hands, she pulled his lips to hers. Her tongue slid wetly over his mouth and Ty's lips parted in surprise. The tip of her tongue darted inside and touched the tip of his tongue, rubbing against it seductively.

Ty almost groaned out loud at the sudden burst of desire burning in his groin. His knees trembled and Lee Ann began to slip from his grasp. Hauling her against him, he locked his mouth onto hers. Nothing else mattered for the next few minutes.

When he turned her mouth loose, Lee Ann unbuttoned his shirt and began to plant kisses against his collarbone. Ty tried to see around her to the bed and eventually moved toward it.

When she was finally lying against the white sheets, staring up at him, he took a moment to really look at her. And she was worth looking at. Her gray eyes glowed with passion and her lips were red and swollen from his kisses.

He wanted her so bad that he ached all over. That's how she always affected him. Yet he wanted to make love to her real slow. The way things were going between them, he might never get the chance to make love to her again, so he wanted this night to last forever.

Lee Ann held her arms out to him and he came down beside her on one knee, reaching for the small buttons on her blouse. He tried to be careful, but his fingers were awkward and one of the buttons came off in his hand.

He stared at it in horror, but Lee Ann only laughed, took it from him and threw it across the room. "It doesn't matter," she whispered, taking his hand and placing it beneath the material against her warm breast. "Nothing matters tonight but this."

Ty felt his insides quicken as his palm covered the soft warm globe. Then Lee Ann helped him unfasten the last of the buttons and slipped the blouse from her shoulders.

She wasn't wearing a bra, that had been evident when he'd touched her just now. And though he'd seen her naked before, he was overwhelmed by her beauty. Her breasts were firm and round, the skin pale with pink nipples that stood straight up, pointing toward him as though beckoning his mouth to them.

Ty couldn't resist, he leaned over and touched one with gentle lips. Lee Ann moaned and pressed his head against her. Understanding what she wanted without her having to speak, he took the nipple in his mouth and rubbed it with the tip of his tongue.

Lee Ann gasped and slid her hands down over his shoulders and around to the front of his jeans. Her fingers found his belt buckle and she began to work it loose.

A moment later, Ty was helping her, and then he was pulling off his boots and slipping the jeans down over his lean hips. He had to wait to remove the rest of his clothes, because Lee Ann leaned up on one elbow to plant a kiss against his hipbone.

He pushed her back against the pillows, unfastened her skirt and slid it slowly down her body, his eyes hungrily devouring each curve as it came into view. The skirt joined his clothes on the floor, and he stared at the triangle of white silk panties.

His eyes moved to her face. There was so much he wanted to say to her. He really cared about her and he wanted her to know that. But before he could speak, Lee Ann took his hand and placed it against silk and lace and the words flew out of his head.

He forced himself to remove the panties slowly, kissing her abdomen, her hips and her inner thighs with slow, delicious deliberation. And then, holding the panties balled in his fist, he rubbed them gently against one cheek. From this day forward, silk would always remind him of Lee Ann.

Her eyes widened. Nothing had ever made her feel so aroused. Her hands reached for him, touched his abdomen, where the hair grew thick and black and slid slowly down the inside of one thickly muscled thigh.

Ty reached for her hand and placed it against his mouth, the tip of his tongue drawing wet circles against her palm. Dropping the panties to the floor, he straddled her, leaned over and pressed his mouth to hers.

Lowering himself against her, he lay there unmoving for long silent moments, their bodies touching from forehead to toe. Then his hands slid up her sides to her face and his head moved so that his mouth could capture hers. He kissed her until she became dizzy. But when he moved to let her breathe, she quickly sought his mouth again.

They moved against each other, touching and kissing, learning each other's most intimate secrets. And the passion between them built slowly, burning like a well-stoked fire.

Time and time again, he brought her to the brink of ecstasy, only to stop and gentle her with tender kisses, nuzzle her neck with warm lips and whisper soft words in her ear. His callused hands skimmed her silky body, letting her passion cool, but letting her know how much he wanted her.

They were both panting, the musky scent of their bodies heavy in the air around them, and Lee Ann thought she might die from the need for him, when Ty pressed his lips against the side of her neck and slid them wetly toward her ear.

"Do you want me?" he breathed throatily.

"Oh, yes," Lee Ann panted. "You know I do."

"I want you to remember tonight," he whispered, his lips tickling her skin. "I want you to remember me and this night for as long as you live."

Alarmed, Lee Ann tried to twist her head to look at him. It sounded as though—

"Shh," he whispered. "Close your eyes and feel—" He drove into her. "Feel me inside you and remember that whatever happens I'll always be part of you...always..."

His warm mouth slid around to hers and he pressed them apart with his tongue, tasting her. His flesh slid against hers as he moved deeply within her, creating his own memories.

And just when Lee Ann thought she couldn't stand any more, the sensations inside her exploded and she held him tightly, crying his name out loud. His voice echoed hers and they rode the tide of explosive sensation to its magic end.

Afterward, he held her curled against him and they drifted to sleep. But sleep wasn't in his plan. When they were both rested, he kissed her breast and Lee Ann pressed her lips to his black hair and the magic began all over again.

Chapter 12

Lee Ann adjusted the hot water and stood beneath it with her head back, letting it cascade over her tired body. She ached all over, but it was a good feeling. Ty had just left after making love to her for what seemed like hours.

She shivered, remembering his hands and lips on her body. If she lived to be a hundred, she'd never forget this night. For the first time, he'd loved her without reservation and she'd given him her heart and soul.

She was now confident that nothing would stand between them. Again, she vowed silently to make things right between Ty and her father. Her father would just have to learn to live with the fact that she loved Ty.

Of course, he hadn't actually told her he loved her, but that didn't matter. She knew, one day, he would. Turning off the water, she slid back the glass partition and reached for a snowy white bath towel.

Ty had gone for coffee and sandwiches. Neither had eaten much that day and both had suddenly discovered that they were ravenous.

In the bedroom, she slipped on a yellow hooded terry-cloth bathrobe and sat down on the end of the bed to blow dry her hair. A moment later, a knock sounded at the door. Her heart lurched at the thought that Ty had returned so quickly.

But it wasn't Ty's warm smile that greeted her when she threw open the door. Tom Purdy, the young cowboy from the party, leaned against the doorjamb, his bloodshot blue eyes pleading with her to let him in.

"Your brother and I were good friends," he said without preamble. "He took me under his wing a couple of years ago, when I first started on the circuit. He was teaching me to be a champion rider, just like him.

"We were traveling together, sharing expenses on the road, when he got killed," he continued quickly, as though fearing she might shut the door in his face before he had a chance to explain why he was at her door at three o'clock in the morning. "I need to talk to you about that."

There was such despair in his expression that Lee Ann could do nothing less than step back and allow him to enter the room. Ty might not approve, but she felt she had to hear Tom out.

She gestured toward a chair. "Please, sit down."

He lowered himself to a chair, dropping the brown felt hat on the floor, his glance not quite meeting hers. Lee Ann pulled the robe more securely around her and tightened the belt at her waist.

It was beginning to occur to her that letting Tom in might have been a very foolish idea. Very few people were out and about at this time of the morning and she really didn't know this young man.

Hiding her sudden uneasiness, she took a seat in the chair nearest the door and said, "Now, tell me what's brought you here."

As though her words had opened a floodgate, the young cowboy twisted his arms over his face and began to cry. "Oh, God, I'm so sorry! It's all my fault—all my fault!"

Startled, Lee Ann grew perfectly still, watching him warily. But there was nothing threatening about the thin shaking shoulders and his cries of remorse.

After a moment, she leaned forward, one hand stretched toward him. "It's all right," she whispered. "I don't know what's upsetting you, but if you think I can help, please, tell me what I can do."

Tom scrubbed at his face with the heels of both hands and ran long unsteady fingers over his shaking mouth. "I'm sorry, ma'am. I didn't mean to…" His words trailed off and the blue eyes again filled with tears. "I just can't stand it anymore—I've got to tell someone."

Lee Ann got up to fetch him a box of tissues and give him a moment to get his emotions under control. She was hoping Ty would return soon, because she didn't know how to deal with this situation.

Tom took the box of tissues and sat staring at it. Finally, he lifted his bloodshot blue eyes and said, "I know who killed your brother."

Lee Ann felt suddenly faint. Here it was. Their search had finally paid off. Tom must have seen one of the drawings and recognized the man in it.

Suddenly, Lee Ann felt afraid. Grasping the back of the chair, she felt her way around it and plopped down on its hard seat, never taking her eyes off Tom's face.

"You're certain you know the killer?" she asked intently.

Tom's lips tightened. He glanced down at his fingers, twisted together like white writhing snakes, and nodded.

"Have you been to the police?"

He darted a quick glance at her face. "No, ma'am."

"Why not?"

His glance slipped sideways. "I was afraid."

"Afraid he'd kill you, too?" she asked quickly.

"No, ma'am." He shifted uneasily. "I was just...afraid."

Lee Ann frowned. "I don't understand."

"It's me," he whispered hoarsely, staring at the wadded tissue lying on the floor at his feet. "I'm the one—I killed your brother."

This young man, barely out of his teens, was confessing to her brother's murder and all Lee Ann could do was stare at him in silence. She couldn't seem to get it straight in her mind. She ought to feel something—threatened by him, perhaps. But all she felt was a sense of confusion, tempered with pity for the young man.

"Why don't you start from the beginning and explain exactly what happened?" There simply had to be another explanation for her brother's death. She just couldn't picture this young man as a murderer.

"I didn't mean to do it, ma'am," he said hastily. "You have to believe me. I didn't know he was going to use that rope." The muscles in his arms and legs began to quiver and his knees jumped. "He trusted me," he whispered, "and I let him down. I'll never forgive myself." His hands hid his face and his head moved slowly back and forth. "I'm so sorry," he whispered, the words muffled by his fingers. "So sorry."

"Wait a minute, Tom," Lee Ann said abruptly, "I don't understand. What rope are you talking about? And how did you let him down?"

Tom took a deep breath and lowered his hands.

All at once, a loud rapping sounded at the door. Tom jumped and stared at it in panic.

Lee Ann froze, her gaze on Tom's frightened face.

"Lee Ann, it's me. Let me in."

"T-that's Ty Yancy," Tom whispered and his eyes widened accusingly as they swung toward Lee Ann's face.

"Yes, it is—but it will be all right," she assured him, rising from the chair. "Just stay where you are," she said when it looked as if he was about to leap to his feet and run to the nearest exit. Which in this case was a window.

"Lee Ann—let me in!"

"I'm coming," she called softly, staring fixedly at Tom. He was half out of his seat when the other man walked into the room.

Ty halted abruptly. "What's he doing here?"

Lee Ann took his arm in a nervous grip and pulled him away from the door so she could close it. "He's confessing to my brother's murder," she said baldly. There was no easy way to put it.

"Bull!" Ty strode across the room to slam the sacks he carried onto the small table near the window.

"Who put you up to this?" he asked, swinging in the other man's direction. "Hank Finton?"

Tom looked helplessly at Lee Ann.

"It isn't funny," Ty continued, "it's sick—coming here and upsetting this woman in the middle of the night! What's the matter with you?

"Haul your carcass out of here, before I throw you out, and don't come back. You got that?" he asked, taking a menacing step in the young man's direction.

"N-no one p-put me up to anything," Tom stuttered, straining away from the other man. "I c-came on my own—to tell her about what h-happened the night before L-Les died."

Ty stiffened. "We all know what happened. He and I had a fight. And I told him I'd kill him if he didn't keep away from me."

Lee Ann gasped, her glance veering toward Ty's bitter face. She knew about the fight, but this was the first she'd heard about a death threat.

"This isn't about t-that," Tom insisted doggedly, then qualified, "at least, not exactly about that."

He was on his feet now, facing Ty across the width of the room. "After you all but knocked him unconscious, he and I left the bar. I wanted to go back to the motel, but—"

Tom darted a glance in Lee Ann's direction. "Les didn't want to, he wanted to go on to another bar, so we did. He drank until the bartender refused to serve him anymore. That's when we went back to the motel. Les was really mad."

"Yeah, so?" Ty asked impatiently, his fists planted on his hips.

"He kept saying how you'd made him look like a fool in front of everyone. He said he was going to get you for that.

"I thought it was just the liquor talking. He always talked like that when he was liquored up.

"I figured he'd go to bed and sleep it off, like he always did. But he didn't—not that night. There was only one chance left for him to win that rodeo, and he was really wired. He was a few points ahead of you, but the bull-riding contest was the next day."

"So?" Ty prodded when the other man fell silent.

Tom stared at the floor. "He said you were good. But that was only because you were just one step away from being an animal yourself."

Ty muttered something beneath his breath and the fists at his sides clenched tighter. He couldn't look at Lee Ann.

Tom continued. "He went to your room and took your rigging—"

"So that's what happened to my rope," Ty muttered.

That day had been unlike any other. At the worse possible time—just a few minutes before his ride—Ty had discovered his rope missing. It had been in his bag the day before. He'd cleaned it after his ride and put it away like always.

Only now it was gone. There wasn't a thing he could do about it, short of pulling out of the competition. And he hadn't for a moment considered doing that. He'd put aside his pride and borrowed a rope from Pete Saddler. He'd used the borrowed rope and given it back to Pete.

And then Les had been killed. The next day, he'd been accused of Les's murder and he'd forgotten all about it.

When the police had let him go, he'd moved on to the next rodeo. That's when he'd thought again about the missing rope, because he'd had to buy another one.

"What did he want with my rope?" Ty asked coldly, the almond-shaped eyes narrowing on Tom's pale face.

"You have to understand," the other man said hastily, "he was drunk, he wasn't thinking clearly—"

"What did he do with it?" Ty repeated dangerously, his fists coming away from his hips.

"H-he used a knife on it," Tom replied, barely above a whisper, his glance on the floor. "He said he'd fix you so you'd remember who you were, that you belonged on all fours in the dirt and that's where he was going to put you."

"Oh, no," Lee Ann whispered, a hand at her throat.

"You little weasel," Ty muttered at the same time, taking a threatening step closer to the cowering man. "You let him cut my rope and didn't say a damned thing about it? Why, I ought to—"

"You don't understand," Tom said hastily. "I sneaked back later, when he was asleep, and took your rope. I didn't want you to know what he'd done—I was afraid if you found out, you might...hurt him bad.

"And I figured," he added, lifting his glance almost belligerently to Ty's angry face, "if you didn't have a rope, you might not be able to ride and Les would win. Everyone knew that you and Les were the only real competitors in the bull-riding event. And after the drinking he'd done the night before, I figured he wouldn't stand much of a chance against you."

"Les was always drunk," Ty snapped. "He drank liquor like it was water."

"My brother wasn't an alcoholic," Lee Ann protested weakly.

"Yes," Ty insisted, still not looking at her, "he was."

Her gaze sought the younger man for confirmation of her words. But he avoided her glance and she realized what Ty had said must have been true. Still...

"Surely, Les must have realized that Ty would notice before the ride that his rope had been tampered with," she whispered, digesting this new bit of information about her brother.

"No, ma'am," Tom answered, "he might not. The bull rope is in nine plats all worked together. Les cut the underside. It wouldn't be easy to see, unless you were giving it a real going-over. And that's usually done right after a competition, so the rosin used on it won't build up and ruin the rope."

He shot a quick glance in Ty's direction. "At least, that's how Les did it. He was a fanatic about keeping his rigging in good shape."

"He's right," Ty said. "I clean the rosin off my rope and glove before I put it away, so it's ready for the next ride. I probably wouldn't have noticed it had been cut."

"I still don't understand how my brother died," Lee Ann said in confusion, her eyes darting between the two men.

Ty's dark glance traveled over the younger man's pale face and quivering lips. "I think I can figure it out. It was my rope Les used that day, wasn't it?"

Tom flinched and nodded. "I just wanted to get it out of your bag so Les wouldn't get into trouble. If the board learned what Les had done, he'd have been disqualified from all competition. After I had it, I didn't know what to do with it. And like a fool, I took it back to the room with me.

"I was standing in the middle of the room, trying to figure out what to do with it, when Les woke up. The rope was in my hand. He saw it and thought it was his.

"He got real upset if anyone touched his rigging. He grabbed the rope and began stuffing it into his bag. I tried to tell him it wasn't his, but he wouldn't listen. He jerked open the door and shoved me outside into the hall and told me I could find someplace else to sleep that night.

"I kept trying to tell him the rope wasn't his—" He shook his head. "I told him the motels were full, thinking he'd let me back inside and I could get the rope when he went back to sleep. He just laughed and said I could sleep on the ground for all he cared. It would teach me to keep my fingers off his stuff.

"I finally went to the arena and bedded down behind the holding pens with some of the other cowboys. I figured the next morning he'd have cooled down and I could tell him about the rope.

"But I couldn't find him early the next morning when I went back to the motel. And no one had seen him. I hung around behind the chutes, thinking he'd come looking for me, when he found out what I'd done. But he never showed.

"It was getting late, so I went back to the motel. But he still wasn't there and I returned to the rodeo. He was getting ready to ride. I wanted to tell him about the rope, but they wouldn't let me on the chute."

Tom turned to Lee Ann. "Honest, ma'am, I didn't think for a minute that he'd gotten the wrong rope. I don't know how it could have happened—"

"I know how it could have happened," Ty said evenly. "Most cowboys use the new synthetic ropes, but I still use the manila-grass rope." He shrugged. "It's a matter of personal taste. Les used the grass ropes, too. He must have had a real bad hangover that morning...."

He stared into the younger man's face as though searching it for the truth. "Les was a headstrong fool and an arrogant son of a bitch. He broke every rule that existed about drinking and riding. But if I thought you had deliberately—"

"I didn't. Honest—it was an accident," Tom protested quickly. "He was my friend."

"What are you going to do?" Lee Ann asked Ty.

"Nothing."

"B-but—"

"He cut the damned rope himself," Ty said angrily. "It was his own damned fault."

"But I didn't speak up and tell the cops the truth about how he died," Tom said. "You could have faced a murder trial."

"Would you have spoken up then?" Ty asked in a hard voice.

Tom opened his mouth to make a quick reply, then closed it without answering. After a moment, he admitted, "I don't know."

"Ty," Lee Ann said, "what about the suspension?"

"I'll go to the board," Tom said. "I'll tell them the truth. If they decide to bring charges against me…" He shrugged.

"What if they suspend you?" Ty asked.

Tom shrugged again. "I'm not that good, anyway. I think Les was coming to that conclusion, too, but he just didn't want to admit that he'd been wrong and taken a failure under his wing.

"I'm sorry," he said again to Lee Ann. "I still feel it's my fault your brother died. I guess I always will."

Bending to pick up his hat, he turned toward the door. His hand was on the doorknob when Lee Ann suddenly said, "Wait! Have you seen the drawing we've been circulating?"

He turned back. "Drawing?"

"Yes." Grabbing the sketch off the dresser, she moved hurriedly toward him. "This one." She handed it to him. "Do you recognize this man?"

Tom studied the man's face for a long moment. He started to shake his head, then stopped and frowned. "I do remember seeing him, at least I think it's the same man. It was the day Les died. He was standing behind the chutes.''

"You don't know his name?'' Ty asked.

"No. I'd never seen him before that day.''

"You haven't seen him since?'' Lee Ann asked.

Tom shook his head. "What's he done?''

"It doesn't matter,'' Ty said.

Taking the drawing from the cowboy, Lee Ann stared down at it in silence.

In the open door, Tom stopped to dart a puzzled glance into the room and then he was gone. Lee Ann closed the door and stood leaning against it.

"Well, that's that,'' Ty muttered.

Hearing the note of finality in his voice, she looked up and asked, "What do you mean?''

"I mean you now have the proof you've been wanting for your father.'' His eyes challenged her. "What do you think his reaction will be, when you tell him the accident that killed his son was one he set up for me and it backfired against him?''

Lee Ann lowered her eyes. Her father would never believe it.

"That is why you're here, isn't it? So you can find the truth and save your father a heart attack or stroke?'' he asked tartly.

What was the matter with him? He sounded as though he hated her.

"What about your accident?'' she asked swiftly.

Ty shrugged.

Lee Ann came away from the door. "You aren't just giving up? You are going to keep looking for the man Cody heard—''

"Talking on the phone to God knows who, about God knows what?'' Ty suddenly demanded. "It doesn't mean a damned thing.''

"But what about the rope he put in the barrel?''

"What about it?"

"Shorty Sims saw—"

"I know what he saw," Ty said impatiently, pushing a hand through the black hair at his forehead. "I'm not cut out to be a detective."

"I know." Lee Ann dropped the drawing to the dresser and hurried to his side. Putting her arms around him, she looked into his face and said earnestly, "But we can't stop now. We're so close—"

"Close to what?" Ty pulled away and strode across the room. "All I want is to ride, go on down the road and ride again. It's all I've ever wanted."

Lee Ann felt everything freeze inside her. Turning to face him, she asked, "What does that mean?"

"Look, your brother's death was an accident. But your father is never going to believe that I didn't have something to do with it, no matter what you, or I, or Tom, have to say. So you might as well face it."

"We'll convince him—"

"How?"

"I—I don't know, but we'll think of something."

"No, *we* won't," Ty emphasized. "I don't give a damn what Wade Newley thinks about me," he snapped. "I don't have to prove my innocence to him—or anyone else," he added with a glare.

"I'm here because I'm a cowboy," he said doggedly, seeing how much he was hurting her, feeling trapped by what he felt for her and what they'd shared earlier that night, but needing her to understand, once and for all, who he was.

Striding across the room, he took her by the shoulders and held her. "You have to understand something about me, Lee Ann, something I've tried to tell you before. This is what I am. You can't make me into something else, something *you* want me to be.

"I'm a rodeo cowboy. That's all I am—all I've ever wanted to be. I don't know why, that's just the way it is.

There's something inside me that makes me what I am. Just like there's something inside you that makes you who you are."

The pain in the gray eyes gazing into his was almost more than he could bear, but he strengthened his resolve and continued, his eyes taking on a glow as he began to speak. "When I'm in the chute, waiting for it to open, and I feel all that raw power between my legs, and I know either I'm going to master this animal, or he's going to master me, it's—" He shook his head. "I can't describe the feeling. It's part fear, part adrenaline, part of every other feeling I've ever had in my entire life.

"And when the chute opens and we burst into the arena and the bull tries every which way to get me off his back— stomp me into the dirt if he can—but I manage to stay on...

"Then the buzzer sounds and I know I've done it. I've gone another round and won. For eight seconds, I've matched wits with an animal that lives by instinct, kills by instinct. And I won."

He shook her lightly. "Can you understand? *I* was in control. There's nothing like it! Nothing can match it. Nothing. It's..." He shook his head again. "It's indescribable.

"Don't you see?" he asked, seeing her glazed expression. "Every time I come out on top, every time I end a ride and climb down on my own, I'm a winner. And I've never had that feeling anywhere else in my life," he added softly.

Lee Ann wanted to say she understood, that she didn't care what her father thought about him, that she didn't mind about his love for the rodeo, that she'd be waiting for him at the end of every ride—but she couldn't.

It did matter, it mattered very much. She was honest enough with herself to know that she wouldn't be able to let him walk away time and time again, never knowing if he'd return to her in one piece, if he'd return to her alive....

She finally faced the fact that rodeo would always be his first love. His mistress. She knew she could have faced a flesh-and-blood mistress with a lot more aplomb than she could face this one.

"Do you care about me at all?" she asked unsteadily.

"I care."

"But not enough to give me the peace of mind in knowing you aren't risking your life every time you leave me."

"I risk my life every time I get behind the wheel of an automobile. Would you have me give up driving?"

"It isn't the same thing!" Lee Ann insisted.

"No," he conceded, "it isn't. But it's my life. It's all I know. I wish I could tell you I'd quit rodeo, but I'd only be lying to you. No matter how many times I get thrown, or how many times I end up in the hospital, until I'm too old, or physically unable, I'll always climb back on for another ride."

It shouldn't have come as a surprise to her, it's what he'd been telling her since they were both kids. But, like a fool, she hadn't wanted to believe him. And like many women in similar situations, she'd had the idea that she could change him.

But real life wasn't like that. You couldn't change people into what you wanted them to be.

She'd thought tonight was her happy ending. She'd been wrong. And she was too emotionally drained after all that had happened for another fight.

Ty let her go and she moved to the bed. Sitting on its edge, she looked up at him and asked, "What will you do?"

"Go on to the next rodeo."

"What about him?" she nodded toward the drawing.

"I'll keep watching for him." The dejected droop to her shoulders almost defeated him. He should have stayed away from her. Why hadn't he?

Because for a little while he'd felt her slipping away from him and he'd tried to keep her the only way he knew how.

He'd made love to her. How did he say he was sorry for wanting her?

"Go home. Forget about me."

Lee Ann was too numb to protest. "My father should be home before long. I'll tell him about Tom." Whether he believed it or not, she was going to tell him the truth. "What about the ranch?"

"It was my uncle's dream," he responded, "not mine. I wouldn't mind having it to come back to, but..." He shrugged.

In other words, if something happened that took it away from him, it was no great loss. Just as it appeared that she was no great loss to him. Suddenly, she wanted to be home.

"Are you going back to the ranch?"

"I'll see that you get home," he answered.

"You don't need to worry about me," she said evenly. "I'm a big girl and I can get home all by myself."

"I don't doubt it," he said. "But I'll take you, anyway."

"It's late."

"Actually," he murmured, looking at the digital display on the TV, "it's pretty early. But we have time for a few hours' sleep before we leave." He moved toward the door. "I'll come by for you about ten."

Lee Ann nodded.

"Lock the door," he called from the other side of it.

Lee Ann got up from the bed like an old woman, shuffled across the floor and snapped the lock into place. She leaned wearily against the door, listening to Ty's soft tread die away.

It felt as though he was walking out of her life forever— and he was. Hurrying to the bed, she flung herself across it, buried her face in the pillows and cried like she hadn't cried in twelve years.

He was leaving her. How could he leave her, when she loved him so much?

Chapter 13

Jennifer shook out her umbrella and rested it against the patio wall. Slipping her purse off her shoulder, she dropped it on a table inside the open glass door as she stepped inside.

"Lee Ann, what's wrong? Are you sick?" she asked as she made her way to Lee Ann's figure huddled in a chair on the glass-enclosed patio.

"No, I'm not sick," Lee Ann answered, staring at the rain falling in a steady sheet on the garden spread out before her. "I just couldn't face going in to the store. My mood matches the weather, and I don't think I could deal with a visit from someone like Nora Peebles today."

Jennifer took a seat on a nearby chair and studied her friend's unhappy face, noting the dull eyes and puffy lids. "I can barely deal with the woman when the weather is at its best," she said. "When Mary told me you'd called to say you weren't coming in, I was afraid something had happened over the weekend."

Lee Ann picked at the edge of her creamy silk housecoat. "It did," she murmured dispassionately, watching her fingers at work.

"Don't tell me you've found the man we've been looking for?"

"Yes and no," Lee Ann answered with a wan smile.

"Yes and no?"

"My brother's death was an accident," she announced without expression. "Another cowboy was involved, but Les wasn't murdered."

"He wasn't?"

"No," Lee Ann answered, studying the rain. "Les caused the accident himself."

"Your brother caused his own death?"

Lee Ann nodded and explained what she'd learned from Tom Purdy.

"Oh, Lee Ann, I'm sorry. How awful. But at least one good thing has come of it, now you know that Ty wasn't involved."

"Yes," Lee Ann agreed, getting to her feet and moving toward the streaming windows spanning the front of the patio. Thunder rumbled overhead and lightning flashed in the distance.

"There's more, isn't there?" she asked softly.

Lee Ann crossed her arms over her chest and nodded. "Ty's gone."

"Gone? Where?"

"On down the road," she said faintly. "That's what he calls moving on to another rodeo." She was trying hard to keep her sense of perspective. She didn't want to burst into tears in front of her friend like a disillusioned schoolgirl.

"Alone?" Jennifer asked.

"Yes."

"Do you want to tell me what happened?"

"I thought I had a chance, Jen," she said in a tortured voice. "I thought that after last night, everything was going to be all right." Her shoulders sagged. "I guess it just wasn't meant to be."

"You mean, he isn't coming back?"

"You were right when you warned me that Ty might not be willing to forgive and forget. He doesn't think the information we got last night will make any difference to my father. And he said it didn't matter to how he felt about Dad."

"Oh, honey, I'm sorry." Jennifer put a hand on her friend's shoulder and gave it a light squeeze.

Lee Ann covered Jennifer's hand with one of her own. "Your hand is so cold. How long have you been out here?" she asked with a frown.

"I don't know." Lee Ann shrugged. "For a while, I guess."

"Come on, let's go inside and I'll make you a cup of hot tea."

"Tea isn't going to cure this, Jen," she said angrily, pulling away from the other woman's touch.

"What's wrong with me?" she asked with a hint of desperation in her voice. "Why do the men in my life find it so easy to walk away from me?

"My father. My brother. Even Paul, my ex-fiancé. They've all left me behind. Is there something wrong with me?"

"No," Jennifer protested vigorously. "There is nothing wrong with you. And I'm certain your father loves you. Did you and Ty have a fight?"

Lee Ann laughed dryly. "No, nothing so extreme as that. He merely explained to me what rodeo meant to him."

"I'm sorry," Jennifer said.

Lee Ann put a hand to her mouth, then took it away to whisper, "He's gone! Just like that—" She snapped her fingers. "He brought me home, left me at the door and walked away...."

"He'll be back."

"No." Lee Ann shook her head. "Not this time."

"What about his own accident? What about the man we've been searching for?"

Lee Ann stared at the rain. "He said he'll keep an eye out for him. We're absolved from all involvement in the search." She swung her head to look at her friend. "But he won't, Jen. He won't keep looking for him, he'll just pretend it was an accident and go on with his life—until the man tries it again—and succeeds in killing him."

"Have you called Cody?"

"No. I figured Ty would call him."

"I don't think he has. I spoke to Cody a little while ago and he didn't mention Ty. So, what are you going to do?"

"I don't know."

"Are you just going to give up?"

"I—" Lee Ann winced as lightning flashed and thunder cracked overhead.

Was she going to give up? She'd given up twelve years ago and her life had become static. Is that what she wanted? Did she want to be the old maid she'd envisioned herself becoming without Ty?

"He doesn't want me, Jen, not as bad as he wants rodeo."

"Doesn't he?" Jennifer's eyes narrowed. "Are you sure about that?"

Into Lee Ann's mind flashed an image of Ty's face as he'd looked down at her moments before his lips had settled on hers and they'd made love. She could have sworn it was love and not only passion she'd seen reflected in his eyes.

"I don't know," she whispered. "I only know that I love him and I don't want him to die like my brother."

"How badly do you want him?"

Lee Ann studied her friend's expression. "You think I should keep looking for the man in the drawing?"

"No, I think *we* should keep looking for him."

"That means I would have to attend the rodeos."

"That's right," Jennifer agreed. "And especially the ones Ty is competing in, because that's where we'll find the man who wants to kill him."

Lee Ann knew Jennifer was right. If they wanted to catch a killer, all they had to do was follow the man's prey. She shivered at the thought of Ty's being anyone's prey, because no matter how he felt about her, she loved him.

"He doesn't want me around." He'd made that perfectly clear when he'd told her to go home and stay there.

Jennifer shrugged. "It's up to you."

Yes, it was. So, why was she letting Ty make that decision for her? He'd walked out of her life. He hadn't the right to decide anything for her.

A militant light entered the gray eyes. "You're right. It is my decision, and I've decided to keep on with the search. Thanks, Jen, for bringing me to my senses."

The other woman shrugged. "Think nothing of it. That's what friends are for. Occasionally, we have to point each other in the right direction. You've certainly done it often enough for me." Putting her arm around Lee Ann's shoulders, she said, "Now, can we have that cup of tea? I know I sure could use it."

After Jennifer left, promising to get hold of Cody and find out where Ty was scheduled to ride and make all the arrangements for them to attend the event, too, Lee Ann settled down for a nap.

At five o'clock that evening, she heard the sound of tires on wet gravel. Hurrying to the front door, her heart fluttering in anticipation, she peered eagerly through the curtains, only to draw back in sudden alarm.

A moment later, she glanced out the window to see her father climb down from his black king-cab truck and stride toward the door. This was an added complication she had hoped to avoid for a while longer.

There were no hugs and kisses when she opened the door and stood back as he entered. Lee Ann couldn't remember a time, even when she was much younger, when they'd been affectionate with each other. Such displays had been discouraged at an early age and she'd learned her lesson well.

"Father," she greeted him, "it's good to see you."

"Thank you, chicken. It's good to be back."

The sound of the truck's engine surprised her. "Did you bring someone with you?"

"I hired a couple of new hands. They'll be staying at the bunkhouse until Smokey and the rest of the men get back from the range."

As he put his briefcase on the hall table, she hung back, wanting to talk to him, but not quite able to gauge his present frame of mind. If she'd learned nothing else in the years she'd lived with him, she'd learned that her father was a master at hiding his emotions. Her brother's death had ripped that mask aside for a short while, but it was now firmly in place.

Clasping her hands before her in a semblance of composure and to hide their trembling, she followed him through the living room to the patio and watched as he strode to the bar and poured himself a hefty glass of bourbon. Turning around, the glass at his lips, he eyed her hesitant figure in the doorway.

"Something bothering you?"

"Yes." He'd given her the opening she needed. "I've learned something about Les's death that I think you should know."

Wade stiffened. Lowering the glass without taking a drink, he stared at her from beneath thick iron gray eyebrows. The handlebar mustache twitched spasmodically, and then he lifted the glass and took a healthy gulp.

"I'm listening."

"I've discovered that his death was an accident. There was someone else involved," she added hastily, sensing he was about to interrupt, "but it was an accident."

"Who else was involved?"

"A young cowboy by the name of Tom Purdy."

"Poppycock!" Tilting the glass, he drained it and turned to pour himself another drink.

"Father—"

"I know Tom. He wouldn't have touched a hair on my boy's head. He worshiped the ground your brother walked on."

"I didn't say he did anything to him—I said he was involved."

"How?"

"Les wanted to hurt someone else—"

"Yancy!" He spat the name at her as though it were a bad taste in his mouth. "This is about Ty Yancy, isn't it?" he bellowed.

And then, before she could answer, he said, "Don't think I wasn't aware of the yen you had for the whelp when he worked for me."

Raising his glass, he made a sweeping gesture, spilling some of the amber liquid onto the floor. "The whole damned county knew you chased after him like a bitch in heat!"

Lee Ann's face burned, but she refused to dignify that statement with a reply. She didn't want to fight with him.

"I know for a fact that my brother's death was his own fault," she maintained stubbornly. "And you would, too, if you'd talk to Tom."

"What is this? How did you meet Tom?"

"Ty came back—"

Wade slammed his glass onto the bar and began to curse. "I'll have him run out of town," he muttered, heading straight for the telephone. "The murdering, lying son of a—"

"He's gone."

"What did you say?" Her father almost skidded to a stop and turned toward her.

"I said, he's already gone. You don't have to run him off. He's gone and I don't think he'll be coming back."

"I'm phoning Nate—"

"Have you been listening to a word I've said?" she asked hotly, losing the battle with her temper. "You don't have to phone the sheriff. I told you, he's gone. Just like I told you there's proof that he wasn't involved in Les's death."

"How do you know this?"

"I spoke with Tom. He told me the whole story. Les was trying to injure Ty by cutting through his bull rope and causing an accident. He accidentally got hold of the rope himself and that's how he died."

"When did you speak to Tom?" He eyed her closely.

"A couple of days ago. I went to a rodeo with Ty." She saw the storm clouds gathering on her father's face.

"You don't like rodeo," he thundered. "I've never been able to get you to attend one—even when your brother was riding."

"I know." She felt her insides rolling. He wasn't going to like what she said next. "I went because of Ty—I love him— and I wanted to help find the man who had tried to kill him."

Wade whirled toward the bar. "What the hell are you talking about? Who tried to kill him?"

"That's what we don't know," she answered eagerly. At least he was listening, he wasn't bellowing like a bull and telling her to stay away from Ty. "You see, someone cut his rope the same way Les's rope was cut and he was injured in a fall. But someone saw the man who did it and we can identify him from a picture Cody drew."

"Who the hell is Cody?" he asked with his back to her, pouring himself another drink.

"Cody is Ty's friend."

She wished he would turn around so she could see his face. He hadn't made any comment on her declaration of love for Ty and that really surprised her. Maybe they had all been wrong about him. He was no longer a young man, maybe he had begun to mellow.

"Dad, I didn't only do this for Ty. I went looking for the truth about Les's death for you, too." That got his attention. He turned to face her.

"For me?" he asked with raised eyebrows.

"Yes, I've been worried about you. It isn't healthy to carry so much anger and hate around inside. I don't want to lose you, too," she whispered.

For an instant, his eyes blazed with a blue light and then a shutter seemed to fall into place. The stern lines smoothed out and his features relaxed.

"It sounds like a lot has been happening while I've been gone. Maybe you'd better tell me exactly what you've been doing."

Lee Ann studied him for a long silent moment. "Are you willing to listen to the whole story?" she asked uncertainly.

"Would that make you happy?"

"Yes."

"All right, let's get comfortable and you can tell me the whole story."

A few hours later, Lee Ann made her way upstairs alone. Her father had gone down to the bunkhouse to make certain the new hands had settled in all right. She was in a state of mild shock. All her life, she'd hoped for a change in her father's attitude.

When Les had been killed, she'd hoped he'd turn to her for comfort, but he'd turned his pain into anger and directed it at Ty, completely shutting her out. One of the reasons she had wanted to prove Ty's innocence was so she could bring the two men she loved together.

It was too soon to tell, but at least now she dared to have a glimmer of hope.

She'd told her father about Ty's bank loan, knowing he would find out, anyway, and she wanted him to hear it from her first, so she could extract a promise from him that he'd do nothing about it. He hadn't exactly promised, but he'd indicated that he'd give careful consideration to what she'd said. He still wasn't giving much away, but at least he was listening to her, and he'd never done that before.

Now, if only Ty would respond in kind, they could find the man who'd tried to hurt him. Once again, she was able to hope there might be a chance for the two of them.

She wanted to believe everything was going to work out. But as she changed into pajamas and climbed into bed, she was honest with herself. Her father had only promised to think about what she'd told him. And Ty was gone. She didn't know where. Nothing had changed between them.

Lee Ann went to work the next day, but only to hire Mary's husband to once again take over the management of the store. She would keep the books and supervise ordering, but Dan and his wife would be in charge. They'd done an excellent job in the past and she was confident that they'd do so again.

She remained on tenterhooks, waiting to hear where Ty would be riding again. Though she'd told her father about the rodeos she'd attended in the past weeks with Ty, she hadn't mentioned that she would be attending a few more.

She didn't relish lying to him now that they'd begun to establish a closer relationship, but she couldn't bring herself to tell him the truth. They were still feeling their way around each other and she didn't want to strain their new bond.

She worried about it all week. On Thursday, the need to make some kind of a plausible explanation for her planning to be gone the last three days of the next week was taken out of her hands. Her father told her that he had a business appointment in Wyoming and he would be gone for a few days.

He left early Wednesday morning, taking his new hired hands with him. Once he was gone, Lee Ann immediately called Jennifer and invited her to the ranch. They hadn't seen much of each other the past several days, and she wanted to tell her friend about her father's change of heart.

"Well, he hasn't exactly had a change of heart," she admitted to Jennifer over dinner that evening. "But he's more receptive than he's ever been. For the first time in years, I'm beginning to think we might establish a closer relationship."

Jennifer kept any skepticism she felt to herself. "Have you changed your mind then, about Ty's being in rodeo?"

Lee Ann played with the pasta on her plate. "No," she finally answered. "I'm still hoping he'll change his mind."

"Lee Ann—"

"No," she interrupted, "let's not discuss gloomy things this evening. Let's eat and drink some wine and play the piano." She smiled a bit desperately.

"Whatever you say," Jennifer agreed, lifting her glass for a toast. "Oh, by the way, I talked to Cody. Ty will be riding in Cheyenne this weekend."

Two days later, Cody and Jennifer drove out to the ranch to pick up Lee Ann for the trip to Cheyenne, Wyoming. This was the first time Lee Ann had seen Cody all week. He'd taken up residence in the town's only boarding house and they'd communicated with each other through Jennifer. She'd stayed away from him deliberately because she hadn't wanted to advertise his presence in town to her father.

After their initial greeting, Lee Ann settled in the truck's back seat and studied the back of Cody's head. "Do you think we're on a wild-goose chase?" she asked.

Cody glanced at her reflection in the mirror. "Do you?"

Lee Ann bit her lip. Now that she was actually here and they were on their way, she kept thinking about what Ty had said last weekend. "Ty won't thank us for doing this. And if my father finds out..."

Cody trod on the brake. "Do you want to go back?"

"No," Lee Ann answered after a moment. "Let's go." Under her breath, she added, "But he's going to be really mad if he finds out we're there."

Pioneer Days Rodeo in Cheyenne was a huge event. People traveled from all over the country to attend. The town was packed and all the motels had been booked solid for weeks.

But Cody had planned for that situation. He carried a couple of tents and sleeping bags in the back of his truck along with some camping equipment.

Lee Ann hadn't given much thought to accommodations, but when they pulled up behind the stock pens and stopped, she began to realize that this rodeo was going to be very different from the others they had attended. It had been a long trip and she was exhausted. A bed, even if it was a bedroll, looked like heaven at the moment.

"Well, this is home for the next few days." Cody stood gazing at the trucks, campers, RV's and tents decorating the scene.

Lee Ann moved up beside him and studied the colorful panorama. "Do you think Ty is here?"

"Yes, ma'am, he's here, all right."

"Should we look for him?" Jennifer asked, coming to stand beside them.

"I don't think that will be necessary. Word has a way of traveling through this crowd." Cody nodded to the people around them. "He'll find us."

"Well, I'm starving. Do you think we could find a meal before we set up camp?" Jennifer asked.

"Yes, ma'am!" Cody responded with alacrity. "A woman after my own heart. Food first and work later."

Lee Ann noted the pink flush on her friend's cheeks as Cody offered Jennifer his arm and thought how right the two of them looked together. A barking dog came racing through the camp and Lee Ann jumped aside as a boy of about ten dashed after it, yelling at the top of his lungs. She stood watching the pair disappear, until her own hunger got the better of her and she turned to hurry after her companions.

Dinner that night was a working meal. They ate in a steak house filled to bursting capacity with the rodeo crowd. Before, during and after dinner, they showed the drawing Cody had made to everyone who would stand still long enough to take a look at it. But no one recognized the man's harsh features.

As they returned to camp, Lee Ann glimpsed a truck that resembled her father's and her thoughts turned to him. She prayed that this would be the weekend they found the man in the drawing and that it would bring to a close the threat to Ty.

Suddenly the question Jennifer had asked a short time ago sprang to mind. *What are you willing to give up?* Her friend had wanted to know if she was willing to compromise.

But there was no compromise. She wasn't trying to be unreasonable, she just couldn't live with a death threat hanging over the head of the man she loved. And that's how she saw rodeo.

A little while later, Cody built a small camp fire near their tents and set a coffeepot over it. He was on his haunches, stoking the fire, when Lee Ann came to sit down beside him. It was after eleven, but she couldn't sleep. Tomorrow Ty would ride and she was on tenterhooks.

"It's chilly tonight."

"Yes, it is." He looked beyond her.

"Jen went to find the ladies' room." Lee Ann answered his unspoken question.

"Cody, do you think he's here?"

"Ma'am?"

"The man in the drawing. Do you think he's here?"

Cody lowered himself to the ground and shoved his hat to the back of his head. "Well, now, there's a strong possibility that he is. Ty's here. And this is a big rodeo, lots of people and lots of opportunity to try something.

"In a smaller rodeo, it's harder to get away with something like what he tried with Ty. But here—" he gestured toward the numerous camp fires "—he's just one of the crowd. And a lot goes on that others don't see."

Lee Ann shivered and rubbed her arms. "He's here," she murmured with sudden certainty, looking into the darkness outside the circles of light. "I can feel him."

"Ty called just before we left Rainville."

Lee Ann's head swiveled in Cody's direction. "He did? You didn't tell him that we were on our way here?" she asked quickly.

"No, but I don't see why you didn't want me to."

"We had a disagreement," she explained hesitantly. "He thinks I should stay home and forget about him."

"Yes, ma'am."

Lee Ann shot him a look. "You can call me Lee Ann, you know." And then she added, "He told you the same thing, didn't he?"

Cody nodded and leaned forward to stir the fire.

"But you brought me along."

"That's right, Lee Ann." He grinned, showing two perfect rows of white teeth. "I didn't pay any attention to him. He knew I wouldn't. Just like he knew you wouldn't stay out of this in the beginning. And that's why he agreed to my plan." He turned bright blue eyes on her face. "He was afraid you'd go off half-cocked—his words, not mine—and get yourself in trouble."

A haughty look masked the leap of joy in her eyes. "Half-cocked, huh?" she asked curtly. "Just wait until I see him. I'll have a few things to say about that."

"Well, you'd better get them straight in your mind, 'cause I think you're about to get your chance."

"What?" Lee Ann's head shot up.

Cody nodded to someone behind her.

"Cody," Ty's deep voice murmured a greeting. "Nice night for a camp fire."

Cody yawned. "It's late, I think I'll turn in." He got to his feet, looked from the man to the woman and realized both had already forgotten his presence. With a grin, he left them alone.

"I thought I told you to stay at home, where you belonged," Ty said grimly.

Lee Ann swallowed with difficulty and found her voice. "A long time ago, you told me the same thing," she said, getting to her feet. "I didn't listen then, either."

Grabbing her hand, Ty pulled her through the camp, around the camp fires, past the tents and campers, away from the sound of strumming guitars and radios blaring country music, and into the darkness.

"Where are you taking me?" Lee Ann asked breathlessly, trying to keep up with his rapid pace.

Ty brought her to an abrupt halt, fumbled with something in his pocket and the next instant a door swung open and light spilled into the night. "Here," Ty said, mounting the steps and hauling her up behind him. "I'm taking you right here."

Lee Ann's breath caught at the double meaning in the words. Noting the burning passion in his glance as he reached around her and slammed the door to the motor home, clicking the lock into place.

And then she was in his arms, her world rocked on its foundation as his mouth took hers in a hungry kiss.

For a long moment, there was only the sound of her heart drumming in her ears as his lips traveled over her jaw to the side of her neck and lower. Yes—yes! a voice cried triumphantly inside her as she locked her arms around his neck and returned his hot kisses.

"Do you have any idea how many times I picked up the phone this week and dialed your number?" Ty asked unsteadily, punctuating the words with small kisses all over her face. "You're all I think about."

His hands were at her waist, fitting her hips to his, sliding up her back, rocking her against him. "I can't let you go again," he whispered, taking her lips in a soul-shattering kiss. "I won't let you go!" he cried, his hands trying to memorize every inch of her quivering body.

Removing the pins holding her hair off her neck, he buried his hands in it. And then he rubbed it against his face, sniffing its haunting perfume.

"Do you know that your scent is in my head, on my clothes." His mouth took hers in a punishing kiss. "Everywhere I go, everything I see, reminds me of you. I can't sleep." He nibbled at her lips, stroking them with his tongue. "I can't eat. I can't ride—my scores haven't been this low since I was a rookie. And it's all because of you, I see your face in every crowd."

Holding her face up to his, he looked at her with such longing that it would have melted even the strongest of resolves, and Lee Ann's was already in a puddle at his feet.

"Say you won't leave me ever again," he pleaded, his lips swooping toward hers. "Say it!" he demanded hoarsely.

Lee Ann looked at him in silence.

"You know I can't give up rodeo, don't ask that of me," he whispered in supplication. "Lee Ann!" His grip tightened on her face, his fingers digging into her soft cheeks. "I need you!"

Tears pooled in the gray eyes tilted toward his.

"It's up to you," he whispered, the light of passion dying a little as each second passed and she remained silent.

All at once, his hands let her go and he turned away. She was breaking his heart. There hadn't been all that many people in his life for him to love. And he loved her more than was good for him.

"It's okay," he said softly. "I understand. Go on back to the others."

"Ty . . ." She couldn't leave him like this. She had to explain. "I wish I could tell you it didn't matter, that I would adjust to your life-style. But I can't!

"Rodeo took my father from me all these years. It killed my brother—it nearly killed you. I'd live in constant fear for your safety. I can't live that way! What if we had children?"

"Is it better to live in denial?" he demanded, turning to face her, his face tight with pain. "Isn't it better to have something," he asked passionately, "even if it's only for a short time, than to have nothing at all?"

Lee Ann couldn't make him understand. Her heart was being ripped to shreds at the thought of losing him. But what was she to do?

She could try to persuade herself that she'd adjust, that things would work out between them, that she'd learn to live with fear. Or she could accept his love under false pretenses, and secretly look for the opportunity to change him.

Either way, they'd both be miserable. She couldn't put either of them through that kind of pain. There had already been enough pain in both their lives.

"I'm sorry," she murmured, dropping her eyes from his unhappy face. She had to get out of here before she burst into tears and made a decision they'd both regret.

"It's all right," he said, unlocking the door and stepping aside. "Here."

Lee Ann looked down at the flashlight he was handing her and that was the last straw. Why couldn't he have been a shoe salesman—anything but a rodeo cowboy?

"Damn it! Why can't you give it up for me?" she demanded. "Why can't I be enough for you?"

"You are," he whispered close behind her. "You're all the woman I've ever wanted, or needed. But I need the space to be me." His voice dropped to barely above a whisper. "That's what you can't understand. You can't separate the man from the cowboy, because they're one and the same. Why can't *you* understand that? Why can't you forget the past and live in the present with me?

"I refuse to be a doormat for your father and what I would become if I went back to Rainville to live in your world. Your father tried to use me against my uncle and he would find some way to use me against you."

He felt tortured as he looked at her. She was only a pawn in her father's game of life, but she didn't know that. Maybe one day soon she'd find out before it was too late for her, for both of them. "If you love me, you must come to me," he said. "I'm sorry, but that's the way it has to be."

He was giving her an ultimatum. He refused to listen to her objections about his way of life, yet he wanted her to give up everything she knew to follow him.

And to what? A life spent constantly on the move, never knowing if he was going to survive from one rodeo to the next?

Twisting the door handle, she staggered outside. Her whole world was caving in on her and she felt as though she couldn't breathe in the dust from its rubble.

This wasn't the way it was supposed to happen! They were supposed to be together. She hated the rodeo! She hated Tyler Yancy! She hated everyone!

"Lee Ann?"

Trying to muffle her sobs, she stuffed the pillow against her mouth at the sound of Jennifer's voice.

"Lee Ann, are you all right?" the other woman whispered from the darkness on the other side of the tent.

Lee Ann pulled the pillow away from her mouth long enough to answer. "Y-yes."

"I was worried about you, but Cody came by a little while ago to tell me you were with Ty. I guess everything is going to work out for the two of you, after all. I'm glad. You belong together."

Lee Ann squeezed her eyes shut and tried to block out her friend's voice. At the same time, she was trying to block Ty's haunted expression from her mind's eye and the echo of his last words from her consciousness.

"Oh, I don't know if this is the right time to tell you, but I think you should know..." Jennifer hesitated. "I don't want you to be hurt—don't be angry with me for telling you this, please."

Lee Ann removed the pillow and listened in growing curiosity. Something told her she didn't want to hear what her friend was about to say. A rustling noise filtered to her ears and she realized Jennifer was sitting up.

"Nora Peebles came into the store Tuesday morning bristling with news," she said loudly. "Her cousin is a secretary at the bank. Nora said—oh, God, I don't know how to tell you this—you were so excited about everything the other evening—"

"Just say it!" Lee Ann demanded impatiently.

"Your father bought Ty's loan."

"I don't believe you," Lee Ann breathed in a tiny voice.

"I'm sorry, honey, but it's true. Cody didn't want me to tell you. He thought you had enough on your plate at the moment, but I just didn't want your father to get away with something so underhanded, after making you believe he'd changed."

"He didn't actually tell me he wouldn't take any action on the loan," she protested. In fact, he hadn't really told her much of anything. He'd merely allowed her to *assume* a great many things.

She'd wanted to believe that he truly cared about her feelings. That he'd put her feelings above those of...greed.

But he'd been lying to her all along, letting her perpetuate the fantasy.

Something inside snapped. All her life, she'd wanted his love and approval and he'd withheld it. The Great Wade Newley had spared no time or effort on her behalf. He'd lavished money on her—as long as she made no emotional demands on him.

She was beginning to see just what the relationship between her brother and father must have been like. Les had struggled to measure up to his father's expectations and at every turn was made to feel inferior. What his son achieved was only important as long as the older man could bask in its reflected glory.

Wade Newley was like an emotional vampire, sucking his son dry. Nothing Les had done had been big enough, good enough, worthy of the Great Wade Newley's attention. And yet Les had struggled to be better, trying to win his father's approval—his love.

That's why Les drank, she realized. That's why he was arrogant. That's why he could never take the pressure of the competition between himself and Ty, even when they were little more than children.

He must have felt that no one could be better than him because then he would have failed to measure up to his father. And if he didn't measure up, he didn't deserve... what? To live?

Poor Les. Rodeo hadn't killed her brother, Wade Newley had killed him, just as surely as if he'd held a gun to his son's head and pulled the trigger.

"Are you angry with me for telling you about this?" Jennifer asked tentatively.

"No," Lee Ann said sadly. "I'm glad you did. It's made several things clear to me."

"Good," Jennifer replied, scooting down in her bedroll, "I wouldn't want to lose my best friend."

"Go to sleep, silly. We've got work to do tomorrow. We're going to find a killer."

"You think so?" Jennifer asked.

"Yes, I do."

After a while, Lee Ann heard her friend's even breathing and knew she was asleep. She was tempted to leave the tent and find Ty, but she didn't know what to say to him.

Would he believe that she'd had a change of heart? That it was her father's treachery that had made her realize how much she loved Ty?

How selfish she'd been, wanting him to give up everything he loved in order to have her. She was no better than her father. She didn't want Ty to submerge his personality into hers. It was because he was who he was that she loved him.

Now she could remember how she'd felt when they were teenagers and Ty had ridden the most dangerous bulls and roped the trickiest calves. How her heart had raced and burst with pride each time she'd watched him at work on the ranch. She wanted him like that, proud and strong and free-spirited. She only prayed that it wasn't too late for her, that she hadn't killed his love with her stupidity.

She was still trying to decide how best to approach him the next morning when she fell asleep. A short time later, the scream of sirens awakened her.

Ty's motor home was on fire.

Chapter 14

Lee Ann was shaking so badly that the coffee someone had thrust into her hands a little while ago sloshed over the sides of the cup. She'd been pacing the hospital's waiting-room floor for over two hours and no one had come to tell her about Ty's condition.

The large double doors suddenly burst open and she twisted in their direction. At last, someone was going to let her know if Ty was all right. But it was only Cody and her spirits took a nosedive.

"Did you find out how the fire started?" she asked as he strode toward her. While she and Jennifer had followed the ambulance to the hospital, Cody had stayed behind to talk to the police and learn what he could about the cause of the fire.

"Gas."

She studied the man's impassive expression. "You mean it was deliberately set?"

"That's what it looks like. Whoever started it didn't even bother to take the gas can with him when he left."

"Oh, God." Her knees gave way and Cody caught her elbow to steady her. Taking the cup from her unresisting fingers, he deposited it in a nearby trash can and led her to a seat.

They were the room's only occupants. Jennifer had gone to try to find out what she could about Ty and hadn't yet returned.

Hunkering down beside her, Cody took both her cold hands in his and began to rub them. "He's going to be all right."

"Have you heard anything?" she asked quickly, her eyes shooting to his face.

"No, ma'am, but I know Ty. He has amazing recuperative powers."

"But fire..." She could imagine, only too vividly, the condition Ty might be in if he'd been doused with gas. The horror of it showed on her face. It wasn't the same as getting bucked off a horse, or thrown from a bull. Broken bones mend easier than incinerated flesh. She shuddered, pulled her hands from Cody's and jumped to her feet.

"We both know who did this," she said unsteadily. "Don't we?" she demanded, striding across the floor to stare out the window at an empty parking lot.

"I knew he was here—didn't I tell you he was here?" She reeled toward Cody. "What if Ty's condition is critical?" The expression on her face became tragic.

"It isn't," Cody insisted, rising to his feet. "He's going to be all right. We just have to keep on believing that."

"W-was Ty inside, when the fire started?"

"No. Either he crawled out on his own, or the arsonist dragged him outside."

"That doesn't make sense."

"Well..." He hesitated. "Ty's clothes had been soaked in gas. I guess it wouldn't matter much either way, once the blaze had started."

All at once, a sound outside the room caught their attention. Two pairs of eyes swung eagerly toward the heavy double doors.

The doors parted and Jennifer stepped into the room. Pausing on the threshold, she glanced from Lee Ann's round eyes to Cody's disappointed scowl. "Sorry," she murmured weakly. "I couldn't find out anything about Ty."

Cody dropped down onto the nearest chair and Lee Ann aimed troubled gray eyes at his face. "No one saw anything?" she asked anxiously, returning to their conversation to stave off disappointment and fear about Ty.

Shaking his blond head, Cody ran an unsteady hand over his gritty face and got to his feet. He paced the width of the room, while Lee Ann paced the length of it. Jennifer stacked the magazines on the small glass-and-chrome table and straightened the chairs.

"I can't stand this," Lee Ann said in a strained voice. "We've got to do something." She turned to Cody. "Did you show the drawing to the police? Did you tell them about Ty's earlier accident?"

"No, I didn't," he admitted slowly.

"What?" Lee Ann stopped short. "Why not?"

"I didn't think about it. But even if I had, there isn't any proof that this had anything to do with that incident."

After a moment, he added reluctantly, "There was some talk at the camp that it might have been drunken teenagers who'd started the fire tonight."

"I don't believe it," Lee Ann said instantly.

"Neither do I," Jennifer said.

"Well, I guess that makes it unanimous, 'cause I don't think so, either," Cody agreed.

"Are the police going to investigate?" Lee Ann asked.

"I'm sure they will," Jennifer said, eyeing the silent Cody. "They have to—don't they?—a crime has been committed."

"Who is he?" Lee Ann slammed an angry fist against the wall and stared helplessly at the room's other two occupants. "Who is this man? And why does he want to hurt Ty?"

"Excuse me," a hesitant voice said from a crack between the doors, "is there someone here named Cody Fargo?"

All eyes turned toward a figure in green, slipping into the room.

"Yes, that's me," Cody responded instantly.

The young man nodded. "Good. Come with me, please."

"Wait!" Lee Ann protested. "Where are you taking him?"

"Someone wants to speak to him," the freckle-faced orderly answered as he and Cody disappeared from view.

Jennifer crossed the room and put an arm around Lee Ann's waist. "It will be all right—"

Suddenly, the door flew open and the same young man stuck his head inside. "Sorry. One of you named Lee Ann?"

"Yes!" Lee Ann jerked upright and peered over her friend's shoulder.

"Could you come with me, please?" he asked.

"Go on," Jennifer urged when Lee Ann hesitated, "I'll wait for you here."

Lee Ann followed the lanky young man down the dim corridor, her eyes measuring the interior of each cubicle they passed.

"Here." The orderly halted to draw back a white curtain and wait for Lee Ann to enter.

She moved forward slowly, her heart pounding. The strong odor of gas mixed with odors unfamiliar to her, stung her nostrils. She was almost afraid to look at the man on the bed.

"Hi." Ty grinned up at her from a sea of white wrapped around his head. "It looks worse than it is," he assured her.

An older man, dressed in the same green as the orderly, turned from a cart filled with packages of needles, plastic bags of IV fluids and other equipment that Lee Ann didn't recognize, to give her a nod of greeting.

"It's a topical analgesic," he explained with a flash of white teeth.

"He was burned?" she asked anxiously.

"First-degree," he answered. "Nothing too serious. For a couple of days, he'll look a bit like a lobster, but that's all. It's the bump on the side of his head that I'm more concerned with."

Now Lee Ann realized that at least a part of the white covering Ty's head was a large square of bandage stuck over his left temple. "What happened?" she asked.

"Looks like a blow from a blunt instrument," the doctor answered.

"Is it serious?" she asked quickly.

"Haven't got the X rays back yet, but I shouldn't think it's too serious. Your friend appears to have a pretty hard head. But, then, that's what you'd expect from someone who does what he does for a living." He smiled and touched Ty's shoulder briefly.

"I imagine we'll keep him in the hospital for twenty-four hours to be on the safe side. By the way, I'm Dr. Jeffries," he added, holding out a hand to Lee Ann.

"I'm—"

"Yes, I know," he interrupted her, nodding toward Ty. "He's been asking—or should I say demanding—that we get you back here, since he regained consciousness."

Lee Ann felt her cheeks grow warm. "I'm sorry if he's been a difficult patient. Maybe you should keep him in the hospital for a few days longer," she suggested solemnly, "until his attitude improves."

The man on the gurney frowned and made a threatening gesture in her direction. The doctor laughed.

"I just might consider doing that," he said, moving toward the door. "Now, if you'll excuse me, you can keep him company, while I go see what's happened to those X rays."

Once the doctor had left, Lee Ann stood looking at Ty. Now that they were alone, she didn't know what to say. Suddenly, she felt self-conscious about her appearance. Dressed in the soft, faded jeans and flannel shirt she'd brought to sleep in, with no makeup and her hair sticking out in every direction, she must look a sight.

"You look beautiful," Ty murmured, as though reading her thoughts.

"I look terrible," she contradicted, pushing the hair back from her face.

"Not to me," he whispered deeply, his eyes devouring her. "Never to me."

"Oh, Ty—"

She wanted to run to him, throw herself against his chest and tell him how worried she'd been about him. That she didn't know what she'd have done if anything had happened to him. Instead, fingers knotted together behind her back, she stood tongue-tied, staring at him.

"I'm sorry about earlier tonight," he said. "I was pretty arrogant, wasn't I? I don't blame you for running away from me."

"I wasn't running from you," Lee Ann said without hesitation. "I think I was running from myself. I've been confused by a lot of things, but I think I'm beginning to get some of them straight in my head. Please, be patient with me."

Now was not the time for what she needed to say, but the time would come.

"You do realize that someone tried to kill you tonight, don't you?"

Ty's glance slid toward the wall. "Yes."

"Do you remember what happened? Did you see who hit you?"

"A few minutes after you left, I went outside. I thought maybe the night air would clear my head. I knew I'd acted like a damned fool—" He broke off to search her face, but she wouldn't meet his eyes. "I heard a noise behind me and I guess I thought it might be you," he admitted. "I turned toward the sound, caught a glimpse of dark shadow—"

"Well, it's just as I thought." Dr. Jeffries pushed past the white curtain and entered the room, holding a set of X rays in one hand. "No fracture, but a mild concussion." He waved the X rays in Ty's direction. "It looks like you'll be out of here tomorrow morning."

He glanced at his watch, raised an iron gray eyebrow and said, "That is tomorrow—tomorrow morning, not today. Do you understand?" he asked Ty.

Ty nodded and a smile of satisfaction momentarily erased the tired lines from the doctor's face. "Good." A nurse stepped from behind the curtain at Lee Ann's back. "I think they're ready to take him upstairs."

He gestured for the young woman to join him and turned to Lee Ann. "Why don't you get some rest and come back later to make sure that we're taking good care of this guy?"

Lee Ann nodded, throwing a quick glance at Ty. It was obvious that he wanted a few minutes alone with her, but she couldn't bring herself to ask the doctor and nurse to leave the room. And she wasn't used to public displays of affection.

"I'll come back later," she promised. "Get some rest and do whatever the doctor and nurses tell you to do."

"Later," Ty murmured and the expression in the hazel eyes sent tingles down Lee Ann's spine.

Back in the waiting room, she found Jennifer and Cody standing on opposite sides of the room, sipping black coffee and staring dismally out the windows. Apparently, neither one had heard her enter the room.

"He's going to be all right," she announced.

Cody turned toward her with a smile, raised his coffee cup in a salute and took a long gulp.

Jennifer dropped her cup into the wastebasket as she moved across the room to her friend's side. "I'm so glad," she said with a faint smile.

As they left the hospital, Lee Ann filled them in on the extent of Ty's injuries. "His burns are no worse than sunburn, but he has a mild concussion. It seems someone hit him over the head before they set fire to the place."

"Did he see who hit him?" Cody asked.

Lee Ann shook her head. "It was too dark. And he thought it was me, until the blow was struck."

"That was the investigating officer, Officer Marsh, who sent for me a little while ago," Cody said. "He'd been to see Ty, but the doctor wouldn't let him in. He told him to come back tomorrow.

"Officer Marsh said one of the campers saw a man running away from the motor home. I showed him the drawing and asked if it resembled the man the witness had described. He looked at it for a long time and asked if he could take it with him."

"But he didn't tell you if it was the same man?" Lee Ann asked.

Cody shook his head. "He probably intends to show it to the witness."

"So, what do we do now?" Lee Ann asked.

"I guess we wait," Cody answered.

"Do you think he'll be safe in the hospital?" she asked uneasily.

"I imagine the police will be keeping a close watch on Ty tonight," Cody assured her.

It was getting light by the time they drove to where their tents were set up. People were beginning to stir. Children played outside with their dogs and the smell of frying bacon and eggs filled the crisp morning air.

"Anybody hungry?" Cody asked.

Lee Ann and Jennifer looked at each other and wrinkled their noses. The bitter taste of hospital coffee was still on their tongues.

"Me, too," he agreed with a crooked smile. "Why don't the two of you get a couple hours of sleep? I'll mosey around camp and see if anyone knows something they didn't report last night."

Both Lee Ann and Jennifer's feet were dragging. Inside the tent, they dropped thankfully onto their bedrolls without even removing their shoes and immediately fell asleep.

A couple of hours later, Cody strolled tiredly into camp and bent to lift the flap on the women's tent.

The first thing his weary glance rested on was a vertical slit down the back of the tent. A moan sounded somewhere to the left of him and he stepped quickly inside.

Jennifer rolled over onto her back with a hand to her face. Seeing the tall figure bending toward her, she cowered with a whimper, the green eyes glazed with fear.

"It's all right," Cody said, kneeling and reaching toward her. "It's only me."

But she continued to shrink from him, her eyes wide with fright, a soft whine coming from between her lips.

Cody sat back on his haunches. His glance swept the tent. "Where is Lee Ann?" he asked. Pivoting on his knees toward Jennifer, he asked again, "Where is Lee Ann?" Grasping her by the shoulders and giving her a shake, he repeated, "What's happened to your friend?"

Jennifer stared up at him, blinked and shook her head, the dazed look fading from the green eyes. "W-what?"

"Lee Ann's gone. Her bedroll is gone. Where did she go?"

Rubbing her jaw, Jennifer's glance dived toward where Lee Ann's bedroll had rested a short time ago. "I don't know," she whispered.

"What's wrong with your face?"

"I—my jaw hurts."

Cody gently removed her hand and stared at the swelling and bruise. "Who did this to you?"

"I don't know," she answered still in a dazed voice. "I remember hearing Lee Ann moving around... I thought she was trying to get comfortable. I looked up and nothing—until now."

"Damn it! Are you okay?"

Jennifer nodded, looking at him with wide eyes. "What is it?" she cried. "What's happened to Lee Ann?"

Twenty-four hours later, everyone was still asking that question. Lee Ann had disappeared without a trace.

Ty left the hospital as planned after being cross-examined by Officer Marsh about his accident and about Lee Ann's disappearance. He could tell them very little about either event.

Of course, the investigation into Lee Ann's disappearance wasn't an investigation—not yet. It hadn't been forty-eight hours since she'd disappeared. And the local police refused to call it a kidnapping, or give official sanction to calling it a disappearance.

But Ty and Cody weren't waiting. Together, they scoured the countryside, talking to everyone who'd talk to them, trying to get a lead on Lee Ann's whereabouts.

The task of phoning Lee Ann's father was left to Jennifer. At first, he'd sounded angry, disbelieving, and then stunned. He told her he'd be on the first available flight to Cheyenne.

Three hours later, Ty was waiting for Wade's plane to land.

The look of concern on Wade Newley's face turned to a scowl the instant he saw Ty. "What are you doing here?" he demanded.

"I think we should concentrate on your reason for being here," Ty said stiffly. "Lee Ann is the only important issue right now."

Wade picked up his suitcase and pushed past the younger man. "I'll get a taxi to the motel."

"I'll take you." Ty stepped in front of the older man, blocking his path. "We have things to discuss."

Wade set his jaw and followed Ty to the exit.

In the truck, Wade glanced at the younger man's stern profile with narrowed eyes. "Don't think I don't know what's been going on behind my back. I know all about your weekend trips with my daughter. You might think you've won the game, but it isn't over yet. I put a stop to your sly tricks once before and I can do it again."

Ty's expression tightened. "I think your memory must have dulled over the years." He lashed the older man's face with a razor-sharp glance. "I seem to recall that it was you playing games. And one of them would have given you my uncle's ranch and left my uncle and me out in the cold, once you had what you wanted from me.

"But you weren't as clever as you thought. You couldn't get Les to play along with the game and I found you out. That's what's been eating you all these years, isn't it?"

Wade stared straight ahead.

"Aren't you the least bit concerned about your daughter's welfare?" Ty asked angrily. He hadn't seen the man in more than a decade, but the ill feeling he'd harbored for him was as strong as ever.

"My daughter's welfare wouldn't be in question if she hadn't gone chasing after you." The man's voice trembled with rage. "You took one of my children from me. Don't think you're going to take this one, too. I'd rather see her—"

"Dead?" Ty finished for him. "Is that what you were going to say? You'd rather seen her dead than with me?" His hands tightened on the steering wheel. "Let me tell you something, old man, if one hair on her head has been touched, I'll see you in hell.''

Ty gave the other man a moment to digest that in silence and then he continued, ''And for the record, I didn't take your son from you—death took him. I had nothing to do with his death—which I'm sure you well know. I spent some time in the hospital recently—''

''I don't give a damn where you've been,'' Wade snarled.

''No?'' Ty shot him a quick glance. ''Well, maybe you should. Because while I was there, I had a whole lot of time to think. My friends have been trying to convince me that someone wanted me out of the way bad enough to resort to murder. I resisted that idea—until now.''

Ty could feel the sudden tension in the man beside him. ''I asked myself, who could possibly hate me so much he would want to see me dead? And you and I both know the answer to that one, don't we?''

Wade didn't answer, but Ty could tell he was listening.

''What I suspect wouldn't hold up in a court of law, because you were miles away when my rope was cut—miles away when my RV was burned. But we both know that you paid someone to do those things for you.''

''Don't be asinine,'' Wade said coldly. ''I'm sure there must be plenty of people besides me who would like to see you lying face down in the dirt.''

''Maybe, but not many of them would resort to murder—or conspiracy to commit murder.''

''If you make such an accusation,'' Wade threatened him, ''I'll bring charges of slander against you. And I'll make certain they stick.''

''Who's got Lee Ann?'' Ty asked through clenched teeth, tired of pussyfooting around. ''What does he want?''

When his passenger didn't answer, he spun the steering wheel and turned onto a dirt road. They'd been heading away from town since they'd left the airport and now they were headed into the mountains.

"Where are you going?" Wade demanded.

"I'm going to take you somewhere deserted where I can beat the living daylights out of you, until you tell me where you've got Lee Ann."

"I don't know what you're talking about," Wade said curtly. "And if you think you're frightening me, think again. Go on, take me clear the hell to the next state if it makes you happy. I won't tell you a damned thing. You want a fight," he added belligerently, "well, I used to be pretty good with my fists. Good enough to knock the pins from beneath you!"

They were several miles from the main highway when Ty stopped the truck and turned to Wade. "Maybe I won't have to touch you, after all," he said purposefully.

"What are you going to do?"

"You're real concerned about your image. I'll bet you'd do just about anything to keep people from knowing what kind of a bastard you really are."

Ty opened his door and climbed out.

"What are you getting at?" Wade muttered, opening his door and stepping out onto the hard-packed dirt road.

"It's been suggested to me that your son's accident was deliberate."

"I know that, you young fool. And I know who engineered it."

"Do you?" Ty eyed him speculatively. "Do you really?"

Wade shifted his weight from one foot to the other and pushed a hand into the pocket of his jeans. "What are you getting at?"

"I have a witness who's willing to testify that your son committed suicide." Ty said, stretching the truth just a little.

"You're a liar!" the older man snarled, doubling his fists. "My son wasn't a coward! I'll see *you* in hell before you tell that pack of lies," he shouted, lunging toward Ty.

Ty dodged him. "I'll see that every paper that has anything to do with rodeo prints the story," he threatened. "And I'll suggest that he did it because he was afraid of the competition—that he was a loudmouthed coward."

Wade was trembling with rage, his florid face an unhealthy shade of red. The stiff hairs at the ends of his handlebar mustache bristled with anger.

"Where is she?" Ty demanded.

"Take a shot at me," Wade suddenly challenged. "Come on, take your best shot. I'll lay you out cold."

"Is that what you want?" Ty asked resignedly. "You want to fight?" Wade was two inches taller and at least fifty pounds heavier, but that didn't matter to Ty. If he wanted to use his fists, he'd be glad to oblige him.

Wade threw the first punch. Ty ducked it and landed one of his own. The other man groaned, grabbed his middle and went down on one knee.

"Where is she?" Ty demanded again, throwing a right to the man's jaw when he refused to answer. "Where is she?" he demanded, slamming a fist against the man's nose and seeing the blood spurt.

Ty stepped back and eyed him with scorn. "How in the hell can you call yourself a father—a man?"

He drew his fist back, planning to put every ounce of power he possessed in this last blow, and Wade raised a hand.

"Enough," he muttered in defeat, wiping his nose with his sleeve. Climbing unsteadily to his feet, he staggered toward the truck. "I had nothing to do with Lee Ann's kidnapping," he muttered harshly. "I was as shocked as everyone else to learn about it."

"Is that the truth?" Ty snapped, following close on the older man's heels.

"I swear it is. The kidnapper called right after Jennifer called me this morning. He said that by now I must know what he'd done and he figured I knew he meant business."

Wade reached into the truck, pulled his suitcase toward him and extracted a clean handkerchief. Holding it to his nose, he turned to face Ty.

"I think you broke it," he charged accusingly.

"What does he want?"

Wade raised a bushy eyebrow and said, "Money—what else? He said he figured that since he'd botched the job on you three times, I wasn't about to pay him. Lee Ann is insurance against that event."

"Three times?"

"He was supposed to see that you had a little accident on your property when you first returned to Rainville. But the damned fool wasted too much time, spraying paint all over everything—so it would look like a gang had moved into the area, he said, and remove any suspicion from me."

"So that was you."

"No—" Wade looked affronted "—that was Mac. And Lee Ann almost stumbled onto him."

"Lee Ann!"

"That's right, smart boy," Wade said with a contemptuous twist to his mouth. "If Lee Ann hadn't chased him away that first night, we wouldn't be here now."

"God!" Ty shook his head. "You're a real piece of work. So, you've been following me all this time."

"No, Mac has been following you since my son's death."

"I didn't kill Les."

"I don't believe you."

Ty stared at him with steely eyes. "Not everyone has as little regard for human life as you." His patience at an end, he asked, "Do you know where he's taken Lee Ann?"

Wade wiped at his nose and eyed the younger man shrewdly. Things could still work out the way he'd planned. If Ty went after the man, Mac might still get the opportunity to kill him. And Wade could deny knowing anything about the previous attempts on Ty's life.

He knew Lee Ann didn't suspect his involvement, Mac had been careful in that at least. And Wade was a well-known, well-respected businessman. If Mac talked, who would believe him, who would take the word of a man—a killer—against his?

"I know where she is," Wade admitted slowly.

"Where?"

"I have a place near Kalispell. There's an abandoned cabin a few miles from mine. He took her there."

There wasn't an ounce of regret or concern in the man's face or voice. His daughter was in the hands of a potential killer and he might have been talking about a stranger.

Ty strode toward the truck. "Get in. I want you to draw me a map of the area. How were you supposed to get the money to Mac?" he asked. "Was he expecting you to bring it to him, personally?"

"I'm supposed to bury it in a certain spot on my property. He'll dig it up."

"How long did he give you?"

"Twenty-four hours."

Ty glanced at him in surprise. "That isn't much time. It looks like he doesn't trust you any more than I do." It wasn't long, but it ought to be enough time to pick up Cody and Jennifer and get a flight to Kalispell, Montana.

"Did you bring the money?" He wouldn't be surprised if the other man said no.

Wade nodded.

"Good. I'll see that your friend Mac gets what's coming to him," Ty promised in a hard voice.

Chapter 15

The flight from Cheyenne to Kalispell went off without a hitch. But Ty kept a close eye on Wade. He didn't trust him an inch. The man was ruthless. And Ty was certain that he cared less for his daughter's life than he cared about exacting revenge on Ty.

In Kalispell, they rented a truck with four-wheel drive. Ty bought a map of the area and they looked for a motel room. They found the perfect place a few miles west of town. It was isolated and it boasted a restaurant.

Inside the unit he'd rented, Ty placed a straight chair in the middle of the room and motioned to Wade. "Sit down."

The man stared at him without moving. "What are you going to do?"

Cody placed a rope in Ty's hand. "I'm going to make certain that you're here when we get back with Lee Ann."

"I'll be here."

"Yes, you will," Ty agreed. "Now sit down."

"I won't stand for this, I'm not some punk you dragged in off the street."

Cody took a step in the older man's direction and Ty moved to his other side. "We can do this the easy way, or we can do it the hard way. It's up to you."

He had no other choice. Wade sat down in the chair. Ty tied him to it amid verbal abuse and muttered threats about what Wade would do to him when this was over.

When the last knot had been tied and tested to make certain it was secure, Ty turned to Jennifer, who stood on the sidelines, hands folded behind her back.

"Don't let him loose while we're gone—not even to go to the bathroom," Ty cautioned. "He isn't to be trusted."

"If all goes well, we should be back in eight to twelve hours. And if we aren't, call the local police and tell them everything that's happened. When they get here, hand him over to them, and give them this."

Ty handed her a copy of the map Wade had drawn of his cabin and the vicinity, including the cabin where Mac had taken Lee Ann. He nodded to Cody and the other man followed him to the door.

"You will be careful?" Jennifer asked, her eyes straying to the back of Cody's blond head.

"We'll be fine," Ty assured her. "You just take care of yourself, and make sure you keep a close eye on our friend over there. Don't let him talk you into cutting him loose. He's unscrupulous. And he has everything to lose when we find Lee Ann and the man holding her prisoner."

"I wish I could go with you," Jennifer said fiercely. "I know you'll do better without me, but..."

"We'll find her," Ty said, touching the woman's shoulder reassuringly. He understood how she felt. It was all he could do to keep from climbing in the truck, speeding to the cabin where she was being held and break the door down so he could tear her kidnapper limb from limb.

He had to keep reminding himself that Lee Ann's life was in danger and he had to go slow if he wanted to ensure her safety.

"Do you think you'll be all right with him?" Ty asked Jennifer. "If you don't think so, say so now, and I'll leave Cody with you."

At that, Cody turned from where he was stowing gear into the truck, but before he could voice a possible objection, Jennifer spoke up. "Don't worry about me. The important thing is that you get to Lee Ann before something awful happens to her."

Both men waved at her as they backed from the parking place and started forward.

Jennifer locked the door, secured the safety chain and turned to stare at Wade Newley.

"Now, then, my girl," Lee Ann's father said smoothly, baring his teeth in a smile, "how much is it going to cost for you to turn me loose?"

Lee Ann huddled in the sleeping bag, watching the man stir something in a pot over the fire in the fireplace. She had no idea where she was, or the identity of the man who'd kidnapped her—other than the fact that he was the man in Cody's drawing.

She wasn't even certain what events had led to her being here. As best as she could piece together, he must have sneaked into the tent while she and Jennifer were sleeping.

Jennifer! Was she all right? The other woman wasn't with them, so he must have left her behind.

Lee Ann felt a bout of dizziness and closed her eyes. When she opened them, it was gone. He must have injected her with something to make her sleep, because she didn't remember a thing about what had happened.

"So, you're awake."

Lee Ann jerked her attention from the yellow-and-red dancing flames and trained her glance on the man watching her. Her breath caught at the back of her throat. His eyes were the purest gray, almost a white, that she'd ever seen. They reminded her of a wolf's eyes.

Hiding her unease, she demanded, "Who are you and why have you brought me here?"

"Oh, I think you know who I am. You and your cowboy have been looking for me long enough."

"How do you know that?" she asked quickly.

"I know a lot of things. I know all about you and your family. I even know that you play the piano."

Fear jolted her insides. She tried to move her hands and realized for the first time that they were tied. Her ankles were bound, too.

"If you're expecting my father to pay you a lot of money for me, you're probably going to be very disappointed."

"Really?" He grinned. "Maybe not."

Lee Ann focused on his face. She was trying to remember if she'd ever seen him before, now that she was looking at the flesh-and-blood man, instead of a drawing of him.

He was really very ordinary-looking, with receding brown hair and a round face. Except for the unusual color of his eyes. He wasn't really what you'd call a big man, a little above average height, with broad shoulders and narrow hips.

Except for being tied and the inference he'd made about knowing things about her that he had no way of knowing, she didn't feel threatened by him. And that was absurd. He'd kidnapped her. He'd cut Ty's rope and probably set fire to Ty's motor home. She ought to fear him.

"Why do you want to hurt Ty Yancy?"

"Who says I do?" he asked, taking a seat facing her on the bench beside the rough wooden table near the fireplace.

"Aren't you the man who cut Ty's rope? Didn't you set fire to his motor home?"

He shrugged and studied his fingernails. "That was business."

"A-are you planning to kill me, too? I can identify you to the police."

At that he gave her a piercing glance and there was something cunning about the look that Lee Ann didn't understand. "I don't think you will," he said confidently.

"No? Why not?"

"Because, if you did, you'd have a lot more to lose than me."

Lee Ann frowned. His cryptic remarks were making her angry. "What is that supposed to mean?"

"Why don't you just lie back and take a little nap until dinner is ready."

"You're going to feed me?"

"What did you think—" he asked with raised eyebrows "—that I was going to starve you? Why should I?" He got to his feet and stood looking at her, the gray eyes suddenly taking on the sheen of pure ice.

"If I wanted to kill you," he said in a conversational tone of voice, "I sure wouldn't take the time to starve you to death."

Holding his hands up so she could get a good look at their size and strength, he said, "These would do the job in less time than it would take to tie a knot in a rope."

Lee Ann shivered. Now she was afraid.

"But I'm not planning on anything like that." He hesitated. "At least, not yet."

Moving around the table to the fire, he picked up a long-handled spoon and began to stir the contents of the heavy iron pot. Glancing over his shoulder as the tantalizing aroma of beef stew filled the air, he asked, "Are you hungry? This is just about done. And I make a mean son-of-a-gun stew, if I do say so myself.''

Lee Ann's stomach lurched. The thought of eating anything this man had cooked made her feel ill.

''I'm not hungry, thank you.''

''Sure?'' he asked, dipping a bowl for himself.

''Yes, I'm sure.''

She watched him shovel the food into his mouth. ''What did you mean,'' she asked curiously, ''when you said I'd have more to lose if I identified you?''

Laying his spoon on the table, he turned to face her. ''You know, I've enjoyed my work these past few weeks, because I had the opportunity to get to know you—well, not exactly know you, but you understand what I mean. You're an interesting woman.''

''Should I feel flattered?'' Lee Ann asked sarcastically, the idea of his watching her and poking into her life making her even more angry.

The gray eyes chilled. Without answering, he got up from the table and moved to the fire, where he picked up a burning stick and turned toward Lee Ann.

She stared at him in horror. What was he going to do with that?

But he only reached in his pocket for a cigarette and lit the tip of it before throwing the stick back into the fire. After pouring himself a cup of coffee from the pot on the stone hearth, he resumed his seat.

''What did you mean it was business?''

With his back against the edge of the table, he watched her and smoked. ''Just what I said.''

''You mean someone paid you to kill Ty?''

''That's right.''

''And me? Did someone pay you to kidnap me?''

''Not yet. That's why we're still here.''

* * *

Cody glanced at the speedometer. "It won't do Lee Ann much good if we end up in jail for speeding."

Ty spared the lighted gage a glance and eased his foot off the accelerator. "Sorry." He eyed the map in his right hand, muttering, "Where the hell is this road?"

"Here, let me see it." Cody took the map Wade had drawn and compared it with the printed map in his other hand. "Have we crossed the Little Bitterroot River?"

"Yes."

"Then it should be the second dirt road on your left."

"We've come over ten miles and it was supposed to be under five."

Ty trod on the brake, bringing the truck to a sudden halt. "Damn him," he raged. "The map's wrong. He's still playing his little games—even when his own daughter's life is at stake. I'll kill him!"

Cody twisted around to peer through the rear window, making certain the horse trailer was intact. They'd borrowed the trailer and two horses from a rodeo cowboy he knew in the area. Wade had told them it would be impossible to drive to the cabin where Lee Ann was being held and it would be slow going on foot.

Turning to face Ty, Cody asked, "What about landmarks? Did we pass the entrance to the Christmas tree farm?"

"I don't know," Ty answered angrily, a hint of desperation in his deep voice. He slammed a hand against the dash. "We're wasting time."

"Let's go back," Cody suggested.

Ty stared at him, gave a sudden jerky nod and whipped the steering wheel hard to the left. The tires spun, kicking up dirt, and the trailer jerked against the bumper in protest as they circled around and headed back the way they'd come.

Driving slowly, Ty watching on one side and Cody on the other, they finally found the road. It was on the opposite side from where Wade had said it would be.

"Do you suppose it was a deliberate mistake?" Cody asked, referring to the discrepancy.

"Everything that man does is deliberate. He's the most cold-blooded bastard I've ever met."

The flat bed of the road they now followed gradually gave way to a steeper grade and soon they were on a winding mountain road. As the sun slipped behind the distant snow-covered mountains, the windows began to fog.

"The temperature is dropping." Cody reached over the seat and grabbed his jacket. After he'd slipped it on, he picked up the thermos at his side and poured a cup of coffee.

"Here." He offered it to Ty.

"Thanks." He took it in one hand and lifted it to his lips.

"Do you think Jennifer's doing all right with Newley?" Cody asked, taking a drink from his own cup.

"I hope so. If he manages to get loose, we could be in big trouble."

Cody threw him a glance. "You think he'd come up here?"

"I think he'd do anything he could to see me dead."

"Why?"

Ty shook his head. "Maybe because I'm not his son."

"From what I knew about Les, he seemed to hate the man."

"I guess they must have had a love-hate relationship. Wade Newley expected his son to be perfect when we were growing up, but perfect in *his* eyes—in the things *he* thought were important. I didn't like Les, but I wouldn't have changed places with him for the world."

"What about Lee Ann? Where did she figure in her father's life?"

"She didn't," Ty answered grimly. "He ignored her."

"How much farther?" Cody asked.

Ty glanced toward the digital clock on the dash. "By my estimation, we ought to be at Newley's cabin in half an hour. From there, we travel on horseback."

Cody looked up at the first faint stars and circle of moon. "It's going to be a cold one—no cloud cover."

"Yeah," Ty answered, his thoughts on Lee Ann. According to Jennifer, she'd been wearing jeans and a flannel shirt. Was she sheltered from the cold? Had she been fed? Given something to drink? *Had he touched her in any way?*

Ty's foot pressed against the accelerator. Lee Ann had now been alone with the man for thirty-seven hours. A lot could happen in that length of time.

"There it is." Cody sat forward and pointed toward a building rising out of the darkness a half mile ahead.

Ty pulled the truck and trailer beneath the trees at the front of the cabin and turned off the ignition. "Newley said everything we need would be in the shed behind the cabin. Let's go."

Fortunately, there was a full moon and that made the trip on horseback over the unfamiliar terrain a little easier. Still, it was rough going. The path was rocky and steep and the horses must have sensed the men's anxiety, because they were easily spooked.

At one point, Ty pulled his animal up short, got down and had a 'talk' with the beast, after which the animal's rolling eyes and nervous twitch disappeared.

"Would that work with the broncs you ride?" Cody asked Ty, clearly impressed.

"I don't know, I've never tried it."

They'd been riding for close to an hour when Ty slowed his horse and motioned for Cody to do the same. "There," he said, pointing above them toward the mountaintop. "Through those trees. See the cabin?"

Cody moved up beside him, his eyes on the small wooden structure in the distance. "What do we do now?"

"Now," Ty answered, dismounting, "we move forward on foot."

They tied the horses to a tree, removed the gear they'd brought and slipped from tree to tree, ascending the mountain. As they drew nearer, they could see smoke rising from the chimney and a yellow glow in the lone window.

"I don't see anyone inside," Cody whispered.

"Maybe he's smart enough to keep away from the window."

"What are you going to do with that?" Cody asked, nodding toward the satchel containing the money Wade had brought to ransom his daughter. "Weren't we supposed to bury it?"

"I'm keeping it close. Mac, Newley's hireling, doesn't know we didn't bury it. He's expecting to find it at the other cabin. If we don't manage to stop him before then, we'll use it as a lever to get Lee Ann free."

It was a cold night and that meant Mac just might have to come outside to get more firewood. Ty was counting on that. He didn't want to wait sixteen hours and then have to try to get the drop on the man in broad daylight.

Creeping to the window, he peered through the grimy glass to an even grimier interior. Directly in line with his vision was a rough wooden table and bench. The bench was occupied by a man hunched over a plate of food. A fire blazed in the fireplace across from him.

Toward the far end of the cabin, a mattress had been thrown on the floor against the wall. A bedroll had been spread over it and Lee Ann lay zipped into it, her eyes closed.

Ty's heart leaped at the sight of her. He wanted to dive through the window straight at the throat of the man shoveling food into his mouth—but he waited. The time wasn't right yet.

Lee Ann appeared to be unharmed. Then her head swung to the side and a dark bruise showed high on one cheekbone. Anger erupted in Ty, until he had to bite the inside of his jaw to keep from crying out loud.

Eyes filled with loathing, he stared at the man's back. He would kill him with his bare hands if he'd done her any lasting damage. And then he'd kill Wade Newley.

His glance swept the room. There wasn't a stack of logs in sight. That was good. That meant Mac would have to come outside before long, if he wanted to stay warm.

And Ty would be waiting for him.

Cody was waiting for Ty near the back of the cabin. "Is she there?" he asked quickly.

"She's there," he answered curtly.

His friend eyed him sharply. "Something wrong? She's okay, isn't she?"

"She better be," Ty answered, making it sound like a threat.

"What's the plan?"

"We wait. Sooner or later, he's got to come outside to get firewood and that's when we grab him."

The sooner or later stretched into an hour and then two. Ty went back to the window several times, and when he found Mac lying hunched over the table, sound asleep, he tried the door. It was barred on the inside.

He was beginning to think they were going to have to wait until daylight to make their move, after all, when the man at the table snorted loudly, gave a gigantic shiver and sat up, rubbing a hand over his face. Ty watched as he threw a glance toward the mattress, got to his feet and went to stir the coals in the fireplace. The fire was almost out.

Ty's gut tightened, just as it did when he lowered himself into the chute and onto the back of a bull. It was time.

Moving back to where Cody waited for him, Ty told him to go around the back of the cabin to the other side of the door. The plan was for the two of them to lasso the man as he came out the door.

In the arena it was called team roping. Cody was the header, he would lasso the man around the neck. And Ty was the heeler, he'd rope the man's legs. Both men were experts at roping and neither expected to miss his target.

Once Cody was in position, Ty peeked through the window to see what their quarry was up to. He was bending over Lee Ann, the side of the bedroll thrown back, and now Ty could see that she was bound hand and foot.

All at once, the man hovering over her stiffened. In an instant, he'd whirled toward the window. Ty ducked low. Had he been fast enough?

Heart pounding, he waited. If he'd been spotted, their plan for getting the drop on the kidnapper was ruined.

After a few minutes, he inched forward to peer over the edge of the window and into the room. Mac was once again standing at the fireplace, poking at the red coals. While Ty watched, he dropped the poker and grabbed a heavy plaid jacket from a nearby nail on the wall. Shrugging into it, he lumbered toward the door.

Ty scrambled to warn Cody. "This is it," he whispered. "Here he comes."

He'd no more than finished speaking when the door swung open and the man's figure moved into view. Ty fumbled with the rope coiled at his side.

He saw Cody inch away from the side of the building, his lasso raised high. Ty moved up to join him. At a signal from him, Cody swung the loop in a widening circle and let it go. An instant later, Ty's lasso spun into view.

Mac gave a startled yelp and grabbed for his throat, at the same time his feet slipped out from under him. He fell to the ground, heavily, struggling to remove the restraints.

Ty was on him in a flash. But the other man was strong and he fought like a wildcat. Using the rope around his own neck, Mac wound it around Ty's and pulled hard.

But having his air choked off only made Ty madder. He doubled his fist and landed a blow to the man's solar plexus, knocking the wind out of him. And when Mac fell onto his back, Ty was on his chest, straddling him like Mac was the meanest of bulls.

Cody had picked up a heavy piece of wood, prepared to knock the man senseless, but Ty was doing all right, so he simply stood by in case he was needed. In a matter of seconds, Mac was trussed like a steer.

Ty climbed to his feet, panting. "There, that ought to hold you," he told the angry man at his feet.

"I should have taken care of you properly when I had the chance," Mac muttered bitterly. "I sure messed up on that."

"Let me tell you something," Ty said grimly, "if you've hurt Lee Ann—"

"She's all right. What do you think I am? I'm a businessman, just like her father." And then he began to laugh.

Ty remembered that laugh and it sent chills down his spine. "Keep an eye on him," he told Cody. "I'm going to get Lee Ann."

She must have heard the commotion outside, because when Ty stepped into the cabin, she was staring wide-eyed at the door.

"Ty?" The fear in her eyes changed to astonishment, then to joy. "Oh, Ty, I was afraid I'd never see you again."

For a long moment, he simply held her, his face pressed against her hair, feeling the living warmth of her in his arms. "Are you all right?" he asked in a quivering voice.

"Yes, I'm fine. Just keep me close from now on." She laughed nervously. "Okay?"

"You better believe it," he said, pulling away to capture her face in his hands and plant a long kiss on her trembling lips.

Lee Ann's lips opened beneath his and Ty deepened the kiss. A long moment later, he drew back, lifted her bound arms and slipped them over his head. Pushing eager hands into the hair at the sides of her face, he whispered, "Is this close enough?"

"No," she answered, her gray eyes darkening with emotion. "Closer."

"I love you."

"M-me, too," she admitted unsteadily, "I mean—I love you, too."

"Did he hurt you?" he mouthed against the bruise on her cheek.

"No, he didn't hurt me."

"What about this?" Ty drew back to touch the bruise with a gentle fingertip.

"I fell. I needed to go outside—you know," she said shyly. "And I was dizzy from the shot he'd given me when he took me from the tent."

"He didn't hurt you in any way?"

His meaning was clear and Lee Ann's blush deepened. "No. He didn't threaten me at all."

"It's a damned good thing," Ty muttered darkly.

"I'm fine," she murmured, her heart skipping beats at the ferocity in his voice, her eyes devouring his beloved face. "How did you find me?"

Ty lifted her arms from around his neck and began to loosen her bonds, keeping his eyes lowered.

"Ty?"

"If you knew how much I love you," he whispered, taking the hands he'd freed and lifting them to his face, kissing each palm, holding one against his shaking mouth.

"I love you, too," she repeated. "I've loved you such a long time. It's a relief to be able to say it out loud."

"I've loved you since you were twelve years old." He looked at her from beneath half-lowered lids. "There's something I want to tell you. That night you followed me to the arena and asked me to take you with me, when I left town—well, I wanted to. I went back later, after my anger had cooled, but you'd gone. I even followed you back to the house, but by the time I got there, I'd come to my senses. What I said then was true. We were only kids."

"I know," she agreed. "And we both still had a lot of growing up to do. But it's nice to know you wanted me."

"I've always wanted you." His eyes slipped away from hers. "I'm sorry about the other night. I was pretty insensitive."

"I'm sorry, too—sorry for trying to make you change your life for me. All I've thought about since you returned is what I want. I never considered your wants and needs."

Ty moved down to release the bonds at her ankles.

"I wanted to make you fit into my life," she confessed guiltily to the top of his dark head. "But now I realize how wrong that was. If we love each other..."

He looked up as she paused and there was no doubt in her mind about how he felt. "We have to make a new life together. One that suits both our needs.

"I wanted you and my father to end your differences, because I thought that would make everyone happy." Her glance dropped. "No, that isn't true, it would have made me happy.

"There's something I have to tell you, Ty," she added quickly. "My father has lied to me. He bought up your note at the bank." She hung her head. "I'm sorry."

"It's all right," Ty hurried to assure her, touching her hair with gentle fingers. "I know my uncle wanted me to have the ranch, but the land isn't what's important to me. You are. I can buy more land."

He didn't know how he was going to tell her about her father's part in her kidnapping. She'd just admitted that her happiness depended on the two of them settling their differences.

"Lee Ann, there's something *I* have to tell you—"

"Is everything all right?" Cody asked from the doorway.

Lee Ann wrenched her eyes from her beloved's face to stare in surprise at the other man. "I didn't know you were here. Is Jennifer here, too?"

Ty looked at Cody before answering, "No. We left her at a motel in town."

"What town?" Lee Ann asked curiously. She still didn't know where she was, the last she knew she'd been in Cheyenne, Wyoming.

"Kalispell," Ty answered slowly. "She's with your father."

"My father is here? Did you call him?" she asked eagerly.

"Jennifer did."

"Thank God it's all over and everyone is all right. When I woke up in this cabin and saw him—" She broke off with a shudder and shook her head.

"Sweetheart," Ty said hesitantly, "there's something I've got to tell you."

Lee Ann glanced from his unhappy face to Cody's. "What's wrong?" she asked them. "Is it my father?"

"Yes. I left him tied up in the motel room. Jennifer is guarding him."

"Tied up?" Shock widened her eyes.

"Yes." Ty shot a look of helplessness toward his friend. How was he going to make her see what the man was really like? "He..."

"Ah, I'll go stay with our friend out here," Cody said uncomfortably, backing out the door, leaving the two of them alone.

"What has my father done now?"

"He paid the man who kidnapped you to kill me," Ty said quickly.

"You mean my father was behind all this?" she said as she gestured around the room.

"Yes," he murmured, taking her cold hands in his and lifting one to his cheek. "I'm sorry."

Now it made sense to her. Now she understood what the man had meant by his cryptic remarks. He'd said she'd have the most to lose if she identified him. She'd lose her father. But it was with great sadness that she admitted that she'd already lost him a long time ago.

"No, it's I who am sorry," she whispered sadly. Turning her face aside in shame, she pulled away from him. Her father a murderer. That's what he was, no better than the man he'd hired to commit the actual crime.

"I love you," Ty said.

"How can you? My family has done nothing but cause you heartache and pain. And now this," she said remorsefully.

"Not true," he protested. "One of you has given me something to live for. Or have you changed your mind about that?"

"No—oh, no!" Lee Ann turned adoring eyes on him. "I love you. Nothing can ever change that."

"Not even my love for rodeo?"

"Nothing," she answered solemnly.

"Then we'll get through this thing with your father together. Just like we'll get through whatever problems arise in the future—that is, if you'll have me."

"Are you asking me to marry you?"

Ty looked around at the cabin's shabby interior. "Not a very romantic setting for a proposal, is it?" he asked with a frown.

Lee Ann put her arms around his neck and lifted her lips to his. "I think it's the most romantic setting in the whole world. And my answer is yes."

*   *   *   *   *

Dark secrets, dangerous desire...

Lovers
**DARK AND
DANGEROUS**

Three spine-tingling tales from the dark side
of love.

This October, enter the world of shadowy
romance as Silhouette presents the third in their
annual tradition of thrilling love stories and
chilling story lines. Written by three of
Silhouette's top names:

**LINDSAY McKENNA
LEE KARR
RACHEL LEE**

Haunting a store near you this October.

Only from

V *Silhouette*®
™
...where passion lives.

The Loop™

Is the future what it's cracked up to be?

This August, find out how C. J. Clarke copes with being on her own in

GETTING IT TOGETHER: CJ
by Wendy Corsi Staub

Her diet was a flop. Her "beautiful" apartment was cramped. Her "glamour" job consisted of fetching coffee. And her love life was less than zero. But what C.J. didn't know was that things were about to get better....

The ups and downs of modern life continue with

GETTING IT RIGHT: JESSICA
by Carla Cassidy in September

GETTING REAL: CHRISTOPHER
by Kathryn Jensen in October

Get smart. Get into "The Loop!"

Only from **Silhouette®**

™

where passion lives.

LOOP1

HE'S AN

AMERICAN HERO

Men of mettle. Men of integrity. Real men who know the real meaning of love. Each month, Intimate Moments salutes these true American Heroes.

For July: THAT SAME OLD FEELING,
by Judith Duncan.
Chase McCall had come home a new man. Yet old lover Devon Manyfeathers soon stirred familiar feelings—and renewed desire.

For August: MICHAEL'S GIFT,
by Marilyn Pappano.
Michael Bennett knew his visions prophesied certain death. Yet he would move the high heavens to change beautiful Valery Navarre's fate.

For September: DEFENDER,
by Kathleen Eagle.
Gideon Defender had reformed his bad-boy ways to become a leader among his people. Yet one habit—loving Raina McKenny—had never died, especially after Gideon learned she'd returned home.

AMERICAN HEROES: Men who give all they've got for their country, their work—the women they love.

Only from

IMHER09

Join award-winning author Rachel Lee as

 explores the dark side of love....

Rachel Lee will tingle your senses in August when she visits the dark side of love in her latest Conard County title, THUNDER MOUNTAIN, SS #37.

For years, Gray Cloud had guarded his beloved Thunder Mountain, protecting its secrets and mystical powers from human exploitation. Then came Mercy Kendrick.... But someone—or something—wanted her dead. Alone with the tempestuous forces of nature, Mercy turned to Gray Cloud, only to find a storm of a very different kind raging in his eyes. Look for their terrifying tale, only from Silhouette Shadows.

SILHOUETTE® Shadows™

MORE GREAT READING FROM BARBARA FAITH

If you enjoyed Barbara Faith's DESERT MAN, you'll want to join her in November as she visits the dark side of love with DARK, DARK MY LOVER'S EYES, Silhouette Shadows #43.

When tutor Juliana Fleming accepted an assignment in Mexico, she had no idea the turn her life would take. Kico Vega—her solemn, needy student—immediately warmed to her presence, but Kico's father, Rafael, showed her nothing but contempt. Until he took Julie as his bride, ravishing her with his all-consuming desire—yet setting in motion Julie's worst nightmare.

Take a walk on the dark side of love with Barbara Faith—only in **SILHOUETTE SHADOWS**